The
Back
Wing

A Harold and Bella
Paranormal Mystery

Novels by Mike Befeler

Unstuff Your Stuff

Death of a Scam Artist

The Mystery of the Dinner Playhouse

Paul Jacobson Geezer-lit Mystery Series

Retirement Homes Are Murder

Living with Your Kids Is Murder

Senior Moments Are Murder

Cruising in Your Eighties Is Murder

Care Homes Are Murder

Nursing Homes Are Murder

The Back Wing

A Harold and Bella Paranormal Mystery

Mike Befeler

M B[signature]

12-15-19

Encircle Publications, LLC
Farmington, Maine, U.S.A.

Cover Art by JC Davis Photo
Cover Design by Davis Creative
Images Copyright © Courtney Literary 2013

Published by: Encircle Publications, LLC
PO Box 187
Farmington, ME 04938

Visit: http://encirclepub.com

Printed in U.S.A.

Dedication

I want to thank my critique group including Becky Martinez, Lori Lacefield, Bonnie Biafore, Jedeane Macdonald, Darla Bartos and Virginia Brost, and my editor Deb Courtney.

CHAPTER ONE 🦇

The day after he arrived, Harold McCaffrey couldn't figure out why he had been assigned to the Back Wing at the Mountain Splendor Retirement Home. It could have been that an administrator confused him with someone named Harry McArthur; or Peter Lemieux, the residence manager, became flustered when a bat flew out of the vent in his office; or a normal bureaucratic snafu might have occurred; or maybe someone just had it in for Harold. Whatever the reason, he ended up in room 493 right between Bella Alred and Viola Renquist. And that was a difficult place for an unsuspecting widower to be.

Harold's second guessing about moving had started during the ride from his long-time home in Denver to the retirement community in Golden, Colorado. He sat in silence as his son, Nelson, drove along I-70. Too many things were piling on top of each other. First, the death of his wife. That had been traumatic enough, and afterwards he tried to become acclimatized to being a widower. Second, he started losing things—his keys, reading glasses and driver's license. Then after a minor accident, he had given up driving. Finally, he left the burner on too long while cooking oatmeal. When foul-smelling smoke had set off the alarm, that had been the last straw. Nelson insisted on taking him to see retirement homes where meals could be provided without the risk of a conflagration.

They had toured half a dozen places of mass aging. One retirement community allowed pets. Now Harold usually had no problems with animals, and he could even tolerate the smell of cat pee and dog poop up to a point, but some little critter had nipped at his ankle and tried to detach part of his cuff. He put an X through that name on the list, as he pushed aside visions of being attacked by a pack of wolves in his sleep.

One retirement home didn't pass the sniff test and was rumored to have bedbugs. That also drew a heavy X. Another lacked a good view. On the tour through a resident room, Harold had peeked out the curtains to see a brick wall across a narrow alley greeting him. And not just the lack of anything green in sight had offended him, but the graffiti on that wall indicating what to place up a particular part of his anatomy didn't appeal to him.

He almost liked one retirement community until he sat down for lunch and was served mystery meat reminiscent of the elementary school cafeteria meal that led to a world-class food fight in his youth.

In leaving his home of forty years, he certainly wanted something to look at besides people stumbling around in walkers and food to eat other than ground up horsemeat.

He had given up hope of finding anywhere to spend his declining years, until he and Nelson had visited Mountain Splendor. It had no rumored bedbugs, no ankle-biting critters, good food and a pleasant view of the foothills in Golden.

A nice woman named Ruth something gave them a tour. She appeared to be his age but spritely, with a good sense of humor, even joking that she once ended up in the wrong room and found two residents shaking the bed in blissful coitus. He figured if she could kid about that event, this place might have a future for him. But then again, he wasn't sure he wanted to leave his house.

As Nelson took the Highway 58 exit off I-70, Harold could stay quiet no longer. "I'm not sure this move is a good idea."

Nelson looked over his right shoulder for a moment and then returned his gaze to the highway ahead. "Dad, we've been over this a hundred times. The house was too big for you with Mom gone. You don't like cleaning, doing laundry or cooking and can't stand takeout food. Having meals provided will be the best thing for you. You checked out everything within a fifty-mile radius and liked Mountain Splendor best. Don't start backpedaling now."

"I suppose you're right." Harold had no intention of being a burden by foisting himself on his son, daughter-in-law and grandson in their home in Broomfield. And he realized he had struggled being in the house alone since his wife Jennifer passed. Still, this relocation to a huge building stuffed full of old farts like himself didn't seem all that appealing. What was he getting himself into?

"What if I don't like it there?"

"Come on, Dad. Mountain Splendor has lots of activities, hiking trails nearby…and three times as many women as men."

Harold rolled his eyes and mentally put his finger in the back of his throat. "Give me a break. I don't need any female companionship."

"You never know. You're still a fit, with-it guy. I know you miss Mom, but you may find someone who interests you again."

"No one can take your mother's place."

Nelson tapped a finger on the steering wheel. "I know that. But there's nothing wrong with going on a date now and then. It has been two years."

Two years. It seemed like an eternity. He'd never get used to being on his own again after fifty years of marriage. So here he was a seventy-nine year old widower going to his last resting place, a six-story building full of walkers, canes and geriatrics. But he didn't have the willpower to fight it any longer. He'd eat his meals, pay his bills and get by. The idea of other women didn't appeal to him. Not that he'd lost his libido. Rather, no one had caught his eye, and he didn't expect anyone to. Some things you just couldn't replicate. After his wonderful marriage to Jennifer, what could compare?

"Dad, are you there?"

Harold let out a deep sigh. "I was thinking of your mother." "And I think of her too. But you still have many good years

ahead. You passed your last physical with flying colors. Your doctor says you're in excellent shape and could live to be a hundred."

Harold did a quick calculation. That would mean twenty-one years in this new place. *How exciting.*

They pulled into the circular driveway in front. The building didn't look that old, but Harold tried to imagine how it would deteriorate in twenty-one years — paint peeling, cement disintegrating, wood warping. Then he thought how he would degrade in that same

3

amount of time. Maybe this building and he were made for each other after all.

Petunias, begonias and roses lined the sidewalk leading to the entrance. Harold had been interested in gardening when Jennifer was alive, but after she succumbed to pancreatic cancer, he had lost his desire to putter in the garden. Frankly, he had lost his desire for everything. He hardly read, spent little time with their previous mutual friends, didn't even get excited by watching Bronco games on the tube. His one activity had been walking. Long walks along the Platte River, into the foothills, up in the mountains. The wind in his face, the sun on his white but still full hair, the exhilaration of reaching the crest of a hill. This was all life held for him now. And he was convinced things wouldn't get any better in this new domicile. He could keep walking, but what did this joint have in store for him? He'd probably be bored to tears.

Into his mind splashed the image of an old, wrinkled man sitting in a wheelchair with a blanket over his lap, staring into space, while drool from a toothless open mouth dribbled down his chin.

Get a grip.

Harold opened the car door as a gentle summer breeze ruffled his hair. He automatically smoothed the out-of-kilter strands. Not that it mattered how he looked. A remnant from the days he had sold insurance. Keep up appearances. No one wanted to buy from a slob. He had learned that his first year in business. Now he didn't have anything to sell. A geezer settling in to bide his time until he could rejoin his wife.

Then a concern struck him. "Did you pack my walking poles?"

Nelson came around the side of the car and smiled at Harold. "You bet. I made sure those were in the boxes shipped over. Everything's up in your new room. I'll stick around to help organize."

Not that he had much to unpack. After sorting through the meager belongings he wanted to keep, he had donated everything else to Goodwill. Nelson, the top notch realtor, would take care of selling the house. Harold had enough savings and social security to pay the retirement home bills. One less responsibility. Keeping the house up had become a chore in the last two years. He had no desire to paint, fix leaky pipes or clean. Now someone else would be responsible for all these things for him. He'd have to wake up, dress and eat meals served to him, but nothing more would be expected of him. He could sit back and relax. He pictured the play *Annie* with Rooster and Lily St. Regis dancing around and singing about "Easy Street." Now he was embarking on his own version of "easy street." *How exciting.*

He caught himself. *Now, don't turn into an old curmudgeon.* No sense becoming Harold, the grouch. He took a deep breath. He'd have to be thankful for what he had — health, all organs working, minimal arthritis, mental faculties still clicking most of the time, eyes and ears functioning at a hundred percent. *Quit feeling sorry for yourself.*

He straightened and squinted at the building again. Six stories of people. Who were they, where had they come from, and why did they end up here of all places? Think of it as a challenge. People to meet. Maybe someone to share stories with. Everyone living here had his or her own history — happiness, tragedy, laughter, sadness. Think of the people he'd get to know. Think of all the old withered bodies limping around in there. He slapped his cheek. *Come on, stay positive.*

"What do you think, Dad?"

If only Jennifer had lived, I wouldn't be in this place. "I think I'm here and will make the most of it."

"That's the spirit."

Harold and Nelson headed up the sidewalk to the main entrance of the retirement home. Harold suddenly pictured an image from the movie, *The Green Mile*, with a long hallway, the footsteps echoing down the corridor as someone shouted, "Dead man walking!"

As they reached the building, a man burst through the automatic door, waving his hands at them. He appeared to be in his forties, wore a neatly pressed gray suit and pumped Harold's hand with enthusiasm. This guy would have made a good insurance salesman.

"Mr. McCaffrey. We've been waiting for you to arrive. I'm Peter Lemieux, the residence manager. I'm here to accompany you up to your apartment."

Don't think I can find it on my own? Keeping the thought to himself, Harold answered, "It's kind of you to greet me at the door."

"Of course." A huge smile crossed Peter's face. Harold realized it was even genuine. This guy enjoyed his job. A good sign. "Come with me."

5

Peter led them to a reception desk. "Mr. McCaffrey, meet Andrea. Andrea, Mr. McCaffrey is our newest resident."

She wiped a strand of blond hair from her forehead, stood and held out her hand. "It's a pleasure to meet you. If you have any questions, stop by or give me a call. Just hit zero on your room phone, and it will ring this desk. You'll meet the other receptionists Stacie, Pam and Brenda. We work as a team, so don't hesitate to call any time, night or day."

Harold took her warm hand and regarded her twenty-something, perky face. It was good to see she could stay cheerful with all the old fogies around this place. If she could do it, he supposed so could he.

"You're like a ray of sunshine." He gave her hand a squeeze.

She reddened slightly and squeezed back. "Thank you. You'll find we all enjoy seeing our residents. Oh, and here's your residents' directory." She released his hand, reached under the counter and retrieved a booklet. "This has a listing for everyone in Mountain Splendor, both residents and staff." She thumbed through and handed it open to Harold. She pointed to the page. "You'll notice we already have your name and room number listed."

Trying to make sure I don't back out? Harold instead said, "How thoughtful."

"Oh, Mr. Lemieux," Andrea said. "I meant to tell you. That detective is speaking with Mr. Salton and wants to talk to you as well about the missing woman."

Peter looked wildly around and leaned toward Andrea. "We... um...shouldn't be discussing that."

She turned beat red. "Oops."

Peter let out a long sigh. "Anyway, I'll look for him after we get Mr. McCaffrey settled."

Harold wondered what was going on in this new home of his. He raised an eyebrow. "Missing woman?"

Peter put his arm around Harold's shoulders to guide him past one set of elevators and down a hallway toward another elevator bank. "Someone apparently wandered off. Nothing to worry over. Now, Mr. McCaffrey, you're in the Back Wing. The elevators we just passed are for the Front Wing. They're color coded as well. Green doors for the Front Wing, Red for the Back Wing."

Must think we're all forgetful old fools. "That will be easy to keep straight," Harold replied.

"And posted in each elevator you'll find the schedule for the day. It includes the times for each of the three meals and all the planned activities. There's also a weekly resident newsletter put under your door on Sunday. It includes everything happening for the next week, so you can pick and choose what interests you."

What if nothing interests me? Harold pushed the thought aside. "That sounds very convenient."

An elevator arrived, the red door opened and a woman stepped out. "Hi, Pamela," Peter yelled. "Meet our newest Back Winger, Harold McCaffrey. Harold, this is Pamela Quint."

They shook hands, and Harold almost grimaced. The old broad had quite a grip. And ice cold. He regarded her more carefully. Her gray hair spiked out behind her as if she'd been flying. "Good to meet you," he mumbled

"Eh? What'd you say?" She held her hand to her ear and tilted her head. "I'm a little deaf."

"Good to meet you," Harold shouted.

She gave a curt nod. "Likewise. I'm sure I'll see you around the Back Wing." She headed toward the reception desk.

Peter, Harold and Nelson entered the elevator.

Harold immediately spotted the huge notice written in large type. An aerobics class would be held in the wellness center at two this afternoon, an art class at four in the activity room and dinner from five-thirty until seven, main course chicken marsala. Although, Nelson had treated him to lunch at Arby's on the way over, his stomach rumbled. At least he would be feasting tonight.

"When we came here to visit before, a woman named Ruth showed us around," Harold said.

"Well…uh…yes. She passed away three days ago."

"Oh." Harold figured he would have to get used to this type of occurrence. He pictured an ambulance pulling up every morning for the daily purge. He let out a deep sigh. One day the pick-up would be for him. How much longer did he have? Was this place the next step on the slippery slope to oblivion?

When they reached the fourth floor, Peter strode out of the elevator and led the way toward Harold's apartment.

The hallway had good clean brown carpet, neatly hung photographs of mountain scenes and freshly painted walls with no dirty hand prints or blood spatter. Harold recognized one picture of Bear Lake in Rocky Mountain National Park. He sniffed. A touch of Clorox but no whiff of puke or rotten food. He looked for any sign of human inhabitation. "No one around?"

Peter came to an abrupt stop. "Well…uh…a lot of night people in the Back Wing. You'll see more residents here later."

Harold looked at his watch. 1:30. "At this hour shouldn't there be people coming back from lunch?"

Peter frowned. "Most Back Wingers don't use the dining room."

"Well, I'm a morning person. Bed by ten and up at six. And I don't plan to prepare any of my own meals."

Peter forced a smile. "That's the beauty of Mountain Splendor. To each his own. You can eat and sleep on your own schedule as you choose. Remember, the dining hall is on the second floor, but be sure to acquaint yourself with the meal hours." He opened the door and ushered them inside the one bedroom apartment.

"Here's your key." Peter pointed to a gold key dangling from a stretch band hung on the inside doorknob. "We find this is a good place to keep it, so when you get ready to go out and reach to open the door, you'll find it."

Great. As if I'm that addled that I couldn't find my key. Then he remembered losing his keys. "I guess that will be a good place to keep it," Harold replied.

Harold's furniture was all in place. He had kept a brown couch that turned into a bed, his favorite easy chair, an entertainment center replete with television, stereo, CD and DVD player and a pole lamp. Along one wall rested stacked cardboard boxes containing his clothes, books, knickknacks and miscellaneous grooming materials. He smiled to himself. And no pills. He might be the only person his age who didn't have one of those little containers with the days of the week to take an assortment of red, green and yellow medication every morning. He patted his firm stomach and resisted the urge to strike a pose showing his biceps. *Healthier than your average geezer.*

Harold strolled into the bedroom. A momentary ache seized his chest when he saw the double bed he and Jennifer had shared. They had never converted to one of those king-sized monstrosities, preferring to snuggle close to each other. Now the memory of her would have to suffice for him. The rest of the room contained a dresser and night table with lamp. Sparse, but all he needed.

He thought back to all the paraphernalia cleaned out of his garage. The old sets of skis. He and Jennifer used to go downhill and cross country skiing. Another thing he had given up when she got sick. After that, the equipment only gathered dust in the corner of the garage. The lawnmower had been easy to part with. He didn't miss one little bit pushing it and hacking at the fumes.

The golf clubs had been difficult to give up, but then again he hadn't played since Jennifer became sick. One of his favorite activities for over fifty years—all the golf games, wagers with his buddies, even a few tournaments, all gone. The desire to hit a golf ball disappeared with that first diagnosis of Jennifer's cancer. He had given his clubs to Nelson who played golf sporadically.

And he had donated all the tools he had once used to build cupboards, repair clogged drains and add a grab bar in the shower as Jennifer lost strength. He bit his lip at the memory of the time she became so weak he had to lift her in and out of the tub.

"I'll leave you two to get settled," Peter announced and then scrambled out the door.

"Well, Dad, what do you think?"

Harold went over and parted the curtains in the living room. His fourth floor view showed a glimpse of foothills between two trees. He could also make out the letter M for the Colorado School of Mines on the side of Mount Zion. *Will I make any friends here or end up a recluse looking out my window all day?* "Not bad. I can see some nature outside."

"Let's get you unpacked," Nelson said.

Father and son spent the afternoon opening boxes and putting things away. Harold had a small but adequate closet to contain his slacks, long sleeved shirts, sweaters, sweat suits, jackets and shoes. He stored his walking poles in the corner of the closet and tucked away other clothing in the dresser.

Within two hours they had everything distributed, and Nelson had torn down the cardboard boxes and lugged them to the recycling bin by the loading dock.

He returned and dusted his hands. "All shipshape, Dad."

Harold sat in his familiar easy chair and surveyed his new domain. "Yup. My home away from home."

"No, Dad, your new home."

What have I done? Harold let out a sigh. "Yes. My new home."

CHAPTER TWO

After Nelson left, Harold resisted the urge to curl up in a ball to take a nap. Instead, he sat in his easy chair reading the James Patterson novel he had started the night before. He couldn't concentrate. He read two pages, and then his gaze lifted from the printed page to the blank white walls of his new apartment. What had he gotten himself into?

He looked at his watch. Almost time to eat. He decided he wouldn't be the first to arrive for dinner. After struggling through a few more pages, he leaned back to contemplate his new existence.

He wondered again if he would make any new friends here. Many acquaintances his age had moved away to Florida or Arizona or upward to their place in the sky, so his old crowd had pretty much dissipated. Also, after Jennifer died, he lost touch with some of the couples they used to have dinner with or join at the theater. He felt out of place with married people, now being a widower. He had gone to the senior center several times for lunch but lost his motivation for that as well. Someone tried to get him to join a widows and widowers group, but the idea didn't appeal to him. Maybe he had turned into an old curmudgeon after all. He remembered seeing some old guys sitting around the senior center, munching on their chow but not making eye contact with anyone. Is that what he had turned into?

There would certainly be many things to do around Mountain Splendor. But could he get up the gumption to join in? From the brochure he had read and the tour he had taken, he knew Mountain Splendor offered an exercise room, swimming pool, Jacuzzi, shuffleboard court; various card groups, concerts and trips. Right now none of these appealed to him. He again resisted the urge to sneak into the bedroom for a quick nap.

Would he drift away into staying in his room except for showing up at mealtime? That would be no life. He was still young, physically fit and possessed all his marbles. He sighed deeply. What would become of him?

Closing his eyes, he watched an abstract pattern of red jiggle across the background of black. He couldn't concentrate, couldn't fall asleep. He was in limbo in more ways than one. *Yuck.*

He opened his eyes and checked his watch again. 5:55. He put the book down, realizing he had become distracted and hardly read at all. He stood, stretched and headed for the door. His hand grazed the knob, and he felt the key hanging there. He removed the stretchy band, locked the door and dropped the key in his pocket. Maybe this was a good system, particularly for distracted geezers.

As he moseyed toward the red elevators, he noticed the hallway still remained deserted. After pushing the down button, he waited in silence. No TV, no radio, no loud voices. Not a peep out of anyone. Then a distant whirr and the elevator arrived. He stepped in, finding he had the cabin to himself. He punched the button for the second floor. As it descended, he looked at the schedule for the next day. Breakfast from six to seven-thirty. Water aerobics at nine. Pottery at ten-thirty. Lunch from eleven-thirty to one. A speech on how to make or modify your living will at two. A cribbage tournament at four. Dinner from five-thirty to seven. What an exciting day in store for him. The elevator didn't stop on the third floor. Harold wondered if anyone besides Pamela Quint and he lived in the Back Wing.

He made his way to the dining room and found it crammed full of geezers and crones, with a heavy weighting on the female side of the equation. Plates rattled, chairs scraped and the aroma of grilled chicken permeated the air. He spotted one table with an open spot. Two women and one man sat there. He approached the table.

"May I join you?"

One of the women and the man continued to shovel soup in their mouths as if they hadn't eaten in a week. The other woman looked up momentarily, waved a hand toward the open chair and took a bite of salad.

Chatty group. "I'm Harold McCaffrey. Just moved here."

Three heads nodded, but apparently the food caught their interest more than he did. He put some ranch dressing on the salad sitting closest to him, picked up a fork and began munching. When the two soup slurpers had finished, the man dabbed his mouth with a napkin, burped and said, "Big news. Did you hear that a woman from the Front Wing went missing today?"

Harold perked up. Andrea at the front desk had mentioned something earlier, but Peter Lemieux had brushed the comment aside.

The salad-eating woman dropped her fork, and it clattered onto her plate. She gasped as her hand flew to a small red birthmark the shape of a leaf on her left cheek. "Anyone we know?"

"No, Sandra, didn't catch her name. She was new, only been here six months, but from your sixth floor."

The other soup eater hacked like she had swallowed wrong and said, "Never go up there. The heights make me dizzy."

At that moment a waiter arrived and placed a plate of chicken, mashed potatoes and peas in front of everyone at the table.

"I love the chicken," the man said.

The one referred to as Sandra said, "That's because you can't even tell the difference between poultry and beef."

"Sure I can. The beef's harder to cut."

Everyone dug in, conversation obviously secondary to stuffing their faces. The room reverberated with clacking plates, banging silverware and the general background of primarily high-pitched voices.

Harold took a bite and discovered the chicken was juicy and tender with a delicious creamy mushroom sauce. He swallowed and surveyed the room—nearly all full tables with mass mastication in full flight. Nearby, four women talked at the same time, waving their hands in the air between bites. Others ate in silence. The common denominator, everyone tore through their food like there was no tomorrow.

In five minutes his tablemates had cleaned their plates. Then they began on the pieces of chocolate cake already on the table.

When Harold realized no one intended to introduce themselves or say anything to him, he asked, "Where do all of you live?"

The man took a last bite of cake and dropped his fork on the table. "I'm from the third floor."

"Front or Back Wing?" Harold asked.

The man scrunched up his nose, and his mouth opened and closed several times like a beached fish. "Front Wing of course. You nuts?"

Harold flinched. "I live in the Back Wing."

It was as if red hot pokers had goosed the three of them simultaneously. They shot upward, dropped their napkins on the floor and dashed for the exit as fast as their old legs could carry them.

Harold sat there with his jaw slack. He used the opportunity to pop in the last bite of chicken. Then he reached for the cake. He had no intention of letting it go to waste even with his companions deserting him.

Off to the side Peter Lemieux was making the rounds of tables and speaking to people. When he approached Harold's table he said, "Eating alone?"

"I had three tablemates here, but they left in a hurry. Very strange. They never introduced themselves. I overheard one woman's name was Sandra. She had a birthmark on her cheek."

"That's Sandra Vickery. Long time resident. I'll be happy to introduce you to some other people."

Harold took another bite of cake, savoring the rich chocolate frosting. "That's all right. I'm almost done with dinner."

Peter moved on, and Harold proceeded to finish his dessert before rising to leave the room. He became caught in a wave of people heading out the door. They all proceeded to the green elevators for the Front Wing. He was the only one who continued on to the Back Wing red elevator bank. Strange.

As he stood by himself ready to push the up button, he changed his mind and hit the down button. When the empty elevator arrived he went to the first floor and strolled outside. The evening sun had turned the fluffy clouds above to orange. He admired his new home. Not bad really. He noticed a path winding through the grounds and began walking, passing a couple his age sitting in a gazebo. They held hands. Ah, young love. He'd had his chance but probably never again. The hollow place in his chest throbbed. He'd never get over missing Jennifer. With a deep sigh, he continued his solo promenade.

The path led him to a back parking area and he spotted a hiking trail in the open space behind the retirement community. He continued on through the late summer dried grass until the clouds had turned from orange to pink. It was nice to be outside as night descended. He would have to continue on this trail during daytime on another occasion.

His thoughts turned to the dinner. What kind of people lived here? From that experience, not very friendly ones. Would he suffer through meals like that three times a day? If the pattern repeated the next day, would he end up sitting by himself with only his salad keeping him company? Or should he always eat in his room? He had the option of preparing frozen dinners in his kitchenette. *Yuck*. That didn't appeal to him. Maybe he'd find more friendly people the next day. And that pleasant woman named Ruth who had given him a tour. Dead. If he did make friends would they go the same way? Get friendly with people one day, and the next day they kick the bucket? What kind of life was that?

He mentally slapped his cheek. *Come on, stay positive. Don't write the place off before you get to know it.* Still, he didn't have that good a feeling about the people here. And a missing woman? Maybe she had become fed up with the unfriendly residents and hit the road without notifying anyone. Would he eventually want to bail out of here?

He turned around and by the time he reached the building, the last wisps of pink clouds had turned to gray. He was fortunate to live in Colorado. All the natural beauty, places to hike and scenery to enjoy. Maybe he could become a hermit up in the mountains. No, he didn't like cold winters where he'd be out for long periods in the snow. He'd get by with his heated apartment and see what happened next.

As he approached the building he spotted a man in overalls picking dead leaves out of a flower bed. Harold stopped and cleared his throat. "Are you the one who keeps all the posies here looking so good?"

The man straightened, and Harold saw they were approximately the same age. "Yeah, I've enjoyed gardening all my life. When I moved here I decided to volunteer to help with the landscaping."

Harold held out his hand. "Harold McCaffrey. I just moved here."

The man clasped his hand with a firm grip. "Ned Fister. I've been kicking around here for several years."

"What advice would you give to a newcomer?"

"You living in the Front or Back Wing?"

"Back Wing."

Ned eyed him warily. "You don't look like a Back Winger."

"Do they have a particular look?"

Ned shrugged. "Some do. Different crowd, although I've never had any trouble with any of them. Now the Front Wing where I live, that's another story."

"How so?"

Ned removed a clod from his overalls. "A number of highfalutin types who think they're better than anyone else. I'm just a common guy who likes to get his hands dirty."

"I'm not much for the high society crowd myself. You seem to be a down-to-earth kind of guy, Ned."

Ned laughed. "Good one."

Harold heard a pop and humming sound like a bee and the cuff of his trousers struck his leg. "What was that?" He looked down. "There's a hole in my pants."

"Tarnation. It's the blasted Perforator again."

"Perforator?"

"Yeah. There's some yahoo who shoots a BB gun at people's pants legs. Look at what he's done to me." Ned displayed the cuffs of his overalls that looked like moths had feasted on the material. "Since I'm out here often, I'm one of his favorite targets."

"Has he ever hit your leg?"

"The only redeeming quality with this jerk—he's a good shot. He hits cloth every time."

Harold looked up toward the hillside where the shot must have come from. "Have you called the police?"

"Numerous times. They haven't been able to catch the culprit. Wear old pants when you're wandering around here."

"I'll remember that."

Ned dusted his hands. "It's getting dark, I better go shower. Nice meeting you, Harold. See you around."

Harold headed to the Back Wing elevators, punched the button and waited for the door to open. Again, no one entered with him. The cab ascended and didn't stop until it reached the fourth floor. When he stepped out, it was as if the world had changed. Doors to apartments were open. People clustered in the hallway, laughing. At the other end of the hall, a woman shouted a greeting to another woman. It reminded him of a college dorm in the evening. Where had all these people been earlier? Obviously, there were a lot of night people living on his floor.

CHAPTER THREE 🦇

Harold awoke. It was still dark, and he could hear two female voices. Was he dreaming? No, the sound was distinct. Mighty thin walls in this place. That's something he hadn't thought of when he'd made the decision to move here. The fourth floor had been so quiet yesterday afternoon that he never considered this might be a problem.

He rubbed his eyes and turned on the light on the night table. Wait a minute. The voices sounded like they came from his living room. He swung his legs off the bed, put on his slippers and in his Denver Bronco pajamas padded into his living room.

Two women sat on his couch wildly gesticulating with their arms. One was pencil thin with frizzy hair and a bony, jutting chin. She was dressed all in black. The other had a pleasant face, highlighted with high cheek bones, and wore a flower print dress that displayed some respectable curves. He gaped at finding his living space invaded. Who the heck were these people and how did they get in?

They gazed up at him, and the skinny one pointed at him, saying, "Who let in the riffraff? This is a private discussion, and we don't appreciate being interrupted. Who are you and what are you doing in our meeting room?"

Harold put his hands on his hips and summoned his most authoritarian insurance salesman voice. "No, the question is what are you doing in my living room?" He realized he didn't look very threatening in his pj's, maybe even laughable, but darn it, this was his apartment.

The flower print woman smiled at him. "We didn't realize someone had moved in, although in hindsight it should have been obvious

18

with all the new furniture. There used to be an old gray sofa and matching chair, but your couch is much more comfortable. Viola and I have been meeting here for the last month. By the way, I'm Bella Alred and my friend here is Viola Renquist. We're your neighbors on each side." She stood, stepped over to Harold and held out her hand.

Remembering the cold hand of the woman he had met the afternoon before, Harold was pleasantly surprised at the warmth of her gentle clasp. He felt an electric spark pass through his body. "Um...ah... pleased to meet you." He noticed that she was trim, with nice legs and quite well endowed. Maybe this place wouldn't be so bad after all.

Bella patted her curled, silver hair. "Since things become kind of crazy in the Back Wing at nights, we've been coming here as a nice quiet place to talk." She returned to the couch.

Viola leaped up. "Is he the one who's providing dinner?" She raced over and grabbed Harold by the shoulders.

He flinched at her vice-like grip. Dinner? What was this crazy woman talking about?

She leaned over and began nibbling on his neck.

He giggled. She didn't have any teeth, and it tickled.

"Viola, don't do that. You're not wearing your false teeth, so it won't do any good. Besides you shouldn't scare the nice man. He belongs here, and you'll have to get your dinner back in your apartment later."

Viola looked wildly around and slunk back to the couch, mumbling, "I don't know what this world's coming to when you can't even meet in peace without being interrupted by some weirdo in pajamas."

"You'll have to forgive Viola," Bella said. "She has dementia."

Viola stomped her foot. "I do not. My brain works fine. It's just that I can't remember anything."

Harold wiped the saliva off his neck with the back of his hand. He'd never been gummed before.

Viola opened her purse. "Now where are my false teeth? Hmmm. They're not in here."

"Did you lose them again?" Bella asked. "Again? I don't remember losing them before."

"Viola, you're always misplacing your teeth. Try to think where you had them last."

"I thought I had them right with me."

Harold noticed something pink and white under his couch. He reached over and picked it up.

Viola snatched it out of his hand. "Give me back my choppers." She thrust them in her mouth and grinned at him, displaying two long fangs on either side of her mouth. "There. That's better."

He winced. "Is that a Halloween costume?"

"No," Bella replied. "Those are merely her night teeth. Don't let them disturb you. So, who are you, and what are your special powers?"

Harold stood as tall as he could with as much dignity as his pajamas would allow, which, unfortunately, wasn't much. "I'm Harold McCaffrey. I moved in here yesterday. I don't have any special powers."

Bella eyed him. "Come now. All the residents of the Back Wing have special powers so don't be bashful."

He thought back over his insurance selling career and all that he had accomplished over his lifetime. He didn't have much to go on there. "My special powers...hmmm...I turned paper into money."

Bella arched an eyebrow, and then a smile crossed her face. "You an alchemist or have transformational ability?"

"Something like that." Harold couldn't take his eyes off Bella. "How did you get into my apartment?"

Bella gave a dismissive wave of her hand. "Oh, I let Viola in. I guess we should be going. I'm sorry we bothered you in the middle of the night. Viola, let's go see what Bailey and Tomas are up to." She stood.

Harold watched Viola jump up, race to the door and let herself out. When he turned back to face Bella, she had disappeared.

"Bella?"

He searched through his bedroom, hall and bathroom. She was nowhere in sight. He scratched his head. She had vanished.

CHAPTER FOUR 🦇

Harold didn't sleep well. All through the remainder of the night he heard strange noises and woke in fits and starts. Once he imagined Bella was in the room watching him. He figured he had been having a dream. Still, the image of Bella returned to his mind over and over. There was something about her...something very pleasing.

Then he remembered her disappearing act. How had she gotten in his apartment, and more importantly, how the heck did she get out? She hadn't walked out with Viola. He let out a deep sigh, chalking it up to his confusion at being awakened in the middle of the night and the trauma of finding strangers in his apartment.

He dressed in slacks and a long-sleeved shirt and headed to the red elevator to go get some breakfast. He pushed the down button and waited and waited. Finally, he sat down on a leather couch as he had no idea how long it would take for the elevator to appear. He figured that in this place if you woke up and didn't know which wing you were in, you could decipher your location by determining if you saw red or green elevators.

At that moment a man shuffled up holding onto a walker, stared at Harold and said, "I wouldn't sit there if I were you."

Harold felt the couch move as if it had mice running through it. He shot upright and turned to inspect it. It seemed to be a slightly different color than when he sat down. What was it with this place?

The man with the walker bumped close to Harold's foot.

Harold looked down and jumped back to avoid being impaled by the front struts of the walker.

"You should put tennis balls on the legs of that thing," Harold said.

"No way. I like it nice and sharp. Name's Kendall Nicoletti." He held out a hairy hand.

Harold shook it and scrutinized his companion. The guy looked as bald as a cue ball but had hair spiking out of the back of his shirt.

"You must be new to the Back Wing," Kendall said. "Meet Alexandra Hooper."

Someone tapped Harold on the shoulder.

He spun around and saw a squat woman standing there. Where had she come from? She wiggled her fingers and smiled at him. "Nice butt."

"Um...good to meet you. I'm Harold McCaffrey." At that moment the elevator arrived and Harold stepped in. "Either of you going down?"

Kendall shook his head, and Alexandra said, "No way."

Harold punched the button for the second floor and looked out at the two people still standing there, watching him. He noticed that the couch he had been sitting in had disappeared. He craned his neck, but the door closed.

He gently slapped his cheek as the elevator descended. Was he starting to show signs of dementia? Was it contagious? Had he caught something from that woman Viola who had invaded his room in the middle of the night?

The door opened, and he headed into the dining area, moseying over to where he'd eaten dinner last night. A woman had taken his chair. The three he had seen before didn't make eye contact with him.

Oh, well. He found a table by himself and ate his scrambled eggs and toast, while periodically looking up to see what others were doing. No one paid the least bit of attention to him sitting there alone. As he completed his last bite, he noticed the man who had never introduced himself at dinner staring at him. The guy quickly averted his gaze. Strange and unfriendly people in this place.

Would this be his fate at all future meals? Eating alone? There had to be someone in this room who wanted to conduct a conversation, exchange ideas, tell jokes or even just chew with others. So far no takers.

Harold scanned the rest of the room. He couldn't spot any of the people he had met from the Back Wing. No Viola Renquist, no Kendall

Nicoletti, no Pamela Quint, no Alexandra Hooper and, unfortunately, no Bella Alred. He could do without the rest of them, but he sure wouldn't mind seeing Bella again. He'd enjoy eating a meal with her. He wondered if she skipped breakfast or ate in her own apartment.

On his way out of the dining room, Harold stopped at the table where he'd eaten dinner. He waited for the occupants to acknowledge him, but not one of them lifted a head to make eye contact. Then an urge he couldn't resist came over him. He leaned toward them and said, "Boo."

The two women gasped. The man dropped his fork. It bounced off his plate sending a spray of egg yellow into his lap.

Satisfied, Harold continued on his way.

CHAPTER FIVE

At lunch Harold entered the dining room, spied the same group of people he'd harassed at breakfast, and thought of scaring them again, but judgment prevailed. Wondering if he would ever make any friends from the Front Wing, he looked around the room at people talking, some to each other and some to their plates of roast beef sandwiches and potato salad. The contrast struck him. This room oozed cold aloofness, compared to the odd but friendly people he had met in the Back Wing.

Then he noticed the gardener, Ned Fister, sitting at a table by himself in the corner of the room. Harold ambled over. "Mind if I join you, Ned?"

Ned looked up from a bite of sandwich. "Harold McCaffrey. Plop your butt down."

Harold took a seat. "Always sit by yourself?"

Ned jerked his thumb toward a table nearby. "I used to be over there with three biddies, but they spent all their time yammering over the new hats they planned to buy. I decided to have a little peace and quiet."

"I hope I'm not disturbing you."

Ned gave a dismissive wave of the hand. "I could tell from our brief conversation last night that you're real people. I'd welcome the chance to discuss something other than headwear." He squinted at Harold. "You don't look like a hat person."

"No, other than the occasional baseball cap."

They had a congenial discussion covering the Broncos (looking promising the next season), social security (small cost of living increase), food at Mountain Splendor (not bad), children (somehow surviving being raised), grandkids (hopefully inheriting the good traits of their grandparents) and the life of a widower (a real pisser). Ned had two kids and two grandchildren and enjoyed their infrequent visits.

Harold put his fork down and regarded his companion. "What do you think of the administration around this place?"

Ned shrugged. "Mixed bag. Most of the people are okay. Peter Lemieux is friendly and helpful, but the head honcho, Winston Salton, acts like he'd pick your pocket if you didn't keep your hand over your wallet."

"Haven't met him yet."

"I'm sure you'll have the displeasure." Ned wiped his mouth with a napkin and rose. "I need to get back to the petunias. A lot of work to do this afternoon, so I might as well take advantage of the good weather." He moseyed out of the room.

After Harold finished his main course, a waiter placed a platter of chocolate chip cookies on his table and scurried off to the next table. Harold selected one, bit into the freshly baked oozing warmth, closed his eyes at the pleasure and licked his lips as the succulent chocolate tingled his tongue. When he opened his eyes, a skinny man with a white moustache stood there.

"You going to eat all those cookies?" the guy asked. "No. I'll have one more and that will do it for me."

"Can Abner Dane have the rest?"

"Sure, who's Abner Dane?"

The man thumped his chest. "It's me. Abner loves chocolate chip. He can eat a dozen at one sitting."

Harold regarded Abner more closely. Wisps of white hair grew out of his head like wildflowers on a mountain slope. His chin also sprouted a few whiskers his razor had missed. "Have a seat and you can eat as many cookies as you want."

Abner dropped into the chair across the table from Harold. "Much obliged. Not enough cookies for Abner at his table. Greedy people tried to eat all of them and didn't remember how much Abner loves chocolate chip." He grabbed a cookie, popped it into his mouth and let out a satisfied sigh.

"You always refer to yourself in the third person?" Harold asked.

He nodded, leaned closer and whispered, "Abner is on a secret mission. He watches everything that goes on here. Many unanswered questions at Mountain Splendor. But Abner will get to the bottom of all the shenanigans. Just you wait." He grabbed another cookie and happily munched on it.

"You ever visit the Back Wing?"

Abner held up his two index fingers to form an X while shaking his head as if he were having a seizure. "Not on your life. Abner doesn't go to the Back Wing. No, no, Abner doesn't. Strange doings back there. Even stranger than what's going on in the Front Wing."

"Oh? What's happening in the Front Wing?"

Abner looked wildly around the room as though someone might be listening. He put a finger to his lips, leaned close to Harold and whispered, "Abner can't divulge the details, but there has been a disappearance. A strange disappearance."

Harold thought back to the two reports he had heard the day before. "Someone at dinner last night mentioned a woman had gone missing."

"Sshh," Abner hissed. "Abner has to be careful. Someone is out to get Abner. The walls have ears."

Since they sat in the middle of the room, Harold thought the ears would need better hearing than residents such as Pamela Quint. "Did you know the woman who disappeared?"

"Abner knows everyone and everyone knows Abner. Peculiar doings around here." He grabbed the last two cookies, stood up and dashed for the dining room exit.

Harold wiped his mouth with his napkin and dropped it on the table. He had obviously encountered the local nutcase.

At dinner Harold did not see Ned Fister, so he ate by himself. The people at the table he had visited the night before continued to avert their gazes, and Abner Dane didn't appear to solicit cookies. After a satisfying but lonely meal of halibut, Harold returned to his floor.

Interestingly, the leather couch he hadn't seen since before breakfast had reappeared, and now it seemed to be a different shade of brown.

Strange. He regarded it warily. He patted it and it seemed to let out a low moan. He took a step toward the hallway when who should be walking toward him but Bella.

She stopped in front of him and put a hand on his arm. "I want to apologize for disturbing your sleep last night."

Harold smiled. "It was a shock, but I enjoyed the opportunity to meet you."

She lowered her eyes demurely. "Likewise."

"I didn't see you at breakfast, lunch or dinner."

"No, like other Back Wingers, I don't use the dining room. I fix something for myself in my kitchenette."

"You're the second person who mentioned that people in this wing don't eat downstairs. Why's that?"

"You'll find out."

Harold rolled his eyes. "Come on, Bella. Don't give me such a cryptic response. I've noticed a lot of strange things around here. I'm trying to figure out what's going on."

She put a finger to her cheek. "I don't know how to put this but...I think you may have been assigned to the wrong wing."

"At least residents here act friendly. I tried to get to know some people from the Front Wing at dinner last night, and they acted downright rude. Then when I mentioned I lived in the Back Wing, they scattered like rodents leaving a sinking barge. This morning they wouldn't look at me. I did have fun by scaring the bejesus out of them though."

"Good for you. They're a snobby bunch."

"But what gives, Bella? How did you get in my apartment, and how did you leave? One moment you were there, and the next you were gone. I still can't figure it out. Then this morning I sat on a couch right here and afterwards it disappeared. Now it's back again but looks different. I'm not used to all this appearing and disappearing."

"Things are a little different in the Back Wing."

"I'll say."

Bella glanced over Harold's shoulder. "Maybe you should speak with Peter Lemieux. He could reassign you to the Front Wing."

Harold straightened. "Nope. I'm staying here for the time being.

Besides, I need to get to know my neighbors better."

"I'm not sure that's a good idea with Viola."

"I don't mean Viola. I mean my other neighbor."

Bella patted his arm. "Oh. That's sweet of you, Harold, but I'm not like other people you know."

"I've gathered that. Now, will you tell me what's going on around here, or do I have to apply my insurance salesman's persistence?"

"Well—"

At that moment the PA system crackled to life. "This is Peter Lemieux. I need to have all residents of the Back Wing meet me in the Back Wing first floor lounge. Repeat, all residents of the Back Wing please come immediately to your first floor lounge."

Harold turned toward the elevator. The couch had disappeared again, and Alexandra Hooper stood by the elevator punching the down button.

Doors banged, and soon a crowd had gathered by the elevator. "This will take forever," Harold said to Bella. "Let's use the stairs."

They entered the stairwell and joined a procession of other people heading toward the first floor.

"You were going to tell me something," Harold said over his shoulder to Bella.

"This isn't the right time. We'll discuss it later."

They emerged from the stairwell and followed the crowd to the lounge. Folding chairs had been set up, but soon people filled all of these. The walls were covered with pictures of animals including a large wolf and bats in a cave. Harold watched as several familiar faces appeared. Someone shouted, "We need more seats in this room. Alexandra, can you do something to solve that problem?"

"Nope," Alexandra called out. "You're stuck."

Peter Lemieux sauntered into the room and waited until people had lined the back wall of the lounge. He cleared his throat. "Thank you all for assembling."

"You providing refreshments?" came a booming voice in the back. "No."

"We could call catering next door." This led to a loud roar of laughter.

Harold leaned toward Bella and tapped her on the arm. "I don't get it. The only building next door is a blood bank."

"Exactly."

"But—"

"Sshh." Bella held her finger to her lips. "Peter's talking."

"— and particularly for coming on such short notice, but we're here to discuss a very serious matter."

"Complaints from the Front Wing again?" someone muttered. "Those people always gripe about us."

Peter held his hand up. "Worse than that. A second woman from the Front Wing has disappeared. The Back Wing is being blamed for both missing people."

"We have nothing to do with those dipsticks," Alexandra roared.

An undercurrent of growls, groans and muttering gave Harold the impression of a group of surly teenagers being denied their music. He looked around the room. No smiles.

Peter cleared his throat. "Listen to me, people, and I…ah…use that word loosely. I need your help in this. I don't have any evidence that anyone from the Back Wing is responsible for the disappearances, but I'm under the gun to find out what's going on. I need your cooperation on this serious matter."

"It's probably some Front Wing yahoo trying to earn some extra poker money," one man said. "Probably selling teeth fillings and body parts."

"Now, now, Tomas. Don't be bitter," Peter replied.

Harold had heard Bella say that name last night. He regarded Tomas—a wiry old guy who had a pinched face as if it had been formed in a vise.

"Let the Front Wingers solve their own problems," Tomas said. "They wouldn't budge an inch if one of us fell over in the entryway. They'd step over our bodies and probably kick us as well. If their people are missing, they can deal with it."

"It's not that simple," Peter continued. "This affects the whole retirement home. All of you know I've been very supportive of your…ah…unique community in this wing. You need to work with me on this. May I have your complete cooperation?"

"Sure, sure," came a muttered response.

"I'd like to see a little more enthusiasm," Peter said. "I'm under pressure to close this wing."

Harold sat up, more alert. *Good grief.* He'd just moved here. Was he now to be kicked out on his heiny? How come he hadn't heard this before he moved in?

"Yeah, that's all we need," one voice groused. "To be tossed out in the street on our keisters."

Peter displayed his diplomatic smile. "That's why we all need to work together on this. I don't suspect anyone from the Back Wing has caused these problems, but I do need your participation and cooperation. Detective Deavers from the Golden Police Department will be here at two tomorrow afternoon. I have two volunteers from the Front Wing, and now I need two representatives from the Back Wing to join a residents' committee to assist with the investigation. Let's see some hands for volunteers."

Harold looked around the room. Not a person budged. Then a strange sensation shot through his arm. Before he knew what was happening, his right hand floated upward. He tried to pull it back, but it wouldn't respond. He grabbed it with his left hand, but it had a mind of its own and continued until it was straight over his head.

Peter pointed to Harold. "Good. We have one volunteer. One more."

Bella nudged Harold. "As long as you're jumping in, I'll join you." She raised her hand.

"Excellent." Peter smacked his lips as if he had just finished a hot fudge sundae. "Harold and Bella will represent the Back Wing. Any questions?"

Harold had lots of question starting with what was he doing here? His hand still remained aloft above his head, as though held by an invisible string.

"Yes, Harold."

His hand finally dropped like a lead sinker into a lake. "Uh...where will we be meeting?"

"In the Front Wing lounge on this floor."

"That's good," Tomas said. "We wouldn't want any of them in our part of the building. They'd leave their cooties all over the place."

"Now, now, Tomas." Peter shook a finger at the skinny little guy. "Don't be condescending with me." Tomas stood and hitched up his pants. "Those snobs won't even make eye contact with us."

"Well, there have been a few incidents, but we won't get into that today. If there's nothing else, meeting adjourned." Peter shot out of the room as if a rabid dog was chasing him.

"Now where are my false teeth?" Viola called out.

"They're on the empty chair next to you, dear," Bella replied. "Good thing no one sat there. That would have been quite a surprise."

Viola snatched up the false teeth and jammed them in her mouth. Then Harold saw it. A dog lifted its leg by the back wall.

"Tomas can't hold it again," Viola grumbled. "We need to get him doggy diapers."

Harold looked where Tomas had been sitting. The chair was empty.

CHAPTER SIX 🦇

Harold raced out of the room and spotted Peter repeatedly punching the up button by the elevator bank as if late for an important engagement.

Harold caught up to Peter and grabbed his arm. "I may have been put in the wrong place."

Peter spun around with his eyes wildly looking around the hallway and let out a deep sigh. "You and me both."

"I mean I'm different from the other people in the Back Wing."

"I know what you mean." Peter wiped beads of sweat off his forehead and jabbed the button again.

"Why wasn't I given a room in the Front Wing?"

Peter finally met Harold's gaze and let out another breath. "A timing issue. Your son asked to get you right in, and you wanted a one bedroom apartment. The only one available was in the Back Wing. You might have had to wait for several months otherwise."

"What happened to the previous resident of my apartment?" Harold asked.

"She flew…uh…went away. Decided she no longer wanted to live in a retirement community."

"If I decide to, will there be an opportunity for me to move into the Front Wing when an apartment opens up there?"

The elevator arrived, and they both got in.

Peter pushed the button for the second floor. "I can look into it. Can't make any promises though."

Harold pressed the button for the fourth floor. "Let me know."

After Peter exited, the elevator continued its ascent, rocked slightly and ground to a halt. Harold stepped out and returned to his room, contemplating the meeting he had just attended and the strange occurrences he had witnessed. He didn't know what to make of all of this. His life had certainly changed since arriving at Mountain Splendor. Should he stay here or insist that his son take him away from this crazy place? Harold took a deep breath and decided he'd give it another day.

At two o'clock the next afternoon Harold entered the Front Wing lounge, similar to the Back Wing lounge but with mountain scenes rather than animal pictures on the wall. A man in his thirties in a brown suit sat next to an old woman with puffy, silver blue hair firmly frozen in place.

Harold sat down as a man his age in a cardigan sweater strode in followed by Bella. At the sight of her, a warm jolt passed through his chest. Once everyone had taken a seat, the young man began. "I'm Detective Deavers. I've been assigned to investigate the two missing women. I'd like each of you to introduce yourselves."

The older man ran his hand through his still full head of white hair. "I'm Atherton Cartwright. Retired lawyer. I'm here to help determine what happened to those two unfortunate women. I'm prepared to utilize any of my vast professional experience and contacts to assist you any way possible, Detective."

The woman patted him on the knee. "Why yes, you will make a superb contribution to this committee, Atherton." She turned toward Deavers. "I'm Martha W. Kefauver, DAR. The W is for Washington. I'm a descendent of our first president." She held her chin up high enough that Harold could see the full wattle of her throat.

"I'm Bella Alred. My illustrious descendents go back far before the American Revolutionary War. They include some of the most enchanting celebrities from early England. Jolly what?"

Harold had to suppress a laugh. He took a deep breath. "I'm Harold McCaffrey. I'm new to Mountain Splendor. This is my third day here. I don't know what I can contribute to this effort, but I'll do what I can."

"And your previous profession, Mr. McCaffrey?" Atherton raised an eyebrow high enough to make his face look lopsided.

Harold looked at his inquisitor and wondered if the turtle neck under the guy's sweater still had the cardboard inside from the original package. "I provided financial protection through insurance policies so widows and widowers could afford to live in a place like this."

Atherton jutted his jaw out. "Ah, I see. An insurance peddler."

Harold gave his best professional smile. "Exactly. I even helped a few lawyers, in spite of themselves."

"Okay, let's get going," Deavers announced. "I asked Peter Lemieux to round up two of you from each wing, and I appreciate your joining me this afternoon. I'd like to let you know what has been uncovered so far in our investigation and enlist your assistance in working with the residents in both wings to help find any further information regarding the disappearance of Hattie Jensen and Frieda Eubanks."

"Why yes, we'll be like assistant detectives." Martha stroked her coiffure, and the whole thing jiggled.

Deavers narrowed his gaze at her. "Not exactly assistant detectives but additional eyes and ears. In a place as large as this, I can only spend so much time interviewing people, but with you being here all the time, you should be able to speak to your fellow residents and provide additional information that I can follow up. In a community such as Mountain Splendor you may be able to hear something that will be extremely useful to the investigation. Are you all willing to help?"

"Oh, yes," Martha replied. "I would be delighted. I always contribute to worthy causes."

"Righto," Atherton added. "I'm willing," Bella said.

Harold nodded. What was he getting himself into now? He thought he had been sent out to pasture to read and watch television.

Now he was helping with a police investigation. He had no training in this line of work. He'd once considered attending a citizens' police academy, but his schedule didn't permit it.

"Now for the facts of the case." Deavers pulled out a notepad and thumbed through it. "First, Hattie Jensen was reported missing the day before yesterday. A member of the staff went to her apartment on the sixth floor of the Front Wing at eight in the morning to make sure she took her medicine. She wasn't there, the bed looked like it hadn't been slept in, and her medicine container hadn't been touched. No indication of foul play but no sign of Hattie either."

"Anyone see her the night before?" Harold asked.

"Good question. She was last seen returning to her apartment after watching a movie in the lounge." He looked at his notepad again. "At approximately nine o'clock."

"Oh, yes. That Fred Astaire and Ginger Rogers film. How that man could dance." Martha fluttered her eyelids at Atherton. "You're quite a dancer yourself, Mr. Cartwright."

He cleared his throat. "Yes, well, I spent a number of years in a ballroom dance club. I still participate whenever possible."

Deavers tapped his pad again. "No one saw Hattie Jensen after that."

"Did she ever go visit friends or family at night?" Harold asked.

Deavers looked more closely at Harold. "She has a cousin living in Englewood. She stays there over Thanksgiving and Christmas but was not scheduled to visit the night she disappeared. No other indications of going out at night."

"Anything missing from her apartment like she had packed a suitcase to go somewhere?" Harold asked.

"Her cousin came and checked everything yesterday afternoon. All of Hattie's things seemed to be there from what her cousin could tell. Her cousin mentioned that Hattie always wore a large diamond ring surrounded by rubies, so she expected that to be with Hattie, wherever Hattie had gone."

"And I assume no staff members reported seeing her in the building or wandering around the grounds," Bella said.

"No. She just vanished." Deavers snapped his fingers. "Now the second case. Frieda Eubanks lived on the fifth floor of the Front Wing. Similar situation. She was last seen after dinner the night before last and was discovered missing yesterday morning when a staff member went to her apartment to return her laundry."

Harold raised his hand.

Deavers waved toward Harold. "And to answer your same questions, she has cataracts and no longer drives at night. And like Hattie Jensen's apartment, her bed didn't appear to have been slept in. With both disappearances we can only conclude that something happened to them at night between the time they returned and would have gone to sleep."

"Unless someone went to the trouble of making the beds," Harold added.

The corners of Deavers's mouth turned up ever so slightly. "Sure you weren't an insurance investigator and not a salesman, Mr. McCaffrey?"

Harold shrugged, "Just drawing a logical possible conclusion."

"You're correct. Someone could have made the bed so it looked like the disappearance took place earlier than it really did. And there is other evidence to support that theory. People were still on both floors returning to their apartments after both women went to their own rooms. Several hours later, both halls would have been deserted. Still, we have no definitive timeframe on exactly when both women went missing."

"Does any evidence indicate whether they left on their own accord or were abducted?" Harold asked.

"Nothing definitive. I would surmise that they did not leave by themselves, but I can't prove it yet."

"Did the two women know each other?" Bella asked.

"The only connection so far is that they occasionally played in the same poker group. Other than that I've found no indication that they associated with each other such as eating meals together. Again, I need your assistance. Please speak to people in both of your wings to see if you can find anyone who might have seen the missing women. I have pictures here for you to show." Deavers handed each of them two four-inch by six-inch photographs.

Harold scanned the pictures that had the names printed below. Hattie Jensen had a thin face, slight smile that showed deep dimples and wore granny glasses. Frieda Eubanks had a square jaw with lips pinched together. Other than gray hair, there was little similarity between the two women. He closed his eyes trying to image these women returning to their apartments and what happened next. He drew a blank and opened his eyes.

"Call me immediately if you have any additional information." Deavers handed a business card to each of the four people. "This has both my office number and my cell. Now, any additional questions?"

Atherton sniffed. "Martha and I will do anything we can to assist you, Detective, but why must we be required to associate with these kind of people?" He waved his hand toward Bella and Harold.

Harold felt the hair on the back of his neck bristle, and he clenched his fists. "What kind of people do you mean?"

"Well it's obvious, isn't it? Different, strange, not like us." Martha raised her wattle again.

Bella's eyes flared. "I'll say we're different. You two act like ignorant, malicious snobs, which we aren't."

Atherton looked above Bella's head. "I beg your pardon—"

"That's okay," Bella gave a devilish smile. "I forgive your intolerance." She turned toward Deavers. "Harold and I will help any way we can. And we'll even put up with these other two. Is there anything else, Detective?"

"No, I think we're done for now. I'll reconvene this group when I have anything else to share with you. In the meantime, let me know what you hear. Don't consider anything insignificant. Sometimes the smallest observation leads to a breakthrough."

Atherton and Martha shot to their feet.

Harold heard a faint sound and saw Atherton's pants zipper descend. "Oh, Mr. Cartwright," Bella cooed. "You're fly is open."

Atherton looked down, reddened and quickly raised his zipper.

Martha Kefauver took a step toward the door and her underpants fell around her ankles. She tripped and almost fell, catching herself on the chair Atherton had vacated. She reached down, pulled up her baggy white panties around her knees and stumbled out of the room. Bella clicked her tongue and smiled at Deavers. "Old people. Sometimes they have wardrobe malfunctions."

"Do you know how those two came to be selected for this committee?" Harold asked.

"Yeah. I was speaking with Peter Lemieux about the idea of forming a residents' group. Mr. Cartwright and Ms. Kefauver were standing nearby and overheard our conversation. They came right over and volunteered."

"And Peter Lemieux agreed?" Harold asked.

"Yes. He felt they could represent the Front Wing."

Bella held out her hand and the detective shook it. "Thanks for including us in the investigation. We'll start talking to people on our wing immediately and give you our full cooperation."

Harold also shook hands with Deavers and then followed Bella toward the elevators for the Back Wing. He couldn't hold back his laughter any longer. "Did you see the look on that old bat's face when she tripped on her undies? It was priceless."

Bella giggled. "I love it when snooty people get their comeuppance. But Martha Kefauver. There's something that doesn't feel right about her."

"Your female intuition?"

"Something like that. She's a phony if I ever saw one."

"There was something strange going on. Atherton didn't leave his fly open. It was almost as if some hidden force pulled it down when he stood up."

Bella took Harold's hand. "Imagine that."

CHAPTER SEVEN

A t dinner Harold found Ned Fister sitting alone again and joined him. "I think we're the only two guys in this room sitting together," Harold said.

"Four times as many women. These old broads wear us out and then keep going themselves. We geezers are a scarce commodity."

"Did you beautify the garden today?"

"That I did. Got the mums planted. Tomorrow on to begonias. I've signed up for an unlimited amount of work around this place."

"Except during winter."

"I do a little pruning and cleanup on nice winter days, but you're right, that's my quiet time of year. I can't complain. I enjoy puttering with flowers. Keeps me alive and kicking as long as the Perforator doesn't start aiming higher."

"He still bothering you?"

"Yeah, he shot me again today. Wiley cuss. I scan the hillside but can't spot the jerk. I think no one's there, and then zing, another hole in my overalls. I guess it's better than being stung by bees."

"I have a question for you, Ned. Two women have disappeared in recent days. I'm sure you've heard people discussing this."

"Darn tootin'. Hattie Jensen, a nice mousey woman and Frieda Eubanks who makes Attila the Hun seem like a pussycat. What a contrast." Ned let out a burst of air as if trying to rid his lungs of some unwanted foreign substance.

"Did you know them well?"

"Nah, but I saw them around enough. Particularly, Frieda. That woman was always after money. Had the nerve to hit me up for fifty bucks one time."

"How'd you handle it?"

Ned picked up his knife and slathered butter on a roll. "I told her I only made loans with collateral. That shut her up."

"You have any ideas why they would disappear?"

"Nope."

Harold twiddled the napkin in his lap. "Any enemies or people who disliked them?"

"I can't imagine anyone having a problem with Hattie. Frieda, on the other hand, pissed people off all the time. I don't think she had many loving fans around here."

"I'm on a committee helping the police investigation along with Atherton Cartwright and Martha Kefauver, who represent the Front Wing. Do you know them?"

Ned gave a derisive laugh. "Everyone knows those two. They make sure to be seen with their snouts in the air as they lord it over the other residents."

"That's the same impression I had. Still, I'm going to have to work with them."

"Good luck. Has Atherton given you his casino pitch yet?"

"Casino?"

"He thinks one should be built in Golden."

Harold shrugged. "That subject hasn't come up."

"And Martha will yammer all day that she practically runs Daughters of The American Revolution. She wants everyone to know that her blood runs red, white and blue. She considers everyone else foreign trash."

Harold chuckled. "She made that abundantly clear when she introduced herself."

"If your American roots don't go back to at least the eighteen century, she has no use for you."

"Well, that will cut me out," Harold said. "I'm second generation."

"Me too. Good thing. Anyway, I'd watch my back around those two." Harold put down his fork. "Oh?"

"I certainly wouldn't want to be on a committee with them. They always have their own agendas which focus on Atherton and Martha."

"I'll keep my eyes open."

After dinner Harold headed to the Back Wing lounge. He could now put up with being snubbed by some of the Front Wingers, since he had made one friend in Ned and was looking forward to seeing Bella that evening. She had told him she would gather the Back Wing residents for a meeting. And sure enough, the place was packed with people as he entered. It had the air of a party, rather than being a discussion of two missing women.

Bella waved Harold to a chair next to her facing the rest of the Back Wingers and then began speaking. "As you know, Peter Lemieux asked Harold and me to represent the Back Wing in a meeting this afternoon with the detective investigating the disappearance of the two Front Wing women."

"No great loss," someone mumbled.

Bella held up her hand. "As Peter told us, the Front Wingers think we did something, so we have to help find out what really happened. We met with Atherton Cartwright and Martha Kefauver from the Front Wing."

A collective groan passed through the crowd.

"I know they can be difficult people, but after the first meeting I think they're a little more humble." Bella winked at Harold.

"Those two probably killed the missing women and took their jewelry," a woman with bright red hair and too much rouge on her cheeks shouted out. "They only care about themselves."

"That may be the case, Bailey, but Harold and I have agreed to talk to all of you to see if we can uncover any clues regarding the disappearances. Harold, why don't you discuss the victims?"

"The missing women are Hattie Jensen and Frieda Eubanks. Hattie disappeared three nights ago and Frieda the night before last. I'll pass around their pictures." He stood and stepped over to the front row and handed the pictures to the woman Bella had called Bailey. She took the pictures and let out a loud belch.

A man two chairs over, who Harold had heard called Tomas at the previous meeting, said, "You'll have to forgive Bailey. She had something too spicy to eat this evening."

Bailey squinted at the pictures and then took a magnifying glass out of her purse to examine them more carefully. "Never seen them before." She handed the photographs to Viola.

"I don't remember them," Viola said.

"You don't remember anyone, Viola," Bella said.

"Well, I remember you, but I don't recognize these two yahoos. Now what the heck did I do with my false teeth?"

"You're wearing them," Bella said.

Viola put her hand to her mouth. "Oh." She passed the pictures on to Tomas.

He took a quick look. "Yeah, I've seen these old broads at bingo. One of them has a big mouth."

Harold returned to his chair and waited for the photos to circulate.

"After everyone has looked at the pictures, give them back to Harold. The detective has asked us to collect any information we can. You can contact either Harold or me, and we'll let the police know."

"That's good," Tomas said. "I don't want to spend time with the fuzz."

"No problem," Bella said. "Harold and I will be the interfaces."

"Can you speak up?" Pamela Quint shouted from the second row. "Sorry, Pamela," Bella bellowed. "I said that Harold and I will be the ones to speak with the detective so none of the rest of you needs to do that. Get any information to us, and we'll take it from there. But, Pamela, you might be able to help by doing a little surveillance of the Front Wing."

"Be happy to," Pamela shouted. "I'll see if I can get in a few people's hair. I love it when they scream."

"Now don't go causing any problems," Bella replied. "Just check things out. You may be able to spot something helpful. But please put in your hearing aids, so you'll catch what people say."

"What?"

"Use your hearing aids, dear," Bailey turned around and poked Pamela.

Harold leaned toward Bella and whispered. "Won't that cause a situation if Pamela goes into the Front Wing? Those people don't seem to want any of us around."

Bella whispered back, "She has her way of visiting. She'll be fine."

A hand waved in the back of the room.

Bella pointed. "Yes, Kendall?"

Harold recognized the man who had almost impaled him with the walker.

Kendall held up one of the photographs. "I've seen the one named Frieda Eubanks before. She uses the workout room. Short stocky woman. I also spotted her two nights ago heading out into the open space behind Mountain Splendor."

"Did you follow her?"

"Nah. I got distracted. A car went down the driveway. I chased it for a while."

"Get yourself a mouthful of tire rubber?" someone asked.

Kendall chuckled. "No, I'm not as fast as I used to be. Couldn't catch the dag-nabbed thing."

"What time was that?" Harold asked.

Kendall scratched the scraggly whiskers on his chin. "Oh, probably one A.M. or so."

"Did you see anyone with Frieda?"

"Nope. After my unsuccessful chase of the car, I went back in the building."

Harold's heart raced. They had a lead. Now he had to figure out what the heck Frieda was doing outside at one in the morning.

"Any other comments?" Bella asked.

Harold scanned the faces. No one else ventured anything. "Thanks again for meeting with us," Bella said. "Let us know anything new you find out."

As people began to leave, someone handed the two pictures back to Harold. He noticed that both photographs had two neat holes on the throats of the women.

CHAPTER EIGHT 🦇

Harold's eyes popped open. He checked the clock on his nightstand. 2:23 A.M. *Great.* He felt wide awake. He turned on the lamp and rubbed his eyes. He knew he wouldn't be able to get back to sleep without walking around for a while. This was the routine he had followed when living alone. He'd wander through his yard during warm weather or pace around his downstairs when the temperature dipped below forty degrees.

Putting on slippers and a robe, he grabbed his key, locked the door and headed toward the elevator. As he exited on the first floor he saw Kendall Nicoletti pushing his walker out the front door. No surprise. Insomnia, it seemed, was a frequent occurrence around this place, especially the Back Wing. Harold followed. A gibbous moon shone over the mountains casting shadows from the building across the wide lawn. A slight summer breeze caused Harold to cinch his robe tighter, and his gaze returned to where Kendall had limped toward the shrubbery. What was he up to?

With a clatter Kendall dropped his walker. Harold thought at first that the man had fallen over. He stared and to his amazement saw a bald wolf emerge from a bush. It stopped for a moment, croaked out a pitiful howl and limped off into the open space.

Harold dashed over to where the upturned walker rested. "Kendall?" He poked around the bush. No one there. He decided he better head into the building to report Kendall's disappearance. Did something happen to him like with the two missing women? What was going on around this place?

He had just reached the portico when something slammed into his face. Looking down he saw a bat flapping around on the ground.

"Harold, what are you doing out here?"

Harold turned to see Bella standing behind him with her arms crossed as if ready to scold a naughty boy in a schoolroom.

He looked back to where the bat had been and saw Pamela Quint sitting on the ground, holding her head. "Sorry about that," she said.

Harold's gaze ping-ponged back and forth between Bella and Pamela.

Pamela stood and dusted off her skirt. "Had a nice visit to the Front Wing but didn't find anything useful regarding the two missing women. I'll keep you two apprised." She headed off into the building.

"What...what?" Harold pointed after Pamela.

Bella took his hand. "Why don't you come with me? I think it's time we had a long chat." She led him to a bench in the garden. They sat down with a view toward the mountains, moonlight on their faces.

"I bet you're confused by all strange things you've seen in the last few days." Bella snuggled against him.

"Something happened to Kendall. And then Pamela..."

"I know. I want to assure you they're both fine." She patted his hand. "As you can tell, those of us living in the Back Wing are kind of different."

"I'll say."

"And I think you're owed an explanation."

Harold took a deep breath. He smelled the aroma of jasmine which reminded him of the garden he used to tend at home—the home he had given up. Then he remembered his first conversation with Bella. "When you appeared in my living room my first night at Mountain Splendor, you asked about my special powers. This all concerns special powers, doesn't it?"

She let out a long sigh. "It does. Kendall changes into a werewolf when the moon is out."

"I thought that only happened with a full moon."

"That's just a myth."

Harold shook his head. He had thought werewolves were a myth, but was beginning to realize nothing could surprise him around this place. "And Pamela changes into a bat."

"Exactly. She's pretty deaf and that affects her sonar. She runs

45

into things like your head. And Viola is a toothless vampire with dementia."

Harold's head reeled but it all fit. "I thought vampires couldn't age." Bella laughed. "Oh, the ideas people have. All those stories with teenage vampires, so strong and virile who keep in the same physical condition for hundreds of years. All fantasy. We people with special powers age just like the rest of you."

"And does Viola have to stay out of the sunlight?"

"Like most of us, she's a night person who usually sleeps during the day, but sunlight isn't going to make her turn into dust or anything. Another myth."

"But she drinks blood?"

"The vampires here like Viola and Bailey Jorgensen drink blood, but they only need it once a week or so at their age. They don't burn off the calories like they once did."

Harold shivered. "When Viola nibbled on my neck, was she trying to bite me?"

"An old habit. Having lost her teeth, she's completely harmless."

"Where does she get blood when she needs it?" Harold slapped his forehead. "I get it. The blood bank next door."

Bella put a finger to her cheek. "I could tell from the questions you asked the detective, you're sharp and notice things. That's why I thought it was time to clarify the situation around here."

Harold thought back to another of his weird experiences and burst out laughing. "And Alexandra Hooper shape-shifts into a couch."

"Right. And Tomas Greeley changes into a stray dog."

"With incontinence problems."

Bella hugged his arm. "Our special powers continue, but we suffer the various indignities of old age as any other members of the aging population."

"And your special powers, Bella?"

She turned her head toward him, and he saw her smile in the moonlight. "I think you've figured out some of those with your deductive reasoning. What conclusions have you reached?"

"Hmmm. That first night you disappeared. I guess you can walk through walls or something."

"Very good. What else?"

Harold chuckled. "You caused my arm to rise to volunteer, and you made Atherton's zipper and Martha's drawers drop. I'd say telekinesis is one of your skills."

"Very good. If I were living in seventeenth century Salem, I would be burned at the stake."

Harold couldn't believe he was having this conversation. He took in another deep gulp of Colorado nighttime air. "But obviously you're a good witch."

"Nothing but the best."

Harold regarded Bella thoughtfully. "Never having met a witch before, I have a question for you."

She gave him a wry smile. "Only one? As intuitive as you are, I thought you would have dozens."

"Well, one to start with. What was it like growing up as a witch?"

"Good question. My mother wanted me to fit in with other people, so I went to public school with all the regular children. I got along pretty well but had a tendency to play pranks on bullies and snobby kids."

"People like Atherton and Martha."

"Exactly. I remember one bully who liked to steal lunch money. He grabbed my lunch bag and ended up with more than he bargained for. After the scorpions crawled all over his body, he ran away screaming and never bothered me again. But I've made it a practice to use my special skills judiciously."

"I'd hate to be on your bad side, Bella."

She shook a finger at him. "Just you remember that."

Harold held up his hands in mock terror. "Don't worry, I will. Did you pursue any occupation after your school days?"

"I thought you only had one question."

Harold chuckled. "I lied. I probably have a thousand."

"I tried a number of different jobs along the way. I had to earn enough to provide Social Security for my old age. Unfortunately, there's no Witches Retirement Fund. I worked for a while at a casino. I enjoyed the night shift and met some interesting people."

"Uh-oh. I could see you increasing the house odds."

"No, actually I had the opposite problem. I ran a roulette wheel. I'd get so excited for some of the young newlywed couples gambling their future funds that my wheel had a propensity to pay off very well. I remember one young man who told me he had recently returned from Vietnam and wanted to go back to college. He emptied his pockets and put twelve hundred dollars on number thirteen. I figured anyone who did that deserved to win. I spun the wheel, put the ball in play and somehow the ball skipped over other numbers and ended up in thirteen. He was ecstatic, took his winnings and raced out the door. Unfortunately, the casinos track winnings and losses per employee to make sure they're getting their fair share. After I had consistently lost money for the house, I was fired."

"Too bad I never played when you were there."

"I would have let you win. I've always been a sucker for kind faces."

"So you never made it in the gambling industry. What else did you do?"

Bella put a finger to her cheek. "Let's see. I did a stint as a marriage counselor since I had gone to college and received a psychology degree. As an aside, I loved screwing up those psychology experiments by distracting people with things moving around where they shouldn't have.

"Anyway, back to marriage counseling. I think I helped a number of people, but I ran into one obnoxious couple who kept arguing in front of me the whole session. Finally, I became fed up and froze them from the necks down. I told them they could stay that way in my office until they worked things out. I came back two hours later, and they were still arguing. They pleaded to be unfrozen, but I refused. It took them six hours before they finally resolved their issues. Instead of thanking me, they filed a complaint, and I was fired from the counseling service."

Harold squeezed Bella's hand. "Some people have no gratitude. But you must have had some sustained career to be able to afford Mountain Splendor."

"I eventually settled on retail. I enjoyed helping shoppers find exactly the right thing they wanted. And I gained a reputation for always being able to locate exactly the right size and color in the stockroom, even when other clerks swore we were out of stock."

"Imagine that."

"So, Harold. In addition to your insurance career, how did you entertain yourself all those years?"

Harold caught himself looking off into the distance. "I used to love golf. I played it on the weekends or with clients during my working years, and four times a week after I retired...up until the time my wife died."

"I'm sorry."

"I haven't played since."

"You'll have to teach me some time," Bella said. "I've never tried the game."

Harold chuckled. "You'd be a natural. I could see you hitting a ball, and it would go straight down the fairway and then mysteriously keep hopping through the grass until it fell right into the cup."

Bella gave him a shocked look. "I wouldn't do that."

"Even if you had a big bet riding on the shot?"

"Remember what I told you of my casino career. I helped others but never benefited from it myself," Bella said, indignantly.

"I'm just kidding."

"I know." Bella rested her head on Harold's shoulder. "What do you think of this boring retirement home now?"

"I have to admit, I haven't lacked for interesting events and people thus far. Thank you for taking me under your wing, so to speak."

"I think we'll make a great team. Now, we have to solve the mystery of what happened to those two missing women."

"Hey, if a beautiful witch and a retired insurance salesman can't get the job done, who else can?"

CHAPTER NINE 🦇

The next day, Harold received a phone call from his son Nelson. "Just a reminder that Jason will be coming to stay with you. Emily and I will drop him off tomorrow afternoon around two."

A surge of warmth pulsed through Harold's chest. He had forgotten that his grandson would be coming for a week, while his son and daughter-in-law went off by themselves for their second honeymoon. "I'm looking forward to it. Also, it will be nice to spend a moment with Emily when you bring Jason over."

There was a pause on the line. "Um, Emily always likes seeing you, Dad, but Jason may not be that enthusiastic about staying with you. He's kind of upset that his mom and I are taking a trip to Hawaii and he doesn't get to go."

The heat in Harold's chest turned to an ice cube. He remembered how a kid felt when foisted off on someone. "So he's concerned that he'll be stuck with his decrepit grandfather and his old cronies."

"I hate to think of it in those terms, but that sums it up."

An idea began to form in Harold's devilish brain. *I wonder.* "What has Jason been reading lately?"

Nelson groaned. "Those ridiculous vampire books that all the teens seem so interested in. Kids flying around biting people's throats, causing mayhem and fighting with werewolves. That kind of trash."

"Good." *It just might work.* "Tell him that he will have a very unique experience while he stays with me."

"What does that mean?"

"I can't go into the details now. Just give him the message. I'll see you tomorrow when you drop him off."

That evening after dinner, Harold began to plan his program for Jason. He thought through all the people he had met on the Back Wing. What would work best with Jason? First, he checked the directory and looked up the room for Bailey Jorgenson. Jason would definitely want to meet her. She lived on his floor at the end of the hallway.

He had barely knocked on the door when a woman in a red silk caftan to match her red hair threw it open, squinted at him momentarily before grabbing his hand and dragging him inside. "It's about time. I knew you'd come to visit me eventually. Bella mentioned you."

Harold entered what looked like a room for a séance. Candles on every surface sent smoke up toward the ceiling. The curtains were closed, and a round red object stood in the center of a table in the living room. Harold didn't know what kind of strange ritual he had stumbled into.

"Take a seat." Bailey gave him a shove, and he landed in a chair. "Give me a moment while I finish dinner." Bailey sashayed over to the table, wafted some of the candle smoke toward her nose, leaned over and sank her teeth into the red object on the table.

Harold looked more carefully. It was a giant tomato.

She slurped at it until only the skin remained. "Ah, good."

"What were you doing?" Harold asked.

"Having my special Bloody Mary." Bailey wiped her mouth on her sleeve. "The last of my supply otherwise I'd offer you some."

Harold coughed as he thought of the coppery taste when he had once sucked on his cut finger. "I'm not into that, but I came here with a request."

Bailey peered at him. "I can't see your face very well. Don't be a stranger. Come on and move closer."

Harold scooted his chair up to the table and leaned toward the candles. "Bella has also told me a little about you, and I thought you might be able to assist me."

"Hmmm. What do you want?"

"Well…uh…my grandson will be spending a week with me starting tomorrow. He reads a lot of vampire books and I thought—"

"Say no more." Bailey waved her arm and her sleeve swept over the table missing one of the burning candles by inches. "I will take him under my wing." She waved her arm back again, this time extinguishing two of the candles.

"But I don't want him to be changed in any way."

Bailey leaned back and laughed. "Don't worry. I'm on a restricted diet and only do takeout now. Let me show you why." She jumped up, approached Harold, bent over and put her fangs to his throat.

He flinched but held his ground.

Immediately, Bailey began sneezing. "I've developed an allergy to skin, so I have to snack in other ways now." She let out a long sigh. "Macular degeneration and allergies. You never know what old age will send your way." She squeezed his bicep. "But you look in pretty good shape. Since I've agreed to entertain your grandson, I think you can do a favor for me tonight."

Uh-oh. "What do you have in mind?"

"I'm going to get Viola in a few minutes." She picked up the tomato skin and dropped it in the trash can in her kitchenette. "Since I've used up the last of my supply, we're going to stock up tonight. Viola has a little memory problem, and I can't see too well, so a big, strong man like you could help us."

Harold wasn't sure what this would entail, but since Bailey had graciously agreed to spend time with his grandson, he supposed he owed it to her to do what he could to assist her. "O...kay."

"Good." She picked up three empty grocery shopping bags, grabbed his arm and pulled him out of the chair, practically wrenching his arm out of the socket. It would take him some time to get used to being around such strong little old ladies. She dragged him out the door and down the hallway until she stopped in front of the apartment next to his and beat on the door.

"Hold your horses, I'm coming," came a shout from inside. The door opened and Viola stood there. "What do you want?"

"Viola, have you forgotten?"

"Forgotten what?"

"We're going for takeout tonight?"

Viola looked puzzled, then a smile lit her face. "Oh, goodie. Can I have any flavor I want?"

"As I've told you before, it isn't exactly Baskin-Robbins, but we do have eight choices. And Harold, here, will help us."

Viola wrinkled her nose and poked a finger in Harold's chest. "You look familiar. Where have I seen you before?" Then she snapped her fingers. "That's right. You showed up in our meeting room."

"That's where I live now."

"Too bad. It was a good meeting room. Now where in blazes are my false teeth?"

"They're not in your mouth are they?" Bailey asked.

Viola ran a finger over her gums. "Nope. No choppers here."

"You had them in your hand in your kitchenette earlier," Bailey said. "Let's take a look." She entered the apartment with Harold following and peered closely at the counter, in the cupboard and then the refrigerator. "Jackpot. You left them here with the tomatoes."

"Why'd I do that?" Viola took the false teeth and popped them in her mouth.

Bailey clapped her hands. "Okay, let's not dillydally any longer. Time's a-wasting."

They took the elevator to the first floor and exited the building. It was an overcast night, and the city lights reflected off the cloud layer. A car needing a new muffler rattled past, and the street became quiet.

"Where are we going?" Viola asked.

"You've forgotten again, dear. Next door. I can't see it clearly but it's that two-story building over there."

Harold led the way until they came to the front of the blood bank. He tried the door. "It's locked. Looks like everyone went home."

"Not a problem." Bailey removed a key from a pocket of her caftan and opened the door. "Quickly. Inside."

The three of them dashed in, and Bailey headed to a refrigeration room. She pulled the door open and snapped on a switch. It looked like a meat locker but instead of chops was crammed full of plastic bags of blood.

How appetizing.

"Ooh, what a buffet!" Saliva ran down the corners of Viola's mouth.

"Don't get too excited, dear," Bailey said. "We each can pick three and Harold can carry two of the bags for us. I always take A positive. It's the second most common type of blood and can only be used by A positive and AB positive recipients."

Viola began fingering bags. "Oh, what shall I try? Maybe an O negative." She removed a bag and handed it to Harold. "And here's an A negative. And an AB positive."

"All right. You have your three." Bailey handed a bag of A positive to Harold and removed two more which she held. "This will last us for three weeks. Here, put them into a shopping bag." They proceeded to put the blood containers into the brown grocery bags.

"Won't this be missed?" Harold asked.

"Some get dropped and misplaced." Bailey gave Harold a push toward the refrigerator door. "Besides, this is a much better way for us than what we did when we were younger." She ran her hand over his throat, and he flinched. "And I encourage everyone I meet to donate blood. I've convinced more people to give blood than I consume. In the long run I'm helping not hurting the supply." She poked him in the ribs. "I expect you to come over here in the morning to donate."

Harold stood up straight. "I've been donating at the local blood bank for the last twenty years. Every eight weeks."

Bailey patted his arm. "That's good. You're a contributing citizen. Come on, Viola, let's go."

Viola closed her eyes and whooshed in a deep breath. "Oh, I just love being in here and looking around. Can't we stay a little longer?"

"No, we can't risk getting caught." After they scooted out, Bailey closed the refrigerator door.

"Brrr." Harold shivered. "I wouldn't want to be locked in there."

They headed toward the front of the building when suddenly a flashlight shone through the glass door.

Bailey pushed Harold and Viola behind a counter, and all three ducked down.

Harold watched the light play against the wall behind them, and then it disappeared. He heard footsteps receding.

Bailey stood up. "Darn security patrol. Let's wait a few minutes to make sure the guard's out of sight."

In moments a car started and with a screech of tires pulled away. "Obviously a young person. Someone our age wouldn't drive that fast. Come on team, time to move out." Bailey pushed Harold and Viola to the door, unlocked it, and once they were outside, relocked the door.

On the walk back, Bailey held her stomach and gave out a loud belch. "Uh-oh, I don't feel too well."

"Did you eat earlier?" Viola asked.

"Yes, I had my special Bloody Mary. I must have had some hot-blooded Hispanic, and my stomach can only handle Scandinavian." Bailey let out a groan, opened her purse, pulled out a bottle of Tums and popped a tablet in her mouth. "I wish they would put names on those bags. Then I could pick a nice safe Johansson or Svenson."

Back at Mountain Splendor they passed the Front Wing elevators. Two women waiting there stared at the three of them holding the brown shopping bags.

"Just deli takeout from the local grocery store." Harold gave his best insurance smile as they continued toward the Back Wing elevators.

CHAPTER TEN 🦇

After breakfast the next morning Harold remembered one other thing he needed to do to prepare for Jason's visit. His teenage grandson had a big appetite and required a constant infusion of snacks. He headed into town to a nearby grocery store. After bypassing the aisles with fruit, carrots and broccoli, he homed in on things a kid would actually eat—purchasing two boxes of granola bars, four packages of cookies and an equal number of bags of chips. *That should tide him over – for a day or two anyway.* When he returned to his apartment, he stashed the supplies in the cupboard of his kitchenette. Now he was ready.

That afternoon Harold waited in his room. He tried reading, but couldn't concentrate and kept checking his watch. His mind kept drifting off to how Jason would react when he met the people in the Back Wing. Finally, the doorbell rang, and he opened the door to see Jason scuffing his foot with Nelson and Emily glaring behind him. The skinny fourteen-year-old had a floppy mop of blond hair and stood five-foot-nine.

"Welcome." Harold waved them inside and gave his daughter-in-law a hug. He had always enjoyed being around Emily from the time that Nelson had started dating her. She had a no-nonsense way about her, an attractive smile and a good sense of humor, although Jason seemed to be testing all of these attributes today.

Jason, wearing jeans, a purple Colorado Rockies T-shirt and tennis shoes, shuffled into the living room wheeling a suitcase behind him.

His gaze didn't leave rug level, and his mouth formed a serious scowl. Jason's face had a smattering of freckles with no signs of pimples that often afflicted others his age.

"You're moving like someone my age," Harold said.

Jason scrunched up his nose. "It's nice to see you, Grandpa, but to be honest I'm not looking forward to staying here."

"Jason!" Emily planted herself in the middle of the room with her arms crossed, the warrior mother in full battle stance.

"I told you before, Mom. You're going off on a trip to Hawaii, visiting beaches and seeing all kinds of neat stuff. Then you send me over here where I have to spend time around a bunch of old people."

"Jason!" Nelson picked up the refrain.

Harold chuckled and put his arm around Jason. "I know this isn't your first choice of living arrangements. Did your dad mention what I said to him?"

Jason kicked at the rug as if trying to dislodge an invisible football. "Yeah. Something about a unique experience, whatever that means."

"I can assure you that you'll have a week here like none before in your life."

Jason gave a classic teenage eye roll. "Big deal. I've never spent a week with old people."

Harold whispered in Jason's ear. "I think you'll be pleasantly surprised. I guarantee you'll not be bored."

"What am I going to do here for a full week? Dad wouldn't even let me bring my video games or iPod."

"Probably a good decision. I doubt whether you'll have much of a chance to use any of your electronic contraptions."

Jason's gaze turned toward the ceiling. "Right."

"I like what you've done with the place." Emily strolled around the living room, ran her hand over his easy chair, looked out the window and returned to where Harold stood.

"Not much to it, really. Nelson moved me in, and now it's home."

"I'm glad you're more positive," Nelson said. "When you arrived you were as eager as Jason to be here."

Harold looked toward his frowning grandson. "And for the same reason. Jason, I didn't look forward to being around old people when I first moved here either. I was pleasantly surprised as you will be."

Jason opened his mouth and stuck his finger in it.

"Jason!" Emily shouted. "Do you want to be grounded for the rest of the summer?"

"Well, jeez. I'm already grounded for the next week."

Harold chuckled. "Ah, the wonders of a surly teenager. Jason, I'll make a deal with you. Give it a try for a day and then you tell me if this isn't, as you would say, a cool place."

Jason waggled his head as if trying to shake away unwanted adults.

"I noticed a very attractive blue couch near the elevator on your floor," Emily said. "Nelson, did you see it?"

"Yeah, I almost tripped over it when we left the elevator."

Emily put a finger to her cheek. "It would look good in our den. I'd like to have one like that."

No you wouldn't. Harold smiled but didn't respond.

Nelson looked at his watch. "We need to get going. Our flight awaits us."

Nelson and Emily each gave Jason a hug. Jason stood as stiff as a board.

"I'll keep him entertained," Harold said. "Have a great trip."

Once the door closed, Jason sauntered over to Harold's entertainment center. "Since I couldn't bring anything, you have any good music?"

"Do you like Perry Como and Frank Sinatra?"

"You're kidding."

"Actually, I am. I prefer the Beatles. I imagine even kids your age still appreciate the Beatles."

Jason's eyes lit up. "Well, yeah. I have *The Beatles: Rock Band* video game. I play a cool guitar." He held his left arm out and began strumming with his right hand while shaking his whole body. Then he slumped. "But my dad wouldn't let me bring that either."

"Just as well. It might shake up some of the people here. Although a number of residents have bad hearing, others don't like loud music."

Jason began looking through Harold's collection of CDs. "All right. You have *Rubber Soul* and *Sgt. Pepper's Lonely Hearts Club Band*."

"I even had those in vinyl at one time, but now I've converted over to CDs."

"At least I'll have something to listen to."

"As I said, I don't think you'll have much time sitting around my living room." Harold waved Jason toward the bedroom. "You can unpack into the bottom two drawers of my dresser, and you'll find some extra hangers in the closet."

"Where do I sleep, Grandpa?"

"The couch here opens into a bed, so you'll have the living room to yourself. Don't be surprised if you have visitors in the middle of the night."

"Huh?" Jason's mouth dropped open.

"Oh, nothing. But see if you notice any unique things when you meet people here."

Jason wheeled his suitcase toward the bedroom. "There you go with this unique stuff again."

Harold followed him. "What'd you bring to read?"

"A vampire book."

"Do those things scare you?"

"Nah. But I like how they bite people's throats and suck out the blood. That's really cool."

Harold smiled. "Ever meet a real vampire?"

"Nope. You got them around here?" Jason laughed. "I can just see that. Vampires in a retirement home."

"You may be surprised." Harold winked.

Jason stared at Harold for a moment and then unzipped his suitcase and began stashing clothes into the two allocated drawers.

Harold left Jason to finish unpacking, returned to the living room, picked up the phone and called Bella. "My grandson has arrived. You want to make an appearance?…Good. See you in a moment."

Bella came through the wall.

Jason returned from the bedroom and did a double take when he saw Bella standing there. "I didn't hear the door open."

"Bella, this is my grandson, Jason. Jason, meet Bella Alred, my neighbor."

Bella held out her hand. "Jason, it's a pleasure to make your acquaintance."

Jason put out his hand and a bouquet of flowers popped into it.

"Why, Jason, how nice of you." Bella took the bouquet and

sniffed it. "What a thoughtful grandson you have, Harold." Jason's mouth hung open.

Harold nudged Jason. "As I used to tell your father, close your mouth, so you won't catch flies."

Jason stared at Bella. "How'd you do that? You a magician?"

"Something like that."

Jason took a step back and tripped over his suitcase. "Hey, I left that in the bedroom." He pushed the suitcase away and looked back. Bella had disappeared back to her apartment. "Where'd she go?"

"You'll see more of her later. You and I used to play Frisbee. You up to a little game outside?"

Jason squinted at his grandfather. "What's going on here?"

Harold picked up a Frisbee he had on top of his entertainment center. "Just keep paying attention."

As they waited for the elevator, Jason said, "Not many people around here."

"Wait until after dinner. This place will be jumping then. Mainly night people live in the Back Wing."

They took the elevator down and went out on the front lawn to toss the Frisbee back and forth for fifteen minutes.

"You still catch and throw pretty good, Grandpa."

"I've stayed in good shape. Get ready for a long one." Harold wound up and let it sail way over Jason's head.

Jason raced off but couldn't get close enough to catch it. As the Frisbee dropped toward the ground, Tomas Greeley came running toward it. He caught it in his mouth and crashed into a bush.

Jason came screeching to a halt next to the bush. "Did you see that, Grandpa?"

"Yeah, quite a catch."

The bush shook and a dog came out with the Frisbee in its mouth. "Where'd the old guy go?" Jason parted the bush. "He's not in there." The dog wagged its tail and dropped the Frisbee at Jason's feet. Jason patted the dog on the head, picked up the Frisbee and threw it. The dog took off, leaped into the air, caught the Frisbee in its mouth and crashed into another bush. In moments Tomas came out of that bush with the Frisbee in his mouth and handed it to Harold. "Thanks for stopping by to join the game," Harold said.

"Any time. See you later." Tomas strolled away.

Jason pointed as Tomas disappeared into the building. "But... but..."

"Don't sound like a motor boat. You want to go play bingo?" Jason rolled his eyes. "That sounds real exciting."

Harold gently elbowed his grandson in the ribs. "You might win some money."

They went into the Front Wing lounge where tables had been set up. A group of Front Wingers sat in the first three rows. The only Back Wingers there were Bella, Tomas and Pamela. They sat at the back of the room. "Everyone, this is my grandson, Jason. Jason you've met Bella, Tomas Greeley played Frisbee with us, and this is Pamela Quint."

Jason gave a reluctant wave and sat between Harold and Bella. "How old are you, Jason?" Bella asked.

"Fourteen."

"Ah, a good age. I learned a lot when I was fourteen."

"Like how to make things appear and disappear?" Jason asked.

"Why, yes. You catch on quickly. Just like your grandfather." Harold excused himself to go buy bingo cards. When he returned, he gave two cards to Jason.

Front Wingers won the first three games and on the next game, Jason had a diagonal of four covered. When B-3 was called, Jason shouted, "Bingo!"

He trotted up to the front of the room to show his card.

Someone from the Front Wing contingent growled, "What's a kid doing here?"

"Whooping your fannies," Tomas hollered.

Jason returned holding a twenty dollar bill.

"Way to go, kid," Tomas said. "Upholding the honor of the Back Wing."

A woman in the row in front of them wearing a blue flowered dress turned around, adjusted her glasses and said to Pamela, "You people don't belong here."

"What! Why you little..." Pamela dropped to the floor, and a bat flew out from under the table aiming for the woman.

The woman shrieked, flapped her hands at the bat and fell against a woman sitting next to her. This caused the table in front of them to tip forward into a couple who spilled their coffee on two women in front of them.

The bat flew into the hair of Martha W. Kefauver, DAR, who flailed her arms and knocked the glasses off a woman next to her. Those glasses fell into a glass of cola, which splashed onto Atherton Cartwright's white sweater. In moments, all the Front Wingers jumped to their feet, waved their hands at the bat and streamed out of the room.

The bat bounced off the wall once and flapped back to the floor under the table where Pamela had been sitting. Then Pamela emerged, straightened her hair and took her seat. "Let's play some more bingo," she shouted.

CHAPTER ELEVEN 🦇

At dinnertime Harold didn't see the gardener, Ned Fister, so he led Jason to a table where they sat by themselves.

"All you can eat here, Jason."

"Cool." He dug into a salad.

A waiter placed two plates of salmon, baked potatoes and corn in front of them. Jason attacked his food as if he had been on a starvation diet.

Harold scanned the room and spotted Atherton and Martha sitting with two other women. They were all spruced up, Atherton in a yellow cardigan and Martha with an orchid in her hair. They seemed to have recovered from the incident with the bat.

"I don't see any of your friends here, Grandpa."

"Nah, a number of them have…uh…special diets, so they don't eat in the dining room. They fix their meals in their kitchenettes. In the dining room you'll find people from the Front Wing and us."

Jason whispered. "The Front Wing people don't seem very friendly."

"You have that right. What I like about the Back Wing — lots of interesting folks. You'll meet more of them after dinner. They're kind of different but have welcomed me into their midst."

"They do some weird tricks."

"You're catching on."

At the other end of the room, someone began tapping a knife against a water glass. In moments, all the conversations ceased.

A man in a suit stood up. "I'm Winston Salton, executive director of Mountain Splendor."

"What's he saying?" a woman nearby shouted.

Winston snapped his fingers, and Peter Lemieux scurried over to hand him a microphone.

"Can you hear me now?"

"Yeah," the same woman said. "Who are you?"

Winston cleared his throat and spoke crisply into the microphone. "Again, I'm Winston Salton, executive director of Mountain Splendor. It's good to see all of you this evening. I hope you're all having a good dinner."

The same woman piped up, "I was until some dipstick started talking through a microphone."

"Well...uh...I want to give you an update on the situation with the two missing women."

Jason leaned toward his grandfather. "Missing women?"

"I'll tell you about that later. Let's hear what the head honcho has to say."

"I heard those two women left because they didn't like the food here," came a voice across the room.

"Let me clarify the situation," Winston continued. "Hattie Jensen and Frieda Eubanks have disappeared. The Golden Police Department is investigating the situation. I can assure you that all the members of the Mountain Splendor administration are giving the police our full cooperation, and we're doing everything possible to locate the missing women. At this point in time, we don't know if they left on their own or were abducted."

"Skipped out of town," one woman said. "Frieda owed me money. I know she's stiffing me."

"I bet they went to Vegas," someone else said.

"Aliens," came another woman's voice. "They got snatched by aliens."

Winston held up his hand. "In addition to the police investigation, we've appointed a four-person resident panel to work with the police and all of you. I'd like to ask Atherton Cartwright to say a few words."

Atherton stepped forward, planted a plastic smile on his face and took the microphone. "Martha Kefauver, who most of you know, and I have been asked to serve on a resident panel along with... uh...two representatives from the Back Wing—"

A collective groan went through the crowd.

"The Back Wingers are responsible for whatever happened to the two women," a voice shouted.

"Like I said, aliens."

Atherton held up his hand. "Please, if I can have your attention. We're doing our best to assist the police. If any of you have seen anything please let Martha or me know. We're dedicated to helping the authorities get to the bottom of what's happened." He showed his teeth again. "Thanks."

"The Front Wing and Back Wing don't get along too well, huh, Grandpa?"

"That's true."

"How come?"

Harold thought for a moment on how to answer. "The people in the Front Wing don't like people who are different from them."

"Kind of like in my school. The jocks and cheerleaders don't like the geeks and dorks."

Harold nodded his head. "Pretty much the same situation."

"What's with these missing women?"

Then an idea occurred to Harold. *Why not?* "Bella and I represent the Back Wing on the residents committee along with the guy who just spoke and the woman he mentioned. How'd you like to help us?"

Jason's eyes grew as large as the Frisbee they had played with earlier. "That would be cool."

Harold looked up to see Winston Salton making the rounds, stopping at tables and shaking hands. When he reached their table, he plastered on his administrative smile and said, "Who's this young man?" He rubbed his hand through Jason's hair, which elicited a grimace.

"My grandson, Jason. He's currently working undercover." Harold winked at the scowling teenager. "I'm Harold McCaffrey.

I'm on the resident team helping the police with the investigation of the missing women."

Winston frowned. "I thought we had only two people from the Front Wing on that committee."

"That's correct. I live in the Back Wing."

Winston craned his neck and stared at Harold as if trying to suck brain matter through his eyeballs. "Really?"

"Yup. I think Peter Lemieux may have put me in the wrong wing, but now I kind of like it. You know, real people in the Back Wing."

Winston gagged and then straightened his tie. "I'll have to speak to Peter."

"That's okay. I'm perfectly happy there. And with Jason visiting, the residents in the Back Wing are much more entertaining than the stuffy Front Wingers. Right, Jason?"

"Yeah, I've met some really cool people so far."

Harold's eyes met Jason's, and they exchanged the visual version of a high five. "Since you're here, Mr. Salton, any news for us insiders?"

Winston looked over his shoulder as if someone might be spying on them. "I don't know if I should say anything in front of the young man..."

"Not a problem. He's fully briefed."

"Well...uh...yes. Someone turned in a handkerchief to the front desk. The police think it belonged to Frieda Eubanks."

"Where'd it come from?" Jason asked.

"In the grass leading into the open space."

Harold sucked on his lip for a moment. "It could have been lost when she disappeared."

"That's entirely possible."

"Did the two missing women know each other?" Jason asked.

Winston peered at Jason as if he were one of the strange residents of the Back Wing. "They were members of our poker club."

Harold tapped a finger on the table, remembering the similar statement made by Detective Deavers. "Hmmm. You have a poker group here. I used to play a lot...well, my wife and I played poker once a week or so."

"I didn't know you and Grandma played poker," Jason said. "Dad has been teaching me. It's a great game."

Winston's eyes darted from side to side. "Mr. McCaffrey, you'll have to participate in our poker club. Tomorrow afternoon at two. Nice to meet both of you." He turned and headed to the next table.

Harold watched Winston for a moment as he glad-handed four women who gave him their rapt attention.

Harold turned toward Jason. "So you like poker, do you? I didn't know kids your age played card games anymore."

"Give me a break. I like all kinds of games."

"You play poker often?"

"Yeah. I've been practicing on a web site." Jason gave a satisfied nod of his head. "I win at Texas Hold'em most of the time."

"How'd you like to join me tomorrow afternoon? It sounds like they're short two players."

"Cool."

CHAPTER TWELVE 🦇

W hen Harold and Jason returned from dinner, the fourth floor reverberated with loud conversations in the hallway, and music blaring from various rooms. Tomas and Pamela danced together near the elevators.

"You were right, Grandpa. These are night people."

Harold pointed to the come-and-go couch. "Don't sit on that."

Jason couldn't resist and galloped over to run his hand over the arm of the couch.

It let out a moan, and Jason jumped back, pointing to a shaking cushion. "I think it's alive, Grandpa."

At that moment Bailey Jorgensen grabbed Harold's arm. "There you two are. I was waiting for you to show up. And this must be Jason."

Jason turned away from the couch, and Bailey bared her fangs. Jason gawked. "Cool. Can I touch those?"

"Sure. And they're my own, not artificial." Bailey stepped close to him.

Jason fingered the protruding teeth. "Wow. Are you really a vampire?"

"Yes, just as Alexandra here is a shape-shifter."

Alexandra Hooper waved from where the couch had stood. Jason smiled at his grandfather. "I like this place."

"Come on." Bailey took Jason's hand. "I have some snacks in my apartment."

Harold followed as Jason peppered Bailey with questions. "Do you sleep in a casket?"

Bailey gave a dismissive wave of her hand. "Heavens no. I like a nice soft mattress."

"Do you have to avoid sunlight?"

"I sleep pretty late because I stay up most of the night, but no, other than wearing dark glasses because of my macular degeneration, the sun doesn't affect me."

"Would putting a stake through your heart kill you?"

Bailey's eyes grew wide. "You better believe it. But the same would happen if someone put a stake through your heart."

"Do you have to avoid garlic?"

"Only because I have a sensitive stomach. I'm not much on spicy blood."

"Does a crucifix scare you away?"

Bailey laughed. "Where'd you get that idea? I even wear one." She pulled a chain out of her blouse and showed a silver cross to Jason and Harold.

Jason stared at it for a moment and then continued. "Is it true that you can't see your reflection in a mirror?"

"It was until I turned sixty. Unfortunately, as soon as I got wrinkles I could see my reflection very clearly."

Jason excitedly hopped from one foot to the other. "Do you cast a shadow?"

"Of course. Except on a cloudy day."

"But you do drink blood?"

"Absolutely. Here's my place. Come on in."

They entered to find Viola taking a container out of the refrigerator. She set it on the counter and removed the lid. "Just in time. I have the special Jell-O shots ready. The green are virgin."

Harold stepped over and saw small red and green jiggling cubes. "Jason, I think you better stick to the green ones."

"Who's this kid?" Viola asked.

"He's my grandson," Harold replied.

Viola squinted at Harold. "And who the heck are you?"

"You've met Harold before, Viola," Bailey said.

"If you say so," Viola stepped over and gummed Jason's neck. He giggled. "Stop! That tickles."

"You'll have to forgive Viola," Bailey said. "She forgot to put in her teeth."

"Oh, dear." Viola looked in her purse. "Where'd those choppers go?" Jason pointed to something on the tray with the Jell-O shots. "Uh, over there?"

"Good job, kid." Viola grabbed the false teeth, stuck them in her mouth and then smiled at Jason.

"This is so cool. Two vampires in the same room."

"You'll get used to seeing us around the retirement community," Bailey said.

"Do you know any young vampires?" Jason asked.

"Nope." Bailey scratched her nose. "The swine flu epidemic a few years ago killed them off. Apparently, if they didn't get the flu back in the 1970s, the new strain wiped them out, so only those of us who are older and had blood tainted with the earlier flu antibodies have survived."

Jason put his hand to his neck. "Do you ever bite someone's throat to make new vampires?"

Bailey shook her head. "Not anymore. I'm satisfied with takeout."

Viola waved her hand. "I remember back in the day when I had my real fangs—"

"Don't get Viola started on some of her stories. She can't remember things very well from the recent past, but her long term memory is good, too good at times. She'll go on for hours recounting the throats she's met."

"As I was saying before being rudely interrupted." Viola stomped her foot. "My first throat experience occurred when I was Jason's age. I had just been bit myself and had a classmate who thought she was hot stuff. Her blood didn't taste special, but it filled me up for a week. Now my favorite flavor is Italian. I remember a vacation in Rome—"

"Yes, we can hear all that later. Right now who wants a Jell-O shot?"

Harold and Jason took a green one each, while Bailey and Viola selected red. They all held them up.

"To friendship," Bailey said.

They plopped the Jell-O in their mouths.

Viola smacked her lips. "Ah, a little French with a smattering of German. Solid European heritage."

"Blood has different tastes?" Jason asked.

"Of course, dear boy. I'm a connoisseur. Bailey doesn't have as sensitive a pallet. She can't tell the difference between Mexican and Canadian."

Bailey rubbed her stomach. "Until afterwards. The tangy ones give my tummy the rumbles."

Viola picked up another red cube. "You don't have to worry. Nothing too spicy here tonight."

At that moment Bella stuck her head in the door. "Here's where you two were hiding. I have someone who wants to meet Jason." She pushed the door open all the way, and Kendall Nicoletti pushed through with his walker.

Harold jumped aside as the spiked tips again came within inches of his shoes.

"Hey, kid. It's still almost a full moon tonight. You want to come howl with me later?"

Jason looked toward Harold. "Can I, Grandpa?"

"We'll see."

"I'll be out by the gazebo in the garden from ten until two. Usually lose my voice after that and come back inside. Stop by if you want." Kendall turned and pushed his walker out the door.

Viola reached for a bottle of red wine standing on the table. "Oh, goody. A full week's supply."

Bella grabbed the bottle out of her hand. "Viola, I've told you a hundred times. That's wine and not blood. One sip and you're out like a pinched-out flame."

"Are you sure? It looks so inviting."

"Stick with the special Jell-O shots."

Viola pouted. "You never let me have any fun."

A man with a crinkly face and a big wart on his nose came up and put a sagging arm around Bella. He wore a flowing purple robe. "How's the most beautiful witch in the room?"

She shrugged out of his grasp. "I'm the only witch in the room."

"Details."

Bella took another step away from the man. "Harold and Jason, this is William Tyson. We all refer to him as Warty."

Warty gave an exaggerated bow.

"Is that name because of the wart on his nose?" Jason asked. "No,"

Bella said. "It's a contraction for Warlock Tyson." Jason's eyes grew wide. "A real warlock?"

Warty hitched himself up to his full five-foot-six. "Yes, kid. Say, do you know any magic?"

Jason shrugged. "A few card tricks."

"Let's see what you can do." Warty pulled a deck of cards out of a pocket of his robe. "Show me your stuff."

Jason stuck his tongue out the side of his mouth and shuffled the deck. "Okay, take a card any card."

Warty put his hands over his eyes, reached in the deck and extracted a card.

"Okay, now look at it but don't tell me what it is." Warty peeked at the card and nodded his head. "Now put it back in the deck, anywhere."

Warty inspected the deck and selected a place for the card.

Jason tapped the deck on the table, shuffled it three times and cut it. "Now tell me the number of the card."

"A six."

Jason counted off six cards from the top of the deck. "Now tell me the suit."

"Spades."

Jason counted off four cards saying, "Clubs, diamonds, heart, spades." Then he turned over the next card to show the six of spades.

"Pretty good, kid. Let me show you some real magic now." Warty waved his hand over the deck and said, "Pick any card and memorize it."

Jason reached into the center of the deck, pulled out a card and quickly looked at it.

"Now put it face down on the table." Jason did as instructed.

"Turn the card over. It's the king of hearts."

Jason flipped the card over to show the ten of clubs.

Warty scratched his chin. "Hmmm." He pulled out a wand from his robe and waved it. "As I said, it's the king of hearts."

The card changed into the queen of diamonds. "Nope, you're still wrong," Jason said.

Warty tapped the wand on the table and inspected the tip. "I think it's rusty." He waved it again. "Now it's the king of hearts."

The card changed into the eight of clubs.

Bella clicked her tongue. "That's why the Witches and Warlock Union kicked you out."

Warty harrumphed. "I'll have you know I still have my union card." He reached in his robe, whipped out a wallet, pulled out an ID card, which he snapped down on the table.

Harold, Bella and Jason all bent over to look at it. Bella picked it up. "Warty, you'll notice these big red letters that say, 'VOID.' You lost your membership because of all your faulty magic."

He grabbed the ID card. "Just a minor technical difficulty. Now, you ready for some of my punch? I brought my special concoction for this party."

Bella turned toward Harold and Jason. "I wouldn't advise drinking any of the punch. Once, Warty tried to get me to drink his so-called love potion."

"I thought you might show more interest in me," Warty sniffled. "Ain't gonna happen. And that crazy punch of yours only made everyone sick to their stomachs."

"I've improved the formula."

Bella rolled her eyes. "Right. It will probably cause people's skin to turn green."

"Not exactly green, but a little yellow."

"Why don't you drink some of your own punch, Warty?" Bella asked. "No way. I never touch the stuff."

Bella pointed toward Bailey's kitchenette counter where a punchbowl rested, gurgling as steam circled toward the ceiling. "Like I said, stay away from Warty's punch."

"You can't get any respect around here." Warty turned. His robe swirled, and he stomped off.

Bella leaned over and whispered to Harold and Jason, "He used to be a very good warlock. I think his arthritis has affected his magic."

Harold watched Warty offer a cup of punch to Bailey. She wisely refused.

Harold looked around the room. He spotted Viola over in the corner, slumped down on the floor. She was hugging the open red wine bottle as she snored. He turned to Bella. "I think Viola ignored your advice."

Bella put her hands on her hips. "I don't know what I'm going to do with her. Memory like a punctured balloon."

"Should we take her back to her room?" Harold asked.

"It's better to let her sleep it off here. She'll try to nibble on your neck if you move her."

At that moment Tomas charged into the room. "Hey, everybody, someone's breaking into the building next door. I was out... uh... taking a walk and saw a guy trying to pick the lock."

"What!" Bailey shouted. "That's our private domain. No one else is allowed in there. We need a posse. Come on Bella, Harold, Jason. Let's go nab this interloper."

Bailey led the way like an Indian brave on the war path. They charged down the stairs and out to the street. The glow from a nearby streetlight illuminated a man opening the door to the blood bank. Bailey charged up and grabbed his arm. "No you don't."

He swung around to hit her, but Bella pointed her finger and the man froze.

"Should I bite him?" Bailey asked.

"Not a good idea," Bella said. "Remember, you'll start sneezing, and your stomach might get upset."

Bailey eyed the frozen man. "Yeah. He looks a little on the spicy side."

"This is so cool," Jason said. "You caught a burglar in action."

Harold pulled out his cell phone and called 9-1-1. "I'd like to report a burglary in progress...it's the blood bank next door to the Mountain Splendor Retirement Home. I see someone trying to break in." He snapped his phone shut. "Come on, everyone. Let's go back to our building and watch for the police."

They all trekked back to where they had a view of the blood bank. Alexandra came out of the retirement home building. "Here's where you all went."

"We can use your assistance, Alexandra," Bailey said. "We need a place to sit while we wait here."

"Sure thing." Alexandra transformed into a leather couch and Bailey and Bella sat down to wait. Harold and Jason perched on the arms.

The burglar still stood frozen with the door partially open at the

The Back Wing

blood bank. When a patrol car pulled up in front of the building, two officers jumped out with guns drawn and raced toward the door.

Bella snapped her fingers and the burglar tripped and fell, still blocking the doorway. One of the officers went up and cuffed him.

As the police led the burglar to the patrol car, Bailey gave a satisfied nod of her head. "Nobody messes with our takeout. Nobody."

CHAPTER THIRTEEN 🦇

Once all the excitement at the blood bank was over, Harold, Bella and Jason headed back into the retirement home. Harold turned to his grandson. "Jason, I thought you, Bella and I might do some investigating tonight."

"What kind of investigating?" Bella asked.

"I figure we should check out the rooms of the two missing women?"

"How will we get in, Grandpa?"

"Oh, I think Bella can solve that little problem for us."

They went to the Front Wing elevator bank and caught a ride to the sixth floor. Harold led them to Room 619. "Here we are. I looked it up in the directory." Harold tried the doorknob but found it locked. "Okay, Bella, your turn to get us inside."

"She pick locks or something?" Jason asked.

"Better than that. Let's try an experiment. I wonder if you can walk through the wall with me." Bella took Harold's hand and pulled him forward.

Harold smacked his nose on the door trim as half of Bella disappeared through the wall, with the other half still visible holding his hand.

She stepped back out. "Oops. Maybe, you can't."

Harold rubbed his nose. "So much for that experiment."

"Sorry. It was worth a try. I'll have to go solo." She waved at them before vanishing through the wall.

In a moment the door opened, and Bella ushered them in.

Once they closed the door, Jason said, "Cool. I wish I could walk through walls like that. It would really freak out the kids at school."

"Special powers need to be used judiciously," Bella said. "I only do it for important reasons."

Jason nodded. "Yeah, you could make quite a burglar."

"Which I'd never do…maybe a little breaking and entering but only to help with the investigation. Now let's see what we can find in here."

The living room had thick plush carpet, a large bookshelf and a blue couch with the same flower pattern as two easy chairs. In the bedroom, a made bed, nightstand, dresser and desk with wooden chair filled the room.

They spread out. While Bella checked the cupboards in the hallway and Jason rifled through books and CDs on the bookshelf, Harold entered the bedroom. He did a double-take. On the night stand stood a picture of Atherton Cartwright with the inscription, "With all my love, Atherton."

"Look at this, Bella," Harold called out.

She stuck her head in the bedroom, and Harold pointed to the offending picture. "It appears our committee member may have had a thing going with Hattie."

"That's interesting. He never gave any indication he knew Hattie and acts so cozy with Martha."

Bella scoped out the closet while Harold sat down at the desk in the corner of the bedroom and began skimming through the paperwork.

"I found a checkbook," Harold said. "Hattie Jensen always paid her bills on the fifteenth of the month. And her bank statement shows a monthly Social Security and pension deposit. She lived within her means."

Bella and Jason came to stand with Harold. "Nothing unusual that I can find," Bella added.

"Lots of books," Jason said, "and all her CDs are pathetic old folk's music."

"Watch who you refer to as old folks," Harold said. "I'm not talking about you, Grandpa. You're with it."

"Why would she either disappear or be abducted?" Bella asked.

Harold opened a manila folder. "Here's a listing of her assets… Hmmm…Wow, some large savings accounts and a healthy stock portfolio. She could have afforded to retire to the Riviera or Tahiti instead of this dump…uh…this place. Maybe someone is holding her ransom for her money."

"Detective Deavers didn't mention any evidence of a kidnapping," Bella said.

"I found a picture album, Grandpa. She has two sons and five grandchildren."

"Let's see if we can find phone numbers for the sons," Harold said. "We can check with them to try to learn more."

"Got it covered. Here's an address book. I'll write the numbers down for…" Jason thumbed through the pages, "Ted and Paul Jensen, one in Minneapolis and the other in Phoenix."

Harold continued looking through the desk. In one cubbyhole he found a portfolio with several documents inside. "Jackpot. Here's her will. She had set up a trust with a living will giving terminal medical instructions," He leafed through one of the documents. "Uh-oh."

"Uh-oh good or uh-oh bad?" Bella asked.

"Uh-oh as in strange. Her will has a date of two weeks ago. She must have recently changed it. Rather than leaving anything to her children and grandchildren, everything goes to the Mountain Splendor Retirement Home."

"That doesn't make any sense," Bella said. "Why'd she do that?"

"I wonder if her children know of this provision. I'll have to give them a call tomorrow to check on it."

After twenty minutes with no additional useful evidence, they got ready to leave. Harold cracked the door open, making sure no one was in the hallway, and they all stepped out and shut the door. They took the stairs to the fifth floor and Frieda Eubank's room.

"Jason, you want to take my hand and see if you can go through the wall with me?" Bella winked at him.

"No way. I saw what happened to Grandpa."

"And here I thought you were an adventurous kid."

"Well, yeah, but not stupid."

Bella laughed and disappeared through the wall. In a moment the door opened. "Please join me inside."

Compared to the tidy apartment they had just visited, this place gave off vibes of pure chaos. Dirty dishes rested on the kitchenette counter, the living room was stacked high with magazines and books, and the bedroom looked like a whirlwind had tossed clothes on the bed and gray rug.

"Where do we start?" Bella asked.

"I don't see any obvious place for financial records. Let's check all drawers and the closet."

Jason opened the closet door and waved his arm. "Yuck. Nothing hung up. Clothes all over the floor."

"This coming from a teenage boy?" Bella gave him a poke in the ribs. "Hey, I hang things up in my room. Not like this mess."

Harold rummaged through a dresser and then the drawer of the nightstand before slamming it shut. "Nothing useful."

"She had to have some paperwork." Bella tossed aside a blouse covered with what hopefully was only spaghetti sauce stains.

Jason dropped to his knees and looked under the bed. "Here we go." He reached out an arm and extracted a metal box. He opened it and pulled out some documents, which he waved in the air. "This help, Grandpa?"

"Let me take a look." Harold took the papers and sorted through them. "Term life insurance policy—expired. Passport—out of date. Passbook for a savings account—closed. And some receipts." He thumbed through the chits. "It looks like Frieda was a regular at the casinos in Black Hawk."

Harold flashed back to a time before his wife Jennifer became sick when they had spent the day in Black Hawk and Central City. Jennifer loved playing blackjack, and she settled in at the tables at the Isle of Capri. Harold played for half an hour, lost his twenty dollars and then wandered off to get a snack. When he came back, Jennifer had won forty-five dollars. They headed up the road to Central City, and Jennifer continued her winning streak at the Fortune Valley Hotel and Casino while Harold hiked around the old mine tailings. After his hike he discovered that Jennifer had won another thirty dollars. She always came out ahead, but Harold rarely did.

"Harold, you seem lost in thought," Bella called out.

"Oh, yeah." He pushed aside the memories and returned to looking around Frieda's apartment. "Let's see what else we can find in this place."

They rummaged through the clothes.

"No pictures or any indication of any relatives," Bella said.

"I've looked through the kitchenette," Jason announced. "The refrigerator was empty except for a six-pack of Coors and an onion. The cupboards only had a few dishes and an open bag of stale potato chips."

Harold found a brochure lying between a dirty sweater and a pair of jeans. It had a picture of a large well-lit building with snow-capped peaks in the background. It touted the advantages of the Sky Ute Casino Resort. "This must have been another of Frieda's gambling destinations."

"That's quite a distance," Bella said. "Way to the south."

Harold shrugged. "I guess she liked to spread her gambling losses around."

"Here's a purse, Grandpa." Jason handed it to Harold, who opened it.

"Hmmm. An expired Visa card, an expired Colorado driver's license, a dollar bill, two quarters and a restaurant receipt."

"Let's make one more pass," Bella said.

They spent another ten minutes. Jason picked up a book that had been tossed on the floor and riffled through it. "Hey look, a piece of paper." He handed it to his grandfather.

Harold unfolded the paper and gasped. "Here's our smoking gun."

Both Bella and Jason stared over Harold's shoulder. The typed note read, "$25,000 or else."

CHAPTER FOURTEEN 🦇

"What should we do with that note?" Bella asked. "Should we give it to Detective Deavers?"

Harold thought for a moment. "If we do that, he'll want to know what we were doing here. I'm sure the police have already done a cursory inspection of this room. They will eventually search more thoroughly and find it, so let's put it back where we found it."

"It has your fingerprints on it, Grandpa."

"Good point." Harold took out a handkerchief and wiped the note before putting it back where he found it. He also swiped his handkerchief over the other items he had touched, the purse and book included.

"I wonder if Frieda received that threatening note or was going to give it to someone else," Bella said. "With her gambling problem, she needed money, but maybe someone she owed money left it for her."

"It could be either way," Harold replied.

"What a difference between the two missing women," Bella said when they stopped in the Back Wing lounge to debrief. "Hattie has an immaculate place and lots of money. Frieda is a slob and probably in debt due to a gambling addiction."

"I don't know how that Frieda person could live in all that mess," Jason said.

Bella arched an eyebrow.

"I know. I know. You're going to give me grief again, being a teenager and all. We're not all slobs."

Bella smiled at Jason. "That's good to know."

Harold paced around the room and stopped in front of them. "The one thing we have linking the two women is their poker group. You up for a little poker tomorrow, Bella?"

"I don't know how to play."

"All right. Jason and I will cover the poker game."

Jason rubbed his hands together. "We'll whup 'em good, Grandpa."

"As long as you promise not to take all their Social Security money."

"Let's discuss what's next," Bella said. "Harold, you and Jason check out the poker club and contact Hattie Jensen's kids. I'll take two action items. First, I want to see if the Mountain Splendor administration knows of the windfall from Hattie's will. Second, I'll try to find out if Frieda has any relatives."

"How you going to do that?" Jason asked.

"Oh, I may go through resident files in the office later tonight." Jason hopped from one leg to the other. "Cool. Can I come too?"

Bella frowned. "No. Since I can't pull you through the walls, I'll do this on my own."

"Aw."

She patted Jason arm. "Besides you need a good night's sleep to play your best poker tomorrow."

"I'm not tired. I'm all hyped up."

Harold nudged his grandson. "And to think at one time you worried you'd be bored here."

"Are you kidding, Grandpa? I never thought you'd be living in such a cool place. Vampires, shape-shifters, witches, missing people." Jason waved his arms over his head. "This is a lot better than being stuck on a sucky trip with my parents."

Harold looked up at hearing a clumping sound and saw Kendall thrusting his walker into the lounge.

"Hey, kid. You ready to come howl with me?"

"Can I, Grandpa?"

Harold looked at his watch. "I suppose for thirty minutes."

"I'll leave all of you to your howling." Bella waved and headed for the elevator.

Kendall shuffled out the building with Jason right beside him.

Harold sat on the steps to wait.

In a few minutes Harold heard a pathetic howl followed by coughing and hacking. Then it started again, ending in a wheeze.

82

The next attempt petered off into more of a groan than a howl. Harold leaned back and stared at the moon. Then a piercing howl shattered the night. What the heck was that? The more vigorous howl continued, punctuated by the ineffectual gurgling one for another twenty minutes.

Then Jason came jogging up to Harold. "All done?" Harold asked.

"Yeah. Mr. Nicoletti got laryngitis, so I had to help him out. He's going to stay out for a while and see if the night air helps his throat."

"You certainly produced a fine howl."

Jason straightened his back and stuck his chin out. "What do you think of a bald werewolf?" Harold asked.

"Okay, I guess. I've never seen another werewolf so I'm cool with the way he looks."

Upstairs Harold pulled out the hide-a-bed and put on sheets and a blanket. After Jason changed into his pajamas and brushed his teeth, he jumped into bed.

"You going to read your vampire book before you go to sleep?" Harold asked.

"Nah. It's too boring."

The next morning Jason wolfed down a waffle, three pancakes, scrambled eggs, fruit, a yogurt and two glasses of orange juice while Harold was content to finish a bowl of oatmeal. Harold shook his head in amazement as Jason went back to get a bowl of raisin bran. After he scarfed down the last bite, he wiped his mouth, patted his stomach and gave a contented sigh.

"That fill you up?" Harold asked.

"For a little while. I'll need something a little later, though. Do they have midmorning snacks around here?"

"No, but I have some granola bars, cookies, chips and juice for you in my kitchenette. Just help yourself when you get hungry again."

"Cool. Let's explore, Grandpa."

"Sure. I haven't seen the whole building myself."

They went down to the first floor, and Jason pointed to a sign. "Hey, an exercise room. Let's check it out."

The room had a treadmill, a StairMaster, an exercise bike and a rack holding weights. It was deserted except for Kendall Nicoletti standing in front of a mirror, holding onto his walker with one hand and curling a small dumbbell in the other hand.

"Hi, Mr. Nicoletti," Jason called out. "Whatcha doin'?"

"My weight work. Since the back legs aren't so hot, I need to keep my front paws...I mean my arms in shape."

Jason picked up the heaviest weights in the room, forty-five pounds dumbbells and squeezed out three curls before he quit. "Phew. They're heavy."

"Hey, stick with the light ones, kid. You want to tone your muscles, not break your back."

Jason put the forty-five-pound weights back and rubbed his left wrist with his right hand. "Anyone else ever use these?"

"Only one person I've seen strong enough for those. Frieda Eubanks."

Harold blanched. "The missing woman."

"That's right. Well, you wouldn't want to mess with her, no siree. That old broad was mighty tough. She'd come in here every day and pump iron. Short squatty woman built like a fire plug and strong as a rhino."

Harold didn't add that she had the housekeeping skills of a packrat. He looked at his watch. "I need to go back to the apartment to make some phone calls. Jason, can you entertain yourself for a while?"

"Sure, Grandpa. I'm going to keep exploring and see if I can find any clues. Nice seeing you, Mr. Nicoletti." Jason saluted and dashed out the door.

"Nice grandson you have there, Harold."

"The best." Harold was amazed at the energy of teenagers. If only he could bottle it for the geezers and geezerettes living here. He headed back to his apartment, picked up the phone and punched in the number for Hattie Jensen's son, Ted, in Minneapolis.

A woman answered, and Harold identified himself as a resident of Mountain Splendor. "I'm sorry that your mother-in-law has disappeared."

"We're all shocked. Ted is waiting to hear again from the police. He's considering coming out to Colorado."

"Do you know anything about your mother-in-law's will?"

"No, but Ted would."

Harold asked for Ted's work number and called it next. An admin explained that Ted was in a meeting but would call back in half an hour.

Next, Harold tried Paul Jensen in Phoenix. This time a man answered. Harold identified himself.

"And why would you be calling me?"

Harold was taken aback by the suspicious tone. "I...uh...wanted to express my concern over the disappearance of you mother."

"Yeah, I'm worried too. Now I'm running late. I need to get to work."

"One question first. Did you know she changed her will recently?"

"What? She never would do something like that. Dad set up a trust years ago, and Mom never wanted to mess with it."

"This may come as a shock to you but she's leaving everything to the Mountain Splendor Retirement Home."

"What? That's outrageous." There was a pause. "And how do you know this?"

Uh-oh. "I...uh...happened to see a copy. I thought you should know."

"Thanks for the heads up." The line went dead.

Harold looked at the phone receiver as if a snake would wiggle out of the earpiece. You never could predict how people would react to bad news.

Half an hour later his phone rang, and he picked it up to find Ted Jensen on the line.

"I'm sorry your mother has disappeared. I spoke with your brother a little while ago but wanted to talk with you as well."

"Yeah, I had a message to call Paul, but he didn't answer. What's up?"

"As I explained to your wife when I called your home earlier, I'm a resident of the Mountain Splendor retirement home. I'm concerned over what has happened to your mother. None of us can explain her disappearance."

"Yeah, that's the strangest thing. She pretty much keeps to herself. I can't figure out how she wandered off. She didn't have dementia or anything."

Harold took a deep breath. "I happened upon a copy of your mother's will, and she recently changed it to leave everything to Mountain Splendor."

"What?"

Harold held the receiver away from his ear. The same tone as his brother's but twenty decibels louder. He brought the mouthpiece back to his face. "Paul said this surprised him as well because your mother wasn't someone who would normally go around changing her will."

"Darn right. Something's fishy. She never mentioned anything, and she always runs any financial decisions by me before she acts."

"Have you spoken with the Golden Police Department?"

"Yes, a Detective Deavers called me yesterday."

"You might want to contact him again. This could be pertinent information."

They said their good-byes, Harold thankful that Ted didn't delve into how he came across the will. It would be better for the family to bring this subject up with the police. And if the cops ever questioned Harold, he'd say he heard a rumor around the retirement home.

At that moment Jason raced into the apartment. "Where's the Frisbee? Tomas Greeley and I are going to play catch in the swimming pool."

"It's on the dresser in my bedroom."

Jason dashed into the bedroom, a drawer banged and something thudded. Jason returned moments later with swim trunks on and Frisbee in hand, before rushing out of the apartment.

Harold tsked. "Kids and dogs."

CHAPTER FIFTEEN 🦇

When Jason returned, he was gasping for breath. "Phew, we started in the swimming pool, but some man got all pissed off and kicked us out. Then we played out on the front lawn. I had quite a workout with Tomas."

"Shouldn't you call him Mr. Greeley?"

"Nah. He said to use his first name. He's a nice guy. He even apologized for getting dog slobber all over the Frisbee."

"That's a good thing. I thought we might take a little excursion since my mission is to make sure you don't get bored."

"Hey, no problem, Grandpa. This place really rocks."

"Do you like trains?"

"Yeah. I used to have a model train."

"I remember that one. Your dad gave it to you one Christmas." Harold thought back to his own childhood, remembering the HO gauge train he played with. "When I was your age, I built a train layout with a tunnel through a mountain, village with railroad crossings, miniature people and houses. The whole shebang."

"Cool. I ran my train around the tree for a week after Christmas and then set it up in my room. Haven't seen it since I started playing video games and using a computer. I think Dad stored it in the basement."

"Did your dad ever take you to the Colorado Railroad Museum?"

"Nope."

"It's close by and I thought we might check it out. We have enough time before our big poker game this afternoon."

While Jason changed into his jeans, Harold called for a cab. Then he and Jason took the elevator down to the lobby. Inside the elevator, Harold scanned the wall for the latest announcements. He found a notice that read, "We've had a complaint of a dog being in the swimming pool. No animals are allowed in the pool area."

Harold shook his head as they went outside to wait for the taxi to arrive.

"You don't drive anymore, Grandpa?"

"No, I gave it up."

"I can't wait to drive. Dad's going to teach me when I get my driver's permit. I'll be an awesome driver." He held up a pretend wheel and turned it from side to side. Then he dropped his hands. "How come you quit driving?"

"I stopped driving at night when my cataracts turned approaching headlights into starbursts, and it was hard for me to read signs. Now that I'm here, I can always catch a cab if I need a ride. A few taxi fares are nothing compared to insurance, taxes, gasoline and maintenance expenses for a car anyway. I had an accident two months ago—"

"I never heard that."

"It's not anything I'm proud of. Fortunately, no one was hurt. I smashed my fender and the back bumper of the car I hit. After that I decided the safest thing would be to give up my keys, so I sold my car."

"That must have been a tough thing to do," Jason said.

"Piece of cake." Harold realized that his grandson was pretty sharp. *Hardest decision I ever made.* No longer driving impacted his independence, but the time had come. He didn't want to risk having another accident and maybe hurting or killing someone.

The taxi arrived, and Harold and Jason climbed into the backseat. "I've never been in a taxi before," Jason said.

"Really?"

"Yeah. My mom and dad drive me everywhere I need to go. But when I get my license, I can go wherever I want without a chaperone." He held his mock steering wheel up again. "Varoom!"

"Then when you're my age, you'll be back to having chaperones again."

—

88

The taxi let them off at the front of the railroad museum. They entered through the gift shop, and Harold paid the ransom of twelve dollars for one senior and one child.

Jason muttered, "I'm not a child."

"Cheer up. It saves your grandpa three dollars. The extra money will help keep you in snacks this week."

They went through a swinging gate into the main part of the museum, an 1880s depot, and looked at the photographs and artifacts lining tables and shelves.

"Wow. Look at all this railroad stuff, Grandpa. Did you ever go on a train?"

"Yes, indeed. I traveled across much of the country on trains at one time or another. Once took the California Zephyr riding one of those dome cars through the Rockies from Denver to California. Great way to see the country. People don't do that much anymore. Have you been on a train trip, Jason?"

"Nope. I've been on kid stuff but not any big ones."

"Today you can climb around on some real trains. The brochure says they have over a hundred cars and engines, narrow and standard gauge, out in the fifteen acres this place covers. You can check them all out."

They stopped at an exhibit of a telegraph office and Harold said, "Back in the old days telegraph lines connected all the stations. The operators had to send messages in Morse code. Try tapping the telegraph key."

Jason pushed it twice. "Wow, this would be difficult. Texting is much easier."

Next they watched a video that described the history of the museum from its inception in 1959. Harold thought back to that year. He won an award for the most insurance sales for the Rocky Mountain Region. Now here he was entertaining his grandson, living in a retirement home and trying to figure out what had happened to two missing women. How his life had changed.

"I'm bored," Jason said, five minutes into the film. "Let's go outside."

They left the building, and Jason climbed onto a steam engine. He jumped up into the engineer's seat and grabbed the control lever.

"Look at me, Grandpa. I'm in charge here."

"And I could be your fireman." Harold followed into the cab and opened a swinging door to see where coal would have been shoveled in. "This thing got blazing hot. Can you imagine working next to it during the summer?" Maybe it wasn't so bad being a retired gentleman after all. Then another thought occurred to him. Like trains were dangerous to work around, had he been stupid to involve Jason in the disappearance of the two women? Was he endangering his grandson?

Jason swung down from the engine, and Harold brushed his worries away as he followed.

Jason pointed to the track. "How come there are three rails, Grandpa?"

"Good question. The engine we were on is narrow gauge, three feet between the rails." Harold pointed to another train nearby. "That engine over there is full gauge with four feet between the rails. In some places they put in three rails so both narrow gauge and full gauge engines could run."

"These different-sized engines get along better than the Front Wing and Back Wing in your retirement home, Grandpa."

Harold chuckled. "You're on the right track."

They climbed aboard a dining car used for events followed by a caboose that held kids' parties.

"You could have your next birthday party here, Jason."

His grandson rolled his eyes. "Give me a break, Grandpa. I'm too old for that."

Harold opened up a brochure he had picked up in the museum. "Well, here's another alternative for you. When you're sixteen, you could become a volunteer at the museum."

Jason grabbed the brochure. "Cool. I could work on fixing up the trains." Then he scowled. "But when I'm sixteen, I'll need to have a paying job. Dad says I'll have to buy gas when I start driving."

"Maybe you could get a job at Mountain Splendor."

Jason scrunched up his nose. "As long as I could work in the Back Wing and not the Front Wing."

Harold remembered wanting to be in the Front Wing when he first arrived. How his own opinion had changed.

They continued to explore the grounds, passing a Garden Railroad that had a small train running through a miniature set of houses and trees. They entered another caboose and Jason climbed up to the seat where a conductor could look out a window to see the train ahead and the tracks behind. From his perch Jason opened a cabinet door and his eyes grew wide. "Look at this, Grandpa."

Harold stepped over to see a Halloween mask of a skull. He flinched at the thought of a body being stashed in a tight space. Had something like that happened to the missing women? Here he was on an excursion, and this mask reminded him of the unfinished business back at Mountain Splendor. Did Detective Deavers's mind work this way? When he went somewhere with his family, did everything remind him of cases he was investigating? As an insurance salesman, Harold had always been able to leave his work behind when he went home.

They circled through the grounds inspecting cattle cars, boxcars and diesel engines. Finally, they entered a warehouse where trains were being restored. One engine and a passenger car stood in the building surrounded by lathes and scattered parts. "How'd you like to put that engine back together?" Harold asked.

"Looks like a lot of work."

Next they visited a brick roundhouse that included a ninety-foot turntable.

"That's something, Grandpa. They could turn a whole locomotive and coal car around on that thing."

Jason ran ahead and climbed aboard a caboose. He scampered around inspecting the wheels and cowcatchers of several steam engines. He acted like a puppy off the leash, dashing from one place to the next.

Harold trailed along behind, not even trying to keep up with his grandson. He inspected an old boxcar, tank car and flatbed car. This brought back memories from his childhood of watching trains speed through crossings. He had placed a penny on a track one time and, after the train had passed, spent fifteen minutes trying to locate the squashed penny. He finally found it off to the side in a pile of pebbles, twenty feet from where he had placed it. Nothing remained of the original image. Only flattened copper.

Harold took in a deep breath and then slowly exhaled. There was something about trains that never left you once they were in your blood. Not an addiction, but a pleasant remembrance of hissing steam and clacking wheels.

They stopped at a Galloping Goose, which looked like a modified automobile with train wheels. "Look at this weird train, Grandpa. This place has all kinds of strange stuff."

Harold enjoyed watching the enthusiasm of his offspring, and the stroll through the extensive grounds provided his exercise for the day. This had been a good trip for both Jason and him.

Finally, Jason loped back to where Harold stood. "You want to climb on any more stuff, Grandpa?"

"No, I think you've tuckered me out."

They returned to the museum and took the stairs down to the basement to find an extensive HO model train layout.

"Whoa, this is huge," Jason said. "Look at the mountains and buildings and tunnels."

Harold put a quarter in a slot and a model train began running along the tracks. It went through a tunnel and emerged on the other side of the display. After it ran its course, Harold put a quarter in another slot and an amusement park lit up with a carousel and Ferris wheel turning.

"This would be so cool to build," Jason said.

Harold regarded all the moving parts. Somehow he couldn't concentrate on the display. Instead his mind drifted off to the missing women. He shook his head. What was happening to him?

They went upstairs and while Jason dashed off to look in the gift shop, Harold stopped at a display of couplers, which were used to connect railroad cars. He inspected an example of the buffer-and-chain coupler, which looked liked two sets of metal discs slapping each other with a metal chain as a tether, then a link-and-pin and finally the Janney coupler that resembled two hands clasping. The Janney, also called an AAR coupler, was always right-handed. Harold curved his fingers, twisted his left wrist and brought his fingers together to simulate the locking mechanism.

This made Harold think. There had to be something that connected the disappearance of the two women at Mountain Splendor. These weren't separate, random events. There had to be a link between Hattie Jensen and Frieda Eubanks just like these couplers connected railroad cars. But what was it? So far being in a poker group appeared to be the only connection. He and Jason would pursue that later this afternoon.

His thoughts were interrupted by Jason tapping him on the arm. "Man, there's a lot of cool stuff, Grandpa. Thanks for bringing me here."

Harold smiled to himself. He had put together the right recipe for his grandson's visit. Vampires, werewolves, shape-shifters, witches, warlocks and trains.

That afternoon Harold and Jason entered the Front Wing lounge to find six people at a large table. Harold only recognized one person — Atherton Cartwright, wearing a baby blue sweater, crisp tan slacks and brown loafers without socks.

"We're substituting for Hattie and Frieda," Harold explained. Taking charge, Atherton announced, "You can buy chips from Melba, here."

The woman with pure white fluffy hair sitting next to Atherton waved her hand. "Blues are ten cents, red five and white one. This is the only time to buy chips. After this, only chips are visible until we cash out at the end. For anyone watching, we're only playing for chips."

Harold reached for his wallet and handed over a ten-dollar bill. "Five dollar's worth for each of us."

Atherton eyed him. "That won't last very long in this group, particularly for the young man."

"We'll see." Harold gathered the chips and divided them with Jason. Then he stacked his by color.

Melba put the money in her purse.

Atherton cleared his throat. "For the newcomers, the deal rotates. We each ante a red chip on every deal. Raises are limited to a blue chip. Three raises per round maximum. You're familiar with Texas Hold'em, I assume."

Both Harold and Jason nodded.

"Good." Atherton shuffled the deck three times and put it in front of Melba to cut. "Ante everyone."

All the players threw a red chip into the pot. Atherton dealt out two cards to each person.

Harold lifted the corners of his cards. Jack of hearts and jack of spades.

Melba tossed in a blue chip, the next three folded, a skinny woman wearing a green eyeshade threw in two blue chips and shouted, "Raise ya."

Jason dropped in three blue chips. "Raise again."

Harold looked at his cards again. What the heck. He pushed three blue chips toward the center of the table.

The woman sitting next to Harold scrunched up her already wrinkled nose and folded.

"I'm in," Atherton announced and tossed three blue chips into the center. One spun for a moment before settling into the pile. Melba called, but the skinny woman folded.

"Now the flop." Atherton dealt out three cards, showing the seven of spades, ten of clubs and jack of clubs.

Melba checked, and Jason pushed a blue chip forward. "Raise." Harold smiled and dropped two blue chips in the pot. "Raise again."

Atherton arched an eyebrow. "Getting to be a healthy pot. I'm game." He put in his two blue chips.

Melba bit her lip. Finally, she pushed in two chips. Jason added another two blue chips. "Raise."

Harold liked this. He felt either he or Jason had a good chance of winning this hand. He added his chip as did Atherton.

Melba tapped her cards and folded.

"Down to only the men for the turn." Atherton winked at Jason.

He dealt out a card and flipped it over to show the king of clubs.

Jason checked, Harold shoved in a blue chip and Atherton and Jason called.

Atherton dealt out the river card, a three of diamonds. "Okay, young man, what's your bet?"

Without batting an eyelash, Jason flipped a blue chip into the pot. Harold called, Atherton raised a blue chip, and Jason called.

Harold looked at the table again. What the heck? "I raise." Atherton and Jason matched the bet.

Atherton gave a wide grin. "Harold, you've been called. Whatcha got?" Harold tuned over his cards. "Three jacks."

Atherton gave a derisive laugh. "Not good enough." He showed a queen and ace of hearts. "Straight." He reached for the pile of chips.

"Just a minute," Jason said. He turned over the four and five of clubs. "Flush."

"But...but...you checked your first bet on the turn," Atherton stammered.

"Of course." Jason raked in the chips. "Sucked you in."

They continued playing with Harold winning a hand, Atherton several but Jason continuing to build his stack of chips.

Finally, Atherton called out. "Restroom break."

All the chairs except Harold and Jason's scraped back, and the six people disappeared faster than Harold could say waterfall.

"What do you think?" Harold asked his grandson.

Jason gave a wide grin. "Pretty easy picking. They don't play that well."

Harold chuckled. "Consider it a contribution to your college fund."

After the break, Harold decided it was time to collect a little information. "Since Hattie Jensen and Frieda Eubanks played in this group, did you ever notice anything unusual about them?"

"When we didn't have a game scheduled, Frieda always wanted to run off to Black Hawk or Central City to gamble," Melba said.

"It would be nice if we had a casino here in Golden," Atherton said. "Would make it convenient for people like Frieda to lose money locally."

"Frieda was a nutcase," Melba said. "She bet like crazy and usually didn't have any cards. She'd lose twenty dollars in an hour. She always tried to borrow more money, but I made it a practice not to give her any. Never would have got it back."

"And Hattie Jensen?" Harold asked.

"She played just the opposite," Melba replied. "Very conservative. It would take her an hour to lose a dollar. She never bet unless she had a sure hand and never bluffed. Consequently, when she bet, I always dropped out unless I had a killer hand. Not much of a player. I could read her like a book."

"Any other observations?" Harold asked.

"Let's quit the chit-chat and get back to the game," Atherton muttered. "Jason, it's your deal."

They played for another hour and then Atherton looked at his watch. "Times up, let's cash in."

Jason ended up with thirty dollars and Harold earned back four of his original five. Jason handed him a five. "Here's what you staked me."

"You ended up twenty-five ahead. Not bad." Harold wondered how his grandson had become such a card shark.

"Cool. When do we play again?"

Atherton glared at him. "Uh…we've decided to set an age limit. You have to be over sixty-five to participate in this game in the future."

Jason grinned at him. "Can't take the competition, can you?"

Without answering, Atherton picked up the deck of cards and stomped out of the room.

"Maybe we could start a game on the Back Wing," Harold said.

"No way. Bella would make the cards change and always win."

CHAPTER SIXTEEN 🦇

After dinner Harold and Jason watched Woody Allen's *Sleeper*, the movie of the night, in the Front Wing lounge. When they returned to the apartment, they found Bella sitting on the couch.

"About time you two showed up." Bella tapped a shoe on the carpet. "Can't you just knock on the door like a normal person when you want to visit?" Harold asked.

"Of course not. I'm not a normal person."

I'll say. "You look pretty normal until you make things appear or disappear."

"Who wants to be normal? I have some interesting information from my exploration last night to share with you, but first I want to hear what you two learned today."

"Hattie Jensen's kids were surprised by the change to her will. Both of her sons had a tizzy fit. They had no inkling she planned to give all her money to Mountain Splendor."

"Maybe someone coerced her into making the change. That would make sense with what I found." Bella paused and smiled.

"Well, don't keep us in suspense," Harold said. "Drum roll, please."

Jason tapped his fingers on the kitchenette counter.

"Thank you, young man. When I looked through the files in the administrative offices, you'll never guess what I found."

Harold put a finger to his chin. "I'd speculate a copy of Hattie's will."

Bella pouted. "How did you know?"

"It's all starting to fall into place. Why would Hattie change her will on the spur of the moment and not notify her children? I think someone in Mountain Splendor administration forced her to make the change, and she didn't want to tell her kids. Where exactly did you find the copy of the will?"

"In a locked file cabinet outside Winston Salton's office."

"How'd you get into the locked files?" Harold asked.

Bella stared at him. "Come on, Harold."

He smacked his forehead. "That's right. The same way you made Atherton's zipper move."

"Exactly. It's amazing how locks have a way of popping open when I speak nicely to them."

"When Grandpa's food stash runs out, can you do that with the snack machine downstairs?" Jason asked.

"I could, but I won't. As I've told you before, I only use my special powers for good causes."

"It's a good cause if I'm starving between meals."

"Jason!" Harold barked.

"Just kidding."

Harold frowned. "We have a change to the will, and the executive director of the retirement community has a copy but not the kids. Pretty fishy."

Jason shifted from one leg to the other, as if he had to use the restroom. "That guy Winston Salton who runs this place seemed pretty slimy when he spoke at dinner the other night. Maybe he strong-armed the old lady to leave all her money to the retirement home and then whacked her."

Harold regarded his grandson. "That's a possibility. We'll have to learn more about Salton and how he runs this operation."

"Oh, I already have," Bella said. "Did you know that even with the high rates we pay, Mountain Splendor is losing money?"

"How can that be?" Harold asked. "With all the people living here, this place should be making a mint of money."

"The files show quite a few unplanned maintenance items in the last year. A water pipe burst that damaged over a dozen apartments, and that wasn't covered by insurance. Then the roof had to be replaced, a new driveway put in, the air conditioning conked out and, oh yes, a complete renovation of the kitchen."

"Who in the administration could give us the scoop on all of this?"

Bella paused for a moment. "Our best bet is Peter Lemieux. He's very supportive of the Back Wing lifestyle and always approachable."

"I'll stop by to see him in the morning," Harold said. "Did you have a chance to check Frieda's resident file?"

"Yes, indeed. It turns out she has no close relatives. Never married and no living parents or siblings."

Harold scowled. "So a dead end there. No one to contact. Now, Jason, why don't you tell Bella what we learned during the poker game."

Jason waved his arms as if he wanted to fly. "This old guy named Atherton Cartwright thinks he's hot sh…hot stuff. I won all his money." Jason gave a satisfied nod of his head. "We heard Hattie Jensen played conservative poker, but Frieda Eubanks gambled erratically and usually lost all her money."

"That sounds consistent with what we saw in their apartments." Bella paced around the living room. "Maybe Frieda owed a large gambling debt. That could explain the threatening note in her apartment."

At that moment there was a knock on the door.

Harold opened it to find Pamela Quint. "I'm looking for Bella."

"Hi, Pamela." Bella waved.

"Come quickly. Tomas is having one of his problems."

CHAPTER SEVENTEEN 🦇

Bella disappeared through the wall into her apartment and met the others in the hall with a bottle in her hand. Harold, Jason and Bella followed Pamela Quint down the hall to a room where Tomas Greeley lay on the floor twitching and foaming at the mouth.

"Oh, dear," Bella said. "One of his fits again. Everyone stand back. Jason, get me a wet washrag." She knelt down as Jason dashed into the bathroom.

When Jason returned, she wiped Tomas's forehead and mouth. She held his head up with one hand and sprinkled some powder from a tiny bottle into his mouth.

Tomas jerked again, and then his eyes popped open.

"There, he's coming to." Pamela stepped over to look at Tomas. "Good work, Bella. You've done it again. I'm going to leave you to look after Tomas. I need to fly...er, explore some more." She scooted out the door.

"Where am I?" Tomas sat up and blinked.

"You had another one of your seizures," Bella replied. "Have you been eating raw meat again?"

Tomas put his hands to his forehead and groaned. "It's all coming back to me now. After I left the retirement home tonight I roamed around in the foothills. I found a bone. There was still some meat on it."

"What kind of bone?" Bella asked.

Tomas coughed and wiped his mouth with his hand. "Not deer or elk. Came from something pretty large. A good-sized leg bone."

Uh-oh. Harold didn't have a good feeling. "Can you show us where you found it?"

"Sure. After I gnawed on it. I left it there."

"Are you thinking what I'm thinking?" Bella whispered in Harold's ear.

He nodded. "We should call the police." Jason's eyes grew as large as silver dollars.

Harold, Jason, Bella and Tomas stood in the lobby, each waiting in silence, until a police car pulled up in front of the building. They all went outside as an officer climbed out of the car. He stood slightly taller than Harold, maybe five-foot-eleven, skinny with a determined set to his jaw. "One of you report finding a suspicious bone?"

Harold stepped forward. "I made the call, but this gentleman here found the bone. He can show you where it is."

Tomas led the way to a path that headed into the open space.

The police officer removed a flashlight from his belt and snapped it on.

The night was cloudy and dark without a breath of breeze. Harold, Bella and Jason walked behind Tomas and the police officer as the flashlight beam bounced off the path ahead. Harold felt a shiver run through his body and admitted to himself that he wouldn't like to be wandering around at this time of night by himself.

Tomas veered off the trail to a flat area below a large boulder and pointed to a disturbed patch of dirt with several bones lying on the surface and one poking up in the dirt. "Right there."

The officer bent over and inspected the bones without touching anything. Then he grunted and stood. "Will all of you please wait over there?" He pointed to a log. "I don't want this area compromised." He extracted his cell phone from his belt and placed a call.

After they sat and the police officer was off the phone, Harold called out. "There are two women missing from the retirement home. Detective Deavers has been investigating."

The policeman nodded. "Dispatch will call him as well as the coroner and the crime scene tech. It looks like some animals have been gnawing on the bones."

Tomas gave a loud gulp.

The police officer turned the flashlight from the bones to shine at Tomas's feet. "Tell me how you happened upon this scene."

"I was out...uh...taking a walk," Tomas began. "Saw the bones. When I mentioned this back at the retirement home, Harold called the police."

The officer's cell phone jangled. He answered it, turned his back, walked several steps away and spoke softly.

"I wonder what happened," Bella said. "Do you think this could be Hattie Jensen or Frieda Eubanks?"

Harold bit his lip. "Very possible."

"This is so cool." Jason bounced up and down on the log. "I've never seen a dead body before."

"And you won't be seeing this one either," Harold replied. "As soon as they tell us we can leave, we're going back to the retirement home."

"Aw, you never let me have any fun." Jason scuffed his foot in the dirt.

Harold gave his grandson his best in-the-dark evil eye. "I think you've had your share of new experiences in the last day or so."

"Yeah, this sure beats a cushy Hawaii trip."

They sat there in silence as an owl hooted in the distance.

Harold replayed in his mind what might have transpired. He tried to imagine one of the missing women walking out here. Had she come voluntarily or been abducted? And then what gruesome act led to her demise? Suddenly the image of Tomas writhing on the floor and Bella ministering to him popped into Harold's head. "How'd you bring Tomas around so quickly?"

"In addition to my checkered career, I volunteered at hospitals for forty years." Bella hugged Harold's arm. "And I learned how to use some special potions I cooked up. I always enjoyed interfering when a doctor said a case was hopeless. Watching the expression on those know-it-alls' faces when the patient miraculously recovered was priceless. And it gave me a perfect opportunity to provide... uh...nourishment for some of my friends."

Harold winced. "You're full of surprises, Bella. But you didn't actually steal blood did you?"

"Of course not. But after transfusions and blood tests, the old blood needed to be disposed of. Let's just say that I helped recycle it."

Jason stuck out his tongue. "Yuck."

"Viola and Bailey have a different reaction. They say, 'Yum.'"

Shortly, the detective and a crime scene tech arrived. Deavers escorted Harold, Jason, Bella and Tomas back to the retirement home and into the Front Wing lounge to interview them.

While Deavers interrogated Tomas, Harold sat in a chair to wait. Something pricked his ankle. He looked down and saw cockleburs all over his socks. He picked them off and dropped them in a trash can.

When Harold's turn arrived, he explained how he had called the police. "And Detective, I've heard some interesting rumors that you might want to check out."

Deavers arched an eyebrow. "Yes?"

Harold leaned forward and in a conspiratorial tone said, "I can't say for sure, but there's a rumor that Hattie Jensen changed her will to leave all her money to the retirement home rather than to her own children. Maybe that has something to do with her disappearance. And Frieda Eubanks may have had some gambling debts. She had a reputation for trying to borrow money from other people at Mountain Splendor. I just thought you might want to know."

"Where did you hear this?"

Harold shrugged. "You know how it is with old people. We have time on our hands and gossip with each other. But my memory isn't that good, so I can't say for sure where I heard the reports."

CHAPTER EIGHTEEN 🦇

The next day while Jason played Frisbee with a now healthy Tomas, Harold made an intelligence-gathering trip to the administrative offices. Lemieux was on the phone but waved Harold into the office.

Harold stepped in, closed the door and took a seat.

Once Peter put down the phone, he graced Harold with a gigantic smile. "What can I do for you, Mr. McCaffrey?"

"Since I'm on the committee representing the Back Wing in regards to the two missing women, I want to mention something to you. Last night we found some evidence that might relate to the disappearances, and I called the police to report it."

"Quick thinking. I heard from Detective Deavers this morning that the police hope to have a forensic dental I.D. later today."

Harold regarded Peter for a moment and then said, "Then we'll know if those were the remains of either of the women. There's something else that's bothering me that I want to discuss. Confidentially."

Peter's head did a short bob. "If that's what you want, I'll keep it to myself."

Harold's stomach convulsed, but not from anything he'd eaten. Could he trust Peter? He seemed friendly enough, but would his loyalty to his boss override his promise of confidentiality? "Okay. Here's the situation. I've heard that Hattie Jensen changed her will to leave all her money to Mountain Splendor."

Peter's eyes grew wide. "Why'd she do that?"

"Exactly my question. Were you aware of this?"

Peter shook his head vigorously. "No, and it doesn't make any sense. She has two children and three grandchildren and always spoke positively of her family. Why wouldn't she leave her money to them?"

"My specific concern. Now the question I need to ask you in the strictest confidence. Would your boss, Winston Salton, have influenced Hattie in any way?"

Peter sputtered. "Winston? Get a resident to change her will? I can't see him doing that. No, why would he?"

"I understand Mountain Splendor has had a number of unplanned expenses this year. Could the financial pressure have caused him to do something drastic?"

"Well...uh...we do have some financial challenges, but we have plans for dealing with them. I can't imagine Winston doing anything underhanded." Peter's chin waggled back and forth. "No, that can't be it."

"I was wondering. Changing a will like that is unusual."

"I agree. I agree. Hmmm. Why would she have done that?"

"I'm sure the police will be asking the same question."

Peter gasped. "And soon after she changes her will, she disappears. That will cast suspicion on all of us."

"If you know anything that would aid the investigation—" Peter looked around wildly. "I need to alert Winston."

Harold held out his hand as if trying to stop a runaway freight train. "Just a minute. Remember. We had this conversation in confidence."

A calm smile returned to Peter's face. "Don't worry, Mr. McCaffrey. I'll keep your involvement to myself. I won't mention your name."

Harold hoped he had taken the right path in speaking openly. He rose. "Thanks for hearing me out." He shook Peter's hand and opened the door.

Winston Salton stood right outside with a scowl on his face.

Harold pushed past, wondering if Winston had overheard any of the conversation.

CHAPTER NINETEEN 🦇

Harold slept late the next morning. He looked at his watch. Darn. He had missed breakfast. He wondered why Jason hadn't awakened him. His grandson never wanted to forego a meal.

Staggering into the living room, he found the rollout bed still in disarray but no Jason. Where had the boy gone?

Maybe Jason went out to play Frisbee with Tomas. He looked up the number in the Mountain Splendor directory. A sleepy Tomas answered.

"Have you seen Jason this morning?"

"Nope. I'm hardly awake myself."

"Sorry to have bothered you. If you see him, let me know."

Next, Harold pounded on the sidewall. After a short wait, a disheveled Bella stuck her head through. "What's all the commotion?"

"I can't find Jason. Have you by any chance seen him?"

She patted her wild hair and glared at Harold as if he were out of his mind. "No. As you can see I haven't been out yet."

Harold let out a sigh. "I know. Everyone here but me is a night person. I'm going downstairs to look for him."

"Give me a minute and I'll join you."

The minute turned into fifteen, but finally Bella popped through the wall again. She wore black slacks and a silver blouse and her hair was neatly combed.

Harold winked at her. "You clean up pretty good."

"Oh, posh. I just had to get my face on. Now let's go find this grandson of yours." They took the elevator to the first floor.

"Let's divide up and check both lounges."

"Fine." Bella nodded in agreement. "You take the Front Wing. I'm not up to seeing any of those people this early."

"Those people? You're beginning to sound like Atherton Cartwright and Martha Kefauver, DAR."

"You know what I mean."

Bella began in the Back Wing while Harold strode into the Front Wing lounge, finding two women he didn't recognize playing cribbage.

Harold approached their table, "I'm looking for my grandson. He's fourteen and almost my height."

"Fifteen-two, fifteen-four and a pair is six," one of the women said and then looked up. "What did you say?"

"My grandson has disappeared, and I'm looking for him. Have either of you seen a boy this morning?"

The other woman squinted at him. "Nope. Not since breakfast. There was a kid sitting with Mrs. Harbeson. He wore a red T-shirt." She picked up the deck of cards and began shuffling.

Harold didn't remember Jason having a red T-shirt, and even so why would he be sitting with a Mrs. Harbeson, whoever she was? He headed back out to the hallway and met Bella coming out of the Back Wing lounge. "Any luck?"

"No. As you'd expect for this time of day, the lounge was deserted except for Alexandra. She was practicing changing into different couch materials and patterns but hasn't seen Jason."

"Someone spotted a boy at breakfast, but I'm not sure it was Jason. Let's check at the reception desk."

They hurried to the lobby.

"Good morning, Andrea," Bella said. "We're looking for Harold's grandson, Jason. Have you seen him this morning?"

"No, Ms. Alred. He hasn't been by here."

"And how long have you been on duty?"

"Since six."

"I can't imagine Jason getting up before six," Harold said. "Could you ring Mrs. Harbeson's apartment for me and let me speak with her?"

"Sure." Andrea grabbed her phone and punched in four digits. "Good morning, Mrs. Harbeson. This is Andrea at the reception desk. Mr. McCaffrey would like to speak with you." She handed him the receiver.

Harold bent over the counter. "Mrs. Harbeson, I'm looking for my grandson, Jason, and someone mentioned seeing a boy at breakfast with you...okay...I understand....did you see any other kids this morning?...no, my grandson is older, fourteen...okay...sorry to have bothered you." He handed the phone back to Andrea. "Thanks."

Bella crossed her arms. "Well?"

"False alarm. It turned out to be her ten-year-old grandson visiting. Let's take a look outside."

Harold and Bella walked around the building and found no sign of Jason. "This isn't like him," Harold said, fidgeting with his hands.

"Maybe he left a note for you."

Harold raised an eyebrow, hopefully. "I didn't think of that. Let's go back and check my apartment."

They took the elevator to the fourth floor. Inside Harold's place, he looked first in the kitchenette finding nothing.

Bella leaned over the roll-out and coughed. "What's that strange smell in here?"

Harold went over to the bed and sniffed. "Now that you mention it. It smells like chloroform." He pulled the sheet back and saw a piece of paper. "Ah, maybe he did leave a note." Harold unfolded it and read, "If you want your grandson back alive, stay out of what doesn't concern you."

CHAPTER TWENTY 🦇

"We need to mobilize the Back Wing. Come with me." Bella grabbed Harold's hand and dragged him out into the hallway. Then she raised her other hand, mumbled something and all the doors on the floor shot open. In a booming voice she announced, "Emergency. Everyone come to the Back Wing lounge."

Several people stuck sleepy heads out doorways.

"I repeat. Emergency. Report to the Back Wing lounge immediately!"

Viola peeked out her open door. "It's still morning. I don't do mornings. What's all the commotion?"

"Get dressed, Viola. We need to mobilize everyone." Bella turned toward Harold. "Go down to the lounge. I'll rouse the other floors." Within fifteen minutes a crowd had gathered in the lounge. Some were dressed in their robes and slippers. Others wore disheveled clothes.

When Bella appeared, she clapped her hands. "Everyone listen up. Someone has kidnapped Harold's grandson, Jason. We need to search every last inch of this facility." She pointed to a sleepy woman. "You, Helga. Take the Front Wing sixth floor. Tomas—fifth floor. Viola— fourth floor." She continued to give out assignments. "And finally, Harold, take the administrative area. I'll check the basement. Now, go!"

Everyone scattered including one dog and one bat.

Harold took two steps at a time up to the second floor and dashed out of the stairwell. He almost knocked over Peter Lemieux.

"What's the rush?"

Harold grabbed the collars of Peter's jacket. "My grandson, Jason, has disappeared. Have you seen him?"

"No."

Harold shook Peter. "I need to check the administration area."

"I was heading there. Let me unlock the door for you." Peter reached for a key and opened the outer door.

Harold raced in and found office doors locked. He turned to Peter. "Can you unlock the offices?"

"Yes, I have a master key." Peter pulled it out of his pocket. "I'm the go-to guy when someone forgets or loses their key."

Peter went through the hallway opening doors, and Harold dashed inside each office to look around, panic mounting at each empty office. No one else was in the administrative area. He found nothing.

"Hold on a second," Peter said. "My phone's ringing." He entered his office and answered.

Harold stood in the doorway, listening, his heart beating rapidly. Where was Jason? What had happened to him?

"Uh-huh...yeah...I'll look into it right away." Peter hung up and turned to Harold. "That was housekeeping. Someone reported people racing around the hallways and knocking on doors. It's complete chaos."

"They're looking for Jason."

"I can assist. We have a PA system to use for emergency evacuations. Let me make an announcement. What's your grandson look like?"

"Fourteen, blond hair, skinny, five-nine." Harold paused to think. "Could be still in his blue pajamas."

Peter went into the hallway and opened a cupboard. Inside was what looked like a ham radio. He pushed a power button, picked up a microphone and cleared his throat. "Attention residents and staff of Mountain Splendor. We have a missing person. Fourteen-year-old Jason McCaffrey." He described Jason. "If you have any information call Peter Lemieux on extension two seven three three. I repeat we have a missing person, fourteen year old Jason McCaffrey..."

Harold could hear the message echoing through the hallway. Would this do any good? Would anyone have seen any sign of Jason? Harold's stomach felt like he had swallowed lead. Two missing women. One apparently buried in the open space. He had to find Jason.

Peter returned the microphone, turned off the machine and closed the cabinet. "There. We'll see if that helps." He turned to Harold.

"We'll do whatever we can."

Tomas appeared, panting loudly. "I found no sign of Jason on the fifth floor."

Bella came running up to Harold. "I've found him." Harold shivered and grabbed her arm. "Is he all right?"

"Yes. Come on."

Bella, Harold, Peter and Tomas raced down the stairs to the basement. Bella pointed to an open door to a closet. "He's in there." She whispered in Harold's ear. "I came to find you immediately. I thought you should be here when he wakes up."

Harold stepped in and saw Jason lying on the floor with a strip of duct tape covering his mouth. His hands and feet were bound with more duct tape. His eyes fluttered.

"Thank god you're safe," Harold said, kneeling by his grandson. Jason thrashed but only made indecipherable noises.

"This might hurt." Harold grabbed the corner of the tape and ripped it off Jason's mouth.

"Ow!"

Harold cringed. "Sorry."

Jason groaned. "Wow, I'm dizzy." Then a partial smile crossed his face." It's good to see you, Grandpa."

"Let me get his arms and legs," Peter said, pulling a Swiss Army Knife from his pocket. He soon had the tape cut and helped Jason to his feet. "What happened, son?"

"My head aches. How'd I get here?"

Harold sniffed the air. "It smells like chloroform. Did you see anyone?"

Jason shook his head. "I had some weird fuzzy dreams but can't remember much."

"It must have been someone pretty strong to get him out of the apartment and all the way down here." Peter reached for his cell phone. "I'm calling the police."

Bella pulled Harold aside and whispered in his ear. "There's something else I found while looking for Jason."

"What's that?" Harold whispered back.

Bella pointed to a large closed door across the hall. "There's a dead woman in the storage room."

CHAPTER TWENTY-ONE 🦇

Peter closed his cell phone. "The police are on their way." Harold sniffed. "Something smells funny."

"Besides the chloroform?" Peter asked.

"Yeah. Can we use your master key to open that storage area?"

Peter pulled out his key and reached for the door. "Sure." He opened it and stepped back. "Yuck. You're right. Something is very ripe." He switched on the light.

With Jason resting in the hall outside and Tomas watching over him, Peter, Harold and Bella stepped into the storage area. Harold shivered. The room, the length of a tennis court, contained three levels of wooden storage bins, five-foot cubes reaching almost to the high ceiling. A bare bulb flickered at mid-court. It had the ambiance of a burial cave.

"What's kept in here?" Harold asked Peter.

"Extra stuff when people move in. Residents can store things here. Didn't you put anything in storage when you arrived?"

Harold shook his head. "No. I gave away everything that couldn't fit in my apartment."

"Wise decision. Most people hold onto stuff but rarely come down here to get anything." Peter gasped. "Whew. This place smells awful."

Harold looked in the first bin. It contained an old rocking chair, two dusty blue Samsonite suitcases, a lava lamp and a set of golf clubs from the Bobby Jones era. The next bin contained a bridge table, folding chairs and several cardboard boxes.

Bella moved quickly past Harold and Peter, went down two rows and pointed. "What's that?"

They followed her.

Harold stared. Two wrinkled, pale white hands stuck out of one of the bins.

Within an hour Mountain Splendor swarmed with various members of law enforcement and a coroner's investigator. Detective Deavers was up to his eyeballs questioning everyone.

Jason rested comfortably on a couch in the Back Wing lounge. An EMT examined him and asked Harold if he wanted his grandson taken to the hospital.

"No way," Jason said. "I'm fine now."

Harold regarded his grandson carefully. "Are you sure?"

A glint appeared in Jason's eyes. "I don't want to miss anything."

Harold figured if Jason felt well enough to kid about this whole situation, he didn't need any further treatment.

When Harold's turn came to be questioned by Deavers, he explained how his grandson had disappeared and how they found the dead body in the storage room.

"Do you know who it is?"

"No, I only saw the hands. That was enough. We skedaddled after that."

"And why did you go into the storage room?"

"After we found my grandson, I smelled something bad and asked Peter Lemieux to open the storage area. Inside, the smell was worse. We looked around and spotted the hands."

At that moment a gurney pushed by a man in white uniform passed by. A white sheet covered a lumpy form.

"Just a moment," Deavers called out. He waved over Peter Lemieux who stood nearby. "I'd like you to take a look to see if you can identify the dead woman."

Peter stepped over, and Deavers lifted one end of the sheet. Peter paled as he put his hand to his mouth. "It's Hattie Jensen."

Deavers nodded. "Okay, we have positive identification now of both missing women."

"B...both?" Peter stammered

"Yeah. We have a match from dental records on the remains found in the open space—Frieda Eubanks."

Overhearing this, Harold's mind raced. What had happened to the two women? One dead in the storage room. The other buried out in the dirt. Who had killed them? And why? How did Jason's kidnapping tie in? Then something clicked from an earlier statement.

When Deavers finished with Peter, Harold stepped over. "Detective, may I have another word with you?"

"Yes?"

"Back when you first met with the residents committee, you mentioned that Hattie's cousin said that Hattie wore a diamond ring. I saw Hattie's hands, and she had no rings."

Deavers smiled. "Good observation." He jotted a note on his pad. "Now regarding your grandson."

Harold recounted their search and finding Jason bound in the closet. "I'll have the crime scene investigator check the closet as well. I'll need to speak with your grandson."

They went to where Jason still lay sprawled on the couch in the Back Wing lounge.

Deavers ambled over. "I need to ask you a few questions." Jason looked up. "Okay."

After the interview, Jason had a huge grin on his face as if nothing had happened.

"You look like you've recovered from your adventure," Harold said.

"Yeah, I feel fine now. It was so cool being questioned by a detective. Too bad I couldn't remember any useful stuff. I'm starving."

One of the Back Wing elevators opened, and Tomas Greeley stepped out with a tennis ball in his mouth. He removed the tennis ball and came right up to Jason. "I need some exercise. You want to throw a few for me?"

"Sure. I need to get dressed and have a snack first."

Jason took the elevator upstairs and retuned shortly in his jeans. He was chewing a granola bar.

"Keep a watch out for anyone suspicious, Tomas," Harold said.

"We don't want him disappearing again."

"You can count on me." He clicked his teeth. "I still have all my teeth and will sink them into anyone who messes with Jason."

The two of them trotted off.

"Boys and their dogs." Harold shook his head

Harold approached Peter Lemieux, who looked like he had seen a dead body, which he had. "Peter, why didn't someone look in the storage area sooner?"

"No reason to go there recently. No one moved in, no one moved out..." He gulped. "And no families cleaning out after a death."

"And no one thought to look there when the two women went missing?"

"Apparently not. Now if you'll excuse me, I need to go to my office."

Peter stumbled away. Moments later Bella appeared. "You get the third degree as well?" he asked.

"Yes. The detective asked what I had seen, why we went into the storage area and what happened to Jason. He was very thorough."

"I wonder what happened to Hattie and Frieda."

"Detective Deavers will figure it out, as well as who abducted Jason." Bella looked thoughtfully off in the distance. "If not, we'll have to assist him."

Harold smacked his forehead. "Dang. In all the confusion I forgot to mention the note left on Jason's bed. I better go get it to show to Detective Deavers."

"I'll come with you."

They took one of the Back Wing elevators to the fourth floor and went to Harold's room.

"Where did you leave the note?" Bella asked.

"I dropped it back on the sheets of the sofa bed."

He unlocked the door and they entered. Harold went to the bed still open in the living room. He gaped. The note was gone.

CHAPTER TWENTY-TWO 🦇

Harold and Bella went down to the lobby to wait for Jason. "None of this makes any sense," Harold said.

"It makes sense to whoever did it."

"Yeah, but why leave the note in the first place?"

"Obviously to send you a message, Harold."

"But then taking it back?"

"After the police showed up, it could have been someone with easy access to resident rooms who returned to grab the note to cover his tracks."

Harold popped up and began pacing. "Like someone on the staff."

"It couldn't be Peter Lemieux. He was with us downstairs."

"And Winston Salton?"

"Did I hear my name?" Salton slithered up.

Harold flinched as the executive director of Mountain Splendor leaned over and put a meaty paw on his shoulder.

"Yes...uh...we wondered what you're doing to make this place safer." Harold gave himself a mental pat on the back for the quick recovery.

Bella winked at Harold. "We're very concerned. Two deaths and a kidnapping. How are you going to keep us out of danger? We're not sure we want to continue living here."

Winston paled. "We're working closely with the police to find who committed these crimes. This has been a most unusual set of circumstances. I assure you nothing like this will happen again."

"I don't know. From now on, I'll wake up every morning wondering if my grandson is still in my apartment."

Bella put her hand to her cheek. "And dear me, I don't think I'll

116

ever be able to go into that storage area again."

Winston reached inside his jacket pocket and pulled out a dozen blue tickets which he divided and handed to Harold and Bella. "Here are some free meal tickets. Take them as a small repayment for the trauma you've both been through. I'm sorry for your inconvenience. Let me know if I can be of any further assistance." He turned and strode away.

Bella handed her tickets to Harold. "Since I don't eat in the dining room, you can have these. It should cover Jason for the rest of his stay. Can you imagine him trying to buy us off with a few meal tickets? The gall of the man."

Detective Deavers came out of the stairwell. "Good. I want to speak with you two."

Bella batted her eyes. "More inquisition, Detective?"

"No further questions at the moment, Ms. Alred. Can you gather the resident committee in the dining room in thirty minutes?"

"I'll invite the others," Bella said.

"Fine. I'll meet you there after I make a few phone calls." He whipped out his cell phone and stepped out of hearing range.

Harold and Bella were the first to arrive. They selected a six-person table and waited for the others to appear. Shortly, Atherton Cartwright strolled in. He wore sparkling white tennis shoes, tan Dockers, a pale blue polo shirt with a white sweater over his shoulders. He sniffed. "You two the only ones here yet?"

"The best part of the committee." Harold grinned. "Where's your partner in crime?"

Atherton's mouth dropped open. "I beg your pardon."

"Ah, there she is." Bella pointed toward the door.

Martha Kefauver swished into the room. She wore a floor-length flower dress and a wide brim hat with an orchid attached. "Well, I don't know why we all have to meet again. Those poor women have been found. But I understand the detective insisted that we get together, so here I am. Nice seeing you, Atherton."

"Likewise, Martha."

The two Front Wingers began conversing as if they hadn't seen each other since the last yacht regatta.

"I wish we had a spot of tea," Bella said.

"Mais, oui, Madame," Harold answered. "Or a flute of champagne."

Deavers strode into the room, all business. He dropped into one of the two empty chairs. "Thanks for meeting with me."

"I don't know why I have to be subjected to this again," Martha huffed. "It's good for you," Bella said. "Don't get your drawers in a knot." Martha's mouth shut like a snapping turtle's.

"All right." Deavers tapped his pen on the table. "Since this group had been assigned to work with the residents after the disappearance of the two women, I want to get you all together, so you can communicate with the other residents. Continue to enlist others who may have any useful information."

"Martha and I will give you our full cooperation." Atherton jutted out his chin.

"And you think Harold and I won't?" Bella glared at him.

Atherton gave a dismissive wave of his hand. "I can't speak for those of you in the…Back Wing."

"To set the record straight, the Back Wing has been instrumental in finding the two dead women as well as locating the kidnapped boy, so don't act so superior." Bella continued to glare at Atherton.

Harold wondered what the jerk's punishment would be this time. He smiled inwardly. He could hardly wait to see what Bella would do to him.

Atherton cleared his throat. "But you people caused so much commotion. There were noises in the hallway, shouting and quite a hubbub."

Martha patted her hat. "To say nothing of a bat that flew in my room when I opened the door. And there's now the smell of dog urine, of all things, in the hallway. It was like a pack of ruffians invaded the Front Wing."

Deavers whacked the table again and everyone jumped. "I don't care about your petty bickering. We have two murders and a kidnapping to look into. Are you people going to cooperate, or do I need to find other representatives?"

"You have the full backing of the Back Wing, including Harold and me." Bella graced him with an angelic smile.

"And as I previously mentioned, I committed the support of the Front Wing," Atherton said through clenched teeth.

"Good. Now here's the skinny I can share with you at this time." Deavers sat back in his chair. "We have positive identification of the bodies of Hattie Jensen and Frieda Eubanks. The coroner will be completing tests to learn more on the cause of the deaths. Again, if anyone saw or heard anything when the women disappeared, notify me immediately."

"Eyesight and hearing aren't a strong suit in this place," Harold said. "That may be, but sometimes what may seem insignificant can be very helpful. Now do you have anything else for me?"

Harold thought for moment. "From what I can determine the two women were very different. It appears that Hattie Jensen was very neat and conservative while Frieda Eubanks was pretty sloppy and may have accumulated some gambling debts. The only common thing between them was they both played poker."

"I agree with what Mr. McCaffrey says," Atherton pitched in. "Frieda lost consistently in our poker games. She even tried to hit me up for a loan one time. Of course, I refused."

"She could have accumulated some serious debt to the wrong kind of people," Harold said. "Have you found any indication of that, Detective?"

Deavers jotted a note on his pad. "It's a direction we're investigating."

Harold thought of what they had found in Frieda's apartment and decided why not? "There were some rumors that Frieda was trying to blackmail other residents. Any sign of that?"

Martha gasped, and Atherton choked.

"We're looking into that. What else?"

"As you know, I'm very concerned that my grandson was abducted. He seems to have weathered the trauma very well, but I don't want that to happen again. And I still don't know why someone took him."

"It may well relate to the murder of the two women. Once we know more regarding the cause of their deaths it may shed light on the situation with your grandson."

Harold wished he still had the note left in Jason's bed, but without it, he had nothing for Deavers to go on. "Someone left a warning note to me, but it disappeared."

"What did it say?" Deavers asked.

Harold gave himself a mental pat on the back for remembering the words. "'If you want your grandson back alive, stay out of what doesn't concern you.' It could have been a warning to me because I was asking questions around the retirement home. Since I'll continue to help as a member of this committee, I'm still concerned for Jason's safety."

"Mr. Salton has agreed to increase the security patrol for the next several weeks, and I'll see that a police officer stops here regularly. Anything else?"

All four heads shook.

"Fine. I need to check with one other person while I'm here." Deavers sprang up and shot out of the room.

"Is there anything else the four of us should cover?" Harold asked.

Martha raised her nose and sniffed loudly. "I can't imagine anything that Atherton and I have to discuss with you two."

At that moment Abner Dane raced into the room waving his hands. "Abner heard that you would be meeting here."

"Uh-oh," Atherton said. "The fruitcake has arrived."

"What are you saying about Abner?" The man stuck his face three inches from Atherton's nose and poked a finger into his chest.

"Stand back." Atherton gave Abner a shove.

Abner stumbled but caught his balance. "Be careful how you treat Abner. He has important information for this committee."

"Get lost," Atherton said.

"Abner knows who killed those two women, but now he isn't going to tell you." He spun on his heels and marched out of the dining room.

"Let's get out of here, Martha." Atherton scraped his chair back, stood, took a step and fell flat on his face.

Harold leaned over the table and noticed that Atherton's shoes laces were tied together.

Martha grabbed the midsection of her dress and scooted out of the room before you could say falling drawers.

120

CHAPTER TWENTY-THREE 🦇

When Harold and Jason were back in the room, Harold tested the lock on the door to make sure it was sound. That would keep the Front Wingers out, and his gut told him they were more danger than the Back Wingers with their unique abilities. He was concerned about the safety of his grandson.

"Maybe we should find a different place for you to stay until your parents come back from their trip."

Jason made a crossing motion with his hands. "No way."

"But it isn't safe here."

Jason clenched his fists. "I'll watch my back. No one will sneak up on me again."

Harold hoped that would be the case.

After dinner that evening as Harold sat in his easy chair looking at his *Smithsonian Magazine* and Jason lay on the rug reading a vampire book, the phone rang.

Harold picked up and heard the voice of Jason's mother, Emily. "You calling from Hawaii?" Harold asked.

"Yes, we're having a wonderful time, but I want to check in with Jason. Is he there?"

"Let me put him on the line." Harold held his hand over the mouthpiece and whispered to Jason. "It's your mother. Don't mention being abducted."

Jason nodded, pulled himself to his feet and took the phone. "Hi, Mom." He stood on one foot and then the other as he listened. "Cool.

I'll have to visit Maui sometime...nope, I'm not bored. Grandpa lives in a great place. I've made new friends...no, there's no one here my age, but I've met some cool older people, like Grandpa, with-it people...yeah, in the last few days I think I've learned more than in my last year at school...yeah, I found someone to play Frisbee with, and this is an exciting place...well, sure the people are old but that doesn't mean that all of them are vegetables, sitting in wheelchairs waiting to die...no way, you wouldn't believe what some of these people can do...yeah, I'll tell you more when you get back" He smiled at Harold. "Sorry, I got carried away."

When Harold rolled his eyes, Jason said, "Bye. Here's Grandpa." He handed the phone back to Harold.

"Jason sounds like he's enjoying himself."

"He's quite a young man, Emily. You'd be amazed at how he has handled himself and how well he gets along with...uh...older people."

There was a pause on the line. "That's funny. He never acted very interested when my parents came to visit."

Harold didn't bother to mention that his in-laws treated Jason like a three-year-old. "Jason has matured. He's made the most of being here and has taken an interest in some of the...uh...more unique residents."

"Probably regaling people with his stories of vampires."

"And vice versa."

"Huh?"

Harold gulped. "Oh, nothing. Jason is interested in people, and the residents in my part of the building have taken a liking to him. It's going well."

"Uh-oh, I better go," Emily said. "Our tour's waiting."

"Good to hear from you, Emily. Give my best to Nelson, and we'll see you next week when you both return tan and rested."

Harold hung up the phone and looked at Jason, who had a huge grin on his face as if he were the cat that had eaten a whole aviary. "What?"

Jason wagged a finger at him. "Grandpa, I never thought you'd be one to hide things from my parents."

Harold shrugged. "They're on vacation. No sense troubling them with what's going on here at Mountain Splendor."

"And you didn't tell them about your friends."

"They wouldn't understand. I think it takes a teenager to appreciate old witches, vampires, werewolves and shape-shifters."

"You fit in pretty good, Grandpa."

"I'm more tolerant than most people my age."

"Well, yeah. You even have a girlfriend who's a witch."

Harold felt his cheeks grow warm. "Bella's not my girlfriend."

"She could be if you want her to be. I've seen her eyes when she looks at you."

A feeling of warmth grew in Harold's chest. Out of the mouth of babes.

CHAPTER TWENTY-FOUR 🦇

Harold slept late again the next morning. He awoke with a start and raced into the living room to make sure Jason was still there. To his immense relief his grandson was still sacked out, one leg outside the sheet and his hair as disheveled as if a cake mixer had been used to tend his locks. Harold looked at his watch. Nine. They had missed breakfast. Not even the blue tickets from Winston Salton would help at this hour.

Jason must have been suffering the aftereffects from being chloroformed and all the excitement of finding another dead body. No sense rousing the lad. Harold tiptoed back to his bedroom, picked up his spy novel and propped himself up in bed.

Harold read and dozed until he heard shuffling sounds and the toilet flushing. He removed the book from his chest, set it on the nightstand, stood and went into the hall as Jason emerged from the bathroom rubbing his eyes.

"Sleeping Beauty has finally come around."

"Morning, Grandpa."

Harold tapped his watch. "Actually afternoon. Five after twelve."

"I didn't think I slept that late."

"You must have been tuckered out. Ready for some lunch?"

"Yeah. I'm starving."

They got dressed and headed down for tuna sandwiches, fruit salad and cookies. Jason finished off two sandwiches, two servings of fruit and half a dozen cookies.

"The food here is pretty good, Grandpa."

"Yes, I've been pleasantly surprised."

"And you don't have to cook for yourself anymore."

124

"That's been a relief. Your grandmother was a good cook, but after she was gone, I mainly zapped frozen dinners."

"I remember having a big Thanksgiving turkey at your house when I was seven or so." He licked his lips. "Great stuffing and pumpkin pie. Hmm, mmm."

Harold smiled as he recalled the chaos of a typical Thanksgiving day, helping Jennifer get the turkey into the oven, whipping the potatoes and carving the bird. She prepared plates full of goodies and afterwards stored everything in bins that filled up the refrigerator. They ate turkey sandwiches for the next week.

Jason grabbed another cookie. "When I got a little older, we went up in the mountains for ski trips most Thanksgiving weekends."

"You still like to ski?"

"Yeah. I go up a dozen or so weekends a year. And I've been waterskiing during the summer. I like both."

After Jason finished the last cookie crumbs, they went down to the first floor so Harold could check for mail. He found two bills and three promotional flyers. Typical, but it was good to know his mail had been forwarded to his new address. As he closed his mailbox and turned around, Detective Deavers walked past, leading Bella by the arm.

"Where are you going?" Harold asked.

Bella gave him a devilish grin. "The good detective is taking me in for questioning."

"Do you want me to come with you?" Deavers stopped. "This doesn't concern you."

Harold winced at the tone of the detective's voice.

"I'll stop by your apartment when I get back." Bella waved as Deavers propelled her toward the parking lot.

"How about a game of shuffleboard?" Jason asked. "There's a court right next to the swimming pool."

Harold realized he had not availed himself of some of the activities at Mountain Splendor. Since he had become caught up in the goings on of the Back Wing, the murders and Jason's visit, he really hadn't done much else. "Sure. I used to be pretty good."

"Prepare to meet your doom."

"You sound pretty cocky, young man."

"Well, yeah. I've been practicing. In addition to playing catch, Tomas and I tried shuffleboard. I whipped him big time."

Harold dismissed the image in his mind of Tomas holding a shuffleboard stick in his teeth. "Okay. Let's get this show on the road." Jason led Harold through the gate of the swimming pool. Half a dozen women in swimming caps splashed around, flapping their hands in the air.

"Must be a water aerobics class," Harold said.

"Either that or they're trying to learn to fly." Jason came to the shuffleboard court and extracted two sticks and eight discs from a storage locker. He set them on the cement surface. "You get to choose the color, Grandpa."

"Black for the avenger."

Jason grinned. "Then I'll be red, the favorite color of the Back Wing. I'll even shoot the first puck."

"They're also called biscuits, Jason. You'll be sending the first biscuit." Jason rolled his eyes. "Thanks for the history lesson." Positioning his stick, he shot the first disc down the court right into the seven-point zone. He pumped his fist in the air. "Yes."

"Not bad for a kid." Harold stuck his tongue out the side of his mouth, pulled back his arm and sent his biscuit sailing down the court and tapped Jason's disc into the minus-ten trapezoid while his black puck remained in the seven-point box.

Jason gawked. "How'd you do that?"

Harold dusted his hands together. "Experience and cunning. Your shot."

Jason tried to knock Harold's puck out of the way, but it missed and flew into the grass at the end of the court.

Pushing aside his concern over Bella, Harold took a deep breath and sent his biscuit into the eight-point zone. After the first frame,

Harold led fifteen to minus ten. He soundly trounced Jason through the complete ten frames.

"You up for another game?" Harold patted his grandson on the back. Jason shrugged out of reach. "Darn right. You were just lucky."

"Let's see how lucky I am the second time."

Jason bore down, and Harold watched the intense concentration on his grandson's face. The score ended closer this time, but Harold

126

still won easily. "Three out of five?" Harold asked.

Jason's shoulders slumped. "Nah. I've had enough."

Harold chuckled. "Cheer up. I didn't tell you before, but I used to be an expert at this game. Even won a few tournaments in my day."

Jason perked up. "I didn't know that. You're a ringer. No wonder you beat me. Good thing I didn't bet with you."

"Yeah, stick with poker for that. And let it be a lesson to you. Be careful who you challenge. Loser has to put the equipment away."

Jason picked up the sticks and discs and carried them to the storage cabinet. As he shut the door, he yelled, "Ow!" and shook his hand.

"What happened?"

"A nail jabbed me."

Harold examined the bleeding finger. "Let's go upstairs, and I'll get you a bandage. Have you had a tetanus shot recently?"

"Well, yeah. I had one at the beginning of the last school year." Up in Harold's apartment he sorted through his medicine cabinet.

"I thought I had a box, but apparently it didn't make the move. Bella's not around, so let me try my other neighbor, Viola."

They went out and Harold knocked on Viola's door. There was no sound. He knocked again. This time he heard a shuffling noise and a snort. The door opened and a wild-haired Viola stood there, squinting at him. "Who are you?"

"I'm your neighbor Harold, and this is my grandson Jason."

She wrinkled her nose before a smile crossed her face. "That's right. What do you want in the middle of the night?"

"Oh, I forgot you sleep late. Jason cut his finger, and I'm looking for a bandage."

Viola's eyes lit up. "Don't keep such things, but I may be able to help. Come in."

They entered a stark living room. A small amount of light filter through the drawn curtains to show a white couch on a white rug. Nothing else.

"I can see that your interior decorator obviously came from the minimalist school of design," Harold said.

Viola grunted. "I don't need much. Let's see this finger." Jason held it out.

"Hmmm. Still bleeding a lot." Viola smiled. "That's excellent."

Second thoughts raced through Harold's mind over making a mistake in bringing Jason to see her. Before he could say anything, Bella thrust Jason's finger in her mouth.

"What are you doing?" Jason tried to pull away, but Viola had a firm grip. "She's sucking on my finger!"

After a moment Viola released it. "Ah, good. As long as you woke me up, I needed some breakfast."

Jason stared at his hand. Steam rose from the injured finger. "The... the hole is gone."

"Yup." Viola stretched her arms, yawned and burped. "Vampire saliva cures wounds. You're as good as new. Thanks for the snack."

Harold had a passing thought—a vampire wound clinic would save Medicare billions of dollars.

CHAPTER TWENTY-FIVE 🦇

Back in their apartment, Jason continued to stare at his healed finger. "I can't believe it. Not a sign of where it got poked." Then his eyes widened. "You don't think I'll turn into a vampire because Viola sucked on my finger?"

At that moment Bella appeared through the wall. "No, you have to be bitten on the neck and sucked nearly dry."

Harold smiled. "Excellent. Our expert has arrived to educate us on the ways of vampires. How was your session with the police?"

"Uneventful. Detective Deavers asked me a lot of questions. It turns out he discovered my fingerprints on the storage bin where Hattie Jensen's body was found. He can be a most inquisitive fellow."

"How did he match your fingerprints?"

Bella smoothed her hair. "My fingerprints were on file from a few years ago."

"You've been arrested before?" Jason chimed in.

"Nothing like that. I went through questioning once and volunteered to give my fingerprints. Nothing serious."

"I sense a story there," Harold said.

"Not much of one. Several of us participated in a little...uh chat by a campfire. Some snoopy neighbor reported it, the police showed up and took us in. Just a misunderstanding, but we were booked, printed and then released."

"Wow." Jason's eyes widened again. "Your coven gathering?"

"Something like that."

"Do you get together with other witches very often?" Jason asked.
"Not any more. I don't like sitting by an open fire very much. The smoke bothers my eyes, and my joints don't like sitting in the cold."

"Can I come if you do meet again?"

"I'll let you know, but we have nothing planned in the foreseeable future."

There was a knock on the door.

Jason opened it to find Tomas Greeley standing there. "Ready?"

Jason slapped his forehead. "In all the excitement I forgot we were going to explore the foothills this afternoon."

"You're too young to have short-term memory loss," Bella said. "I think Viola has rubbed off on you."

"Nah, I think it's from the chloroform yesterday."

"I don't know if it's safe after what happened," Harold said.

Tomas thumped his chest. "No one will mess with Jason with me around."

"Won't you get hungry and thirsty if you're going on a hike?" Harold asked.

"I have a backpack with a water bottle and snacks for him." Tomas said, holding it up. "We're set for a long jaunt."

"Just don't find any bones on this trip," Harold replied.

"Let's go." Jason dashed out and slammed the door behind him.

"Jason's certainly a fine boy," Bella said.

"He has overcome his sulkiness with all the entertainment around this place. Quite a change from when he arrived here complaining that he was stuck with old people."

"I think we've given him a whole new perspective on the aging process."

"Definitely exposed him to lots of different kinds of people." There was another knock on the door.

"This apartment has become meeting central." Harold stepped over and opened the door to find a scowling Detective Deavers standing there.

"Is Ms. Alred here?"

Bella waved from the living room. "Yoo hoo, Detective."

He stepped inside. "We weren't done speaking at the police station. How did you get out of the interrogation room?"

Bella turned so Deavers couldn't see her face and winked at Harold. "When the other police officer knocked on the door and asked you to take a phone call, I thought we had finished. You must have left the door unlocked, so I took my leave. Simple as that."

Deavers let out a burst of air as if trying to rid his lungs of Denver's brown cloud. "The door was locked. There's no way you could have gotten out of there."

Bella shrugged. "If you have other questions I can answer them right now."

"One last item. How do you suppose your fingerprints ended up in the storage bin where Hattie Jensen was found?"

"Harold, Peter Lemieux and I went into the storage area because of the foul odor we smelled. We all saw the woman's hands sticking out of the storage bin. I imagine in my shock, I touched the side of the bin."

Deavers looked at her skeptically. "That's it for now. I still can't figure out how you got out of that room."

"As you get older, young man, you won't sweat the small stuff."

Deavers snapped his notebook closed. "I wonder what would happen if you were locked in jail."

Bella gave him her most angelic smile. "I wouldn't advise that. Jails aren't a good place for women my age."

"I've aged ten years in the last three days being around this place." Deavers left the apartment, closing the door none too gently.

"Intense young man," Bella said.

"What did you do this time, Bella?" Harold asked.

"As I told the nice detective, I waited and when no one came back to the room, I left. No sense sitting there being bored."

"Your through-the-wall shenanigans won't sit well with the police."

"No one saw me come out of the wall. Besides, Detective Deavers needs a few things to think over."

"He already has his hands full."

Bella's mouth curled into a coy smile. "That's why we're here to help him."

CHAPTER TWENTY-SIX 🦇

Not to be left alone with Bella for a spare moment, Harold sprang up as someone pounded on the door. He opened it to find Alexandra Hooper looking up at him.

"Bella in there by any chance?"

"How'd you track her down?"

"She wasn't in her apartment, so I figured I'd try here." Alexandra looked around Harold's shoulder. "Hi, Bella. I have some information to report."

Harold waved her in, and Alexandra entered and immediately went over to the couch and ran her hand over it. "Nice sofa. I'll have to try this model sometime." Then she dropped down and bounced on it for a moment.

Bella stepped over to her. "You learn something?"

"Oh, yes. As you suggested, I've spent most of the last day in the Front Wing lounge. That hunk, Atherton Cartwright, even sat in my lap this morning. I wanted so much to reach out and pat his tush, but I didn't. I'll have you know I behaved myself."

Bella's eyes sparkled. "I'm glad you showed some restraint, Alexandra."

"He spoke on his cell phone while sitting there. He thought no one could hear him. And you know what he said?"

"Probably not placing a sell order with his broker." Bella tapped her foot.

"No." Alexandra spoke in a conspiratorial tone. "But something you'll find interesting. He talked about Hattie Jensen."

Bella and Harold both leaned forward as if someone had whacked them on the backs. Bella shook Alexandra's shoulders. "What did

132

he say?"

Alexandra gave a smug nod. "He mentioned expecting she had bequeathed him a sizable amount of money in her will."

"What!" Harold stood as erect as a totem pole. "She left all her money to Mountain Splendor. It seems multiple people were after Hattie's money. What was Atherton up to? Could you tell who was on the phone?"

"Of course. He was leaning back against me...I mean the couch... so I heard everything clearly. It was that snooty woman, Martha Kefauver. They discussed how they would share the money now that Hattie had met her maker. Atherton said he had dropped hints of marrying Hattie, and she had fallen for it hook, line and stinker." Alexandra giggled. "Atherton was the stinker of course. It's obvious he was leading Hattie astray while still playing cozy with Martha. Can you believe the gall of that cad? You just can't find a good man in this place anymore." She smiled at Harold. "Present company excepted."

Bella moved closer to Harold and took his arm. "From what you overheard, do you think Atherton killed Hattie?"

Alexandra regarded Bella thoughtfully. "It's possible either he or Martha took care of Hattie. They obviously wanted her money."

"This still doesn't make sense," Harold said. "With Hattie's money going to Mountain Splendor, Winston Salter was my main person-of-interest, not either of those two. We now have an expanded suspect list. I wonder if Detective Deavers is aware of any of this."

"I don't know," Bella said. "When he questioned me, he never asked about Atherton, Martha or Winston."

"You've uncovered some really important information," Harold said. Alexandra's cheeks reddened. "Just trying to help out."

"Bella, we need to speak with Deavers right away," Harold said.

"Exactly. We may have to set him straight." Bella stepped over to the window and looked out. "Good. His car's still in the parking lot. Let's go wait for him."

"I think I'll go back to the Front Wing lounge," Alexandra said. "See if I can hear any more good poop."

The three of them took the elevator down. Alexandra entered the Front Wing lounge and transformed into an upholstered couch.

Harold and Bella checked the lobby area, and not spotting Detective Deavers, proceeded to the parking lot. Harold tried the door handle on Deavers's car and found it locked. "I guess we can wait here."

"No sense standing up. Let's sit inside." Bella looked around. "Good. No one in sight." She passed her hand through the window, popped the lock, pulled her hand out and opened the door. After plopping down in the driver's seat, she waved to Harold. "It's all unlocked. Come around to the passenger's side."

Harold circled the car and let himself in. "Detective Deavers isn't going to be pleased that we're in here."

"Oh posh. We have important information for him. We'll let him have a little conniption fit and then set the record straight."

Harold looked around and concluded no one had seen them enter the car. "Does anyone ever suspect you're a witch, Bella?"

"Not very often. Most people are so wrapped up in normal rationality that they don't consider the possibility of beings like me. I don't try to shock people. I prefer a low profile."

"Like sneaking out of police interrogation rooms, entering police cars and causing drawers and zippers to drop?"

"There are exceptions. As long as we're here, let's look at all these gadgets." She pointed to a radio and a laptop mounted between the two seats.

"I don't think we should mess with anything."

"You don't want me to turn on his siren?"

"I'm sure that would bring him running, but no."

Bella looked toward the building. "Oh, goodie. Here comes our man." Deavers strode up to his car and came to a skidding stop when he saw Bella and Harold inside. He grabbed the door handle and pulled it open. "What are you doing here?"

"Waiting for you, Detective." Bella gracefully swung her legs out and stood. Harold exited his side and came around.

"How did you get in my car?"

Bella batted her eyelashes at him. "It was unlocked, and we were tired, so we decided to sit down until you appeared. We have some information for you."

"I always lock my car."

Bella wagged a finger at him. "I think you're becoming forgetful like many of our residents. Mountain Splendor must be rubbing off on you." He held his ground like an offensive lineman for the Denver

Broncos and crossed his arms. "I left my car locked."

Bella gave a dismissive wave of her hand. "Be that as it may, we have important news for you. Atherton Cartwright and Martha Kefauver from our residents committee have been conniving together. Atherton had been romancing Hattie Jensen with the intent of inheriting some of her money."

Deavers arched an eyebrow. "And the source of your information?"

"A little couch...er...bird told us. But you don't have to believe us. I'd suggest you check it out for yourself." Deavers whipped out his pad and made a note.

Harold tapped the side of the car. "And you already know this, but Hattie Jensen changed her will to leave all her money to Mountain Splendor. The executive director, Winston Salter, stands to benefit from this. You should grill him."

Deavers rolled his eyes. "Great. That's all I need in this mess — two amateur sleuths getting involved with their pet theories."

"Why, Detective, we were asked to represent the Back Wing and find any information we could." Bella grinned. "We're practically deputies."

"I'll look into what you've given me. Thanks...I guess." He got in his car, started the engine and lowered the window. "My car *was* locked." He stepped on the gas, screeched out of the parking place, and shot out of the lot like Pamela Quint if her sonar had been working.

CHAPTER TWENTY-SEVEN 🦇

As Harold and Bella returned to the building, they passed the Front Wing lounge, where a foursome of women were playing bridge. To their side rested the brown couch that didn't fit in with the rest of the decor.

"Alexandra should be catching up on all the latest bridge gossip," Bella said. "We'll have to debrief with her later."

"With Jason and Tomas still out hiking, I think I'll take a little stroll myself," Harold said. "I'm going upstairs to grab my walking poles. You want to join me?"

"That would be lovely. I need to change my shoes."

Harold collected his walking poles and stood in his living room thoughtfully looking out the window at the parking area. This place reeked of unanswered questions and suspicious activities. Detective Deavers had his hands full. Nothing had been resolved yet.

Bella tapped him on the shoulder. "All set."

He jumped and spun around. "I'll never get used to you coming and going through the walls. I'd hate to try hiding from you."

"Just you remember that." She put two fingers to the bridge of her nose and then pointed them at him. "I have my eyes on you."

"I'm not the one you should be spying on. Why don't you try Atherton Cartwright, Martha Kefauver or Winston Salton? They're much more suspicious that I am."

"True. But I also like to keep tabs on my neighbors. Let's get going."

They took the pokey little elevator to the first floor and headed out into the greenbelt. A breath of wind punctuated the sunny, warm day.

"Nice trail here," Harold said. "I haven't had a chance to go very far on it yet." He planted his walking pole and propelled forward.

"I've never tried walking poles," Bella said. "Why do you use them?"

Harold's eyes lit up. "Let me give you my pitch. First of all, they give you an upper body workout as well as your legs."

"That makes sense."

"They also take stress off of my old hip and knee joints. I want to minimize the effects of arthritis as long as I can."

"I haven't had any trouble with arthritis other than when I sit too long at campfires in the middle of the night."

"You're lucky. They also help with balance. I remember one time before using walking poles coming down a trail and suddenly finding myself face down in the dirt. It happened so quickly I never had a chance to get my hands up."

"Oh, my," Bella patted his arm.

"But since using walking poles, I haven't done another face plant. It's also estimated that you burn off twenty percent more calories using them than regular walking."

Bella gave him the once over. "Obviously it's working. You've stayed trim and fit."

Harold looked at his companion. "You likewise, and you haven't even had to resort to using walking poles."

"I don't eat that much."

"And the final advantage of walking poles." Harold waved one in the air. "Self-defense. They can be used to fend off wild creatures of the animal or human variety."

"Spoken like a true insurance salesman."

"Yep. It's in my blood."

They wound their way up into the foothills for half an hour and came to a spot with a view back toward the Mountain Splendor building.

"All those people down there going about their business," Harold said. "And somewhere in there may be a murderer or two."

"It's interesting. You see a building and don't think of all the emotional drama that may be going on inside."

Bella stretched her arms. "Every building has a story as does every individual."

"Enough philosophy. Let's head back."

As they retraced their steps, Bella asked, "How often do you take walks?"

"I try to exercise for an hour every day," Harold said.

"I don't get out that often, but I'll be happy to join you any time you want to go out for a jaunt. Now let me try these poles of yours." Harold took the loops off his wrists and handed the poles to Bella.

She grabbed the handgrips and took off at full stride. Harold caught up with her. "What do you think?"

"They remind me of giant wands."

"Do you use a wand, Bella?"

"Not any longer. I used one when I was younger, but a finger will suffice or just thinking a spell now that I'm...more mature."

"That's a good way to state it. More mature. I'll have to remember that."

Bella handed the poles back to Harold. "I may have to get a pair of these. Where do you buy them?"

"At any sporting goods store. You'll find all kinds of models from twenty to two-hundred dollars."

Bella whistled. "That much for two sticks?"

"I have the more expensive type. Titanium tip, spring loaded for less pressure on the arms. It's one of my few extravagances."

She raised an eyebrow. "No sports car or villa on the French Riviera?"

"No. I have simple tastes."

"Good. I'm not much for people with affectations."

Back at Mountain Splendor they passed the Front Wing lounge. The bridge game had broken up, and the brown couch had disappeared.

"Let's stop by Alexandra's apartment and see if she's learned anything new," Bella said.

Alexandra was home and welcomed them into her apartment, crammed full of chairs and couches.

"Why all the furniture?" Harold asked.

Alexandra waved her hand. "I need lots of different models to practice with. I've perfected leather, upholstery, fabric, and micro-fiber. I can do any color and shape. But I can't do sectionals. I'd need a split personality for that."

"We stopped by to find out if you learned anything interesting in the Front Wing lounge," Bella said.

"Oh, I did. One of the women playing bridge, Rachel Kunz, lambasted Frieda Eubanks."

"What was her problem with Frieda?" Harold asked.

"Rachel described Frieda as a no good, money-grubbing so-and-so, who tried to borrow money from her and even threatened her with blackmail. Rachel didn't say what the blackmail was about. Apparently she didn't want to divulge that to her bridge group."

"Didn't they ask?"

"Oh, they hinted around, but Rachel became very evasive. She changed the subject after that."

"I think I'll have to make the acquaintance of Rachel Kunz," Harold said. "I may be able to pick up more information if I speak with her in confidence."

"Have at it," Alexandra said. "She's in room 315. After the game she planned to work on some knitting. Making socks for her grandkids. Just be careful. She also mentioned that she didn't like aggressive men. She stabbed Atherton Cartwright with a knitting needle one time when he got fresh with her."

Bella looked at Harold. "Atherton has been making the rounds."

"Apparently he's quite the ladies man," Harold replied. "I'm surprised he hasn't made a pass at you, Bella."

She gave him an innocent smile. "I think he prefers women he can push around. He obviously underestimated the knitting needle wielding Rachel Kunz. Be careful when you approach her, Harold."

CHAPTER TWENTY-EIGHT 🦇

Harold took off to speak with the vicious Rachel Kunz. After knocking and waiting a minute, the door opened six inches revealing a five foot tall, dowdy woman. She pointed a knitting needle and eyed him warily. "Yes?"

"Ms. Kunz, my name is Harold McCaffrey. I'm a new resident here at Mountain Splendor. I'd like to speak with you."

"Yes?" She waved the knitting needle as if it were a sword.

The door didn't open any further, and her expression didn't change. Harold realized he would have to improvise. "I understand you're a bridge player. I'm trying to meet people who play."

She flung the door open, and a glint appeared in her eyes. "A bridge player. We're always looking for new blood. Come in."

Harold might have expected that statement from someone living in the Back Wing, but here? He stepped into the apartment and did a double take. Every surface displayed pictures of cats—Siamese, Persian, Maine coon, tortoise shell and even a gray tabby. The walls had oil and watercolor paintings of cats in meadows, on cushions, in windowsills. The bookshelf held hundreds of cat miniatures. He felt as if he had entered a cat museum.

"In addition to bridge, you must be a cat aficionado," Harold said.

A huge smile coursed over her wrinkled face. "Oh, yes. I love cats of all kinds." Then the grin faded. "But Mountain Splendor won't let me keep a cat in my apartment. They have these archaic rules—no pets."

"That's a shame." Harold sniffed the air. He could swear he smelled a background odor of cat pee. Maybe Rachel sprayed it around instead of air freshener. "I understand you knew Frieda Eubanks."

Rachel's face turned into a snarl, and she waved a knitting needle, missing Harold by inches. "That awful woman."

"In addition to my interest in bridge, I'm on a committee that has been asked by the police to help with the investigation into Frieda's death. I'm always interested in hearing what people knew of her before she disappeared."

"Whatever happened to her, she deserved it in spades...as well as clubs, diamonds and hearts. She was a despicable woman."

Harold arched an eyebrow. "Oh, did she do something to you?"

"Why she...no, I guess I shouldn't speak badly of the dead. May I offer you some coffee or tea, Mr. McCaffrey?"

"Black coffee would be great."

"If you wait a moment, I have some brewing."

Harold heard a sound that he could have sworn was a cat meowing. "Thank you. May I use your bathroom in the meantime?"

Rachel waved toward the hallway. "By all means."

Harold went down the short hall to the bathroom, entered and closed the door. He sniffed again. Definitely cat smells. The shower curtain was closed. He pulled it back and looked inside. A cat litter box sat there with a black stain in one corner. He waited a moment, flushed the toilet and left the bathroom. He stuck his head in the bedroom as a flash of white disappeared under the bed.

This brought a smile to his face.

Back in the living room, Rachel handed him a coffee mug covered with the picture of a black and white cat's face. She clicked his with another mug showing a brown short hair cat, yawning and displaying sharp white teeth. "Cheers."

They sat down facing each other.

Harold took a sip. "Thank you." He had figured out what Alexandra had overheard and had made a decision on how to proceed. "I hate to be blunt, but was Frieda Eubanks threatening to blackmail you over the cat you keep here?"

Rachel coughed and laid her mug down. Her eyes watered, and she coughed again into her closed fist. "What cat?"

"Look. I'm not going to tell anyone. It's fine with me that you like cats and have one in your apartment. But I'm trying to find out what happened to Frieda Eubanks, and I think you could give me some insight into her character."

Rachel slumped back into her chair and covered her eyes with her hands. "Yes, the obnoxious woman threatened to rat me out to the retirement home administration. She wanted me to pay her five hundred bucks to keep her mouth shut."

"Did you agree to the threat?"

"I told her to give me a day to round up the money. In the meantime she disappeared. Good riddance."

Harold considered her carefully. Could she have killed Frieda? His intuition told him no. He couldn't see her actually using the knitting needle as a weapon. "If she blackmailed you, do you think she did the same thing to other people?"

"It's entirely possible. She was after money any way she could get it."

"Did you know Hattie Jensen?"

Rachel bit her lip. "Not very well. What a contrast to Frieda. Hattie was a sweet lady and very demure. A little slip of a woman, couldn't have weighed more than a hundred pounds."

Then a thought occurred to him. "Would it be possible that Frieda also tried to blackmail Hattie?"

"Could be, although I don't know what deep dark secrets Hattie had that would have tempted Frieda to seek money from her. But I guess we all have secrets." Rachel stared at him. "What's your secret, Mr. McCaffrey?"

Harold thought of witches, vampires, werewolves and shape-shifters. Instead, he smiled and whispered, "I used to be an insurance salesman. Don't tell anyone."

She nodded. "You can call me Rachel, and I'll keep your secret if you keep mine."

"It's a deal. And you can call me Harold. So, Rachel, how have you kept the cat from being discovered by the Mountain Splendor staff?"

She rubbed her thumb against her fingers. "I give nice tips to the housekeeping people so they haven't told their boss."

"I see. Money makes the world go around."

"Well I do have to look out for Snookums. I might as well introduce you two." She clicked her tongue and in a moment a white Persian cat sauntered into the living room. "Harold, do you like cats?"

"I had a Siamese when I was a kid. We didn't have cats after I got married because my wife had an allergy to cat hair."

"That would be an awful affliction."

The fur ball approached and rubbed against Harold's leg. He reached down and scratched it under the chin, leading to a loud rumbling purr.

"You're now officially friends. She's trained to hide under the bed when anyone comes in my apartment unless I give her the all clear signal." Rachel went into the kitchenette, opened a cupboard, removed a bowl with brown pellets and placed it on the floor. Snookums dashed over and began gobbling like crazy.

A loud knock sounded on the door. Pandemonium ensued. Snookums shot off for the bedroom scattering pellets in her wake. Rachel madly grabbed the bowl, scooped up the stray pieces and shoved all the evidence into the cupboard. Before Harold could offer to help, everything had been hidden.

Rachel righted herself, patted her hair and calmly opened the door. Detective Deavers stood there staring over Rachel's shoulder at Harold. "Mr. McCaffrey, we need to talk."

CHAPTER TWENTY-NINE 🦇

"**Y**our place or mine?" Harold said to Detective Deavers.

"We could stay here at Mountain Splendor, but I can take you into headquarters, if you prefer." Deavers gave him a crooked smile.

"That's okay. We can speak here."

"Let's go to your apartment where we can talk in private." Harold turned to Rachel. "It was a pleasure meeting you." She smiled. "Stop by again anytime."

As they waited at the elevator, Harold asked, "How'd you find me in Rachel Kunz's apartment?"

"I am a detective."

Harold and Deavers did the elevator shuffle and eventually reached the fourth floor of the Back Wing. Harold unlocked his apartment door as the detective said, "I'd hate to be in a hurry to get from one wing to the other in this place."

"We old people like taking our time. We don't have to rush around like you young whippersnappers."

"Don't give me that. With all the shenanigans going on around this place, I'll never think the same about old people again." Deavers gave a wry smile.

"You and me both, Detective. You and me both. Now, would you like to take a seat or do you want to grill me in the kitchenette?"

Deavers stepped into the living room and plopped down on the couch. "Let's make ourselves comfortable."

"Can I get you something to drink, Detective? I have coffee, tea, orange juice and some kind of cola."

Deavers gave a dismissive wave of his hand. "Nope. I'm fine."

Harold sat down, wondering what the detective was up to.

Deavers opened his notebook and tapped it twice. "Mr. McCaffrey, you've been very cooperative in assisting my investigation, but I have one question for you. Do you often go into the Front Wing?"

What was the devious mind of Deavers getting at? "Uh, yeah, I've been there a number of times. Why do you ask?"

"Can you explain why your fingerprints would be in Hattie Jensen's apartment?"

Harold flinched. "How did you even match my fingerprints?"

"They were in the system."

Harold snapped his fingers as he remembered. "That's right. I worked at a homeless shelter for several years. They required fingerprints."

"There you go. Anyway, your fingerprints on file matched ones found in Hattie Jensen's place. Care to share how they got there?"

Harold looked up toward the ceiling, inspecting the insulated tile for a moment, and then forced a smile. "I bet it was during the tour."

"Tour?"

"When my son brought me here for a visit, a nice woman named Ruth took us all through the facility. Since I wanted a one-bedroom apartment, she took me up to a resident's room on the sixth floor of the Front Wing. Ruth said the woman who lived there had given her permission to look around. It was a very neat apartment with a roll top desk in the bedroom. Ruth insisted that I touch the desk to feel how smooth the wood was. Yes, that must have been it." Harold silently congratulated himself. Deavers had no way to prove his story a fabrication since Ruth had died.

Deavers regarded Harold warily. "That would explain one set of your prints found in Hattie Jensen's room but not all of them."

"Let's see." Harold's mind raced, trying to remember what he had touched when they had been snooping in Hattie's apartment. "I accidently knocked some papers off the desk, picked them up and put them back. Then Ruth showed me an album of photographs of the resident's children and grandchildren. She had a very attractive family."

Detective Deavers grunted.

Harold couldn't tell if the detective bought his yarn or not. He wasn't going to admit that he, Bella and Jason had been snooping around Hattie Jensen's place. That would only land him in deeper yogurt.

Harold was saved by the bell, or rather the chirp, as Deavers's cell phone sounded. He snapped it open and put it to his ear. "Yeah?... you've got to be kidding. I'll get right outside." Deavers raced for the door.

"What's happening?" Harold asked.

"There's a jumper standing on the top of this building, threatening to throw himself into the parking lot."

CHAPTER THIRTY

A crowd of gawkers had gathered in the parking lot. Harold ran down the walkway until he had a view up toward the top of the building, where a man perched on the edge of the roof. Harold immediately recognized the rumpled shirt and wild hair of the cookie-munching Abner Dane, who had also tried to speak to the residents committee. In the distance the sound of a siren could be heard.

Abner teetered on the edge of the roof, waved his arms and shouted, "Look out below. Abner is going to jump."

"Don't jump," a woman shouted.

"Jump," someone else in the crowd called out.

A chorus of, "Jump," and "Don't Jump," continued as if members of the mob were rooting for opposing football teams.

Detective Deavers stepped to the front of the crowd and looked up. "You don't need to do that. Help is on the way."

"Abner doesn't want help. He killed the two missing women and will put an end to it all." Abner leaned forward, and people in the crowd gasped.

"What do you mean you killed the two missing women?" Deavers shouted.

"Yes. Abner did it. He hid the bodies." Abner waved his arms. Harold wondered what Abner was talking about. One body had been found in the open space and the other in the storage area in the basement of the retirement home.

"Where did you hide the bodies?" Deavers asked. "Abner isn't going to say any more. He's going to jump."

Harold had a wild idea. What the heck, it couldn't hurt. "Wait,

Abner. You can't do this before you have a cookie."

Abner straightened up. "What kind?"

"Your favorite. Chocolate chip." Harold whispered to Detective Deavers, "Keep him talking. I have an idea." As an ambulance careened up the driveway, Harold raced back into the building. Taking stairs two at a time, he dashed to the fourth floor, thankful that he had kept in shape. He raced into his apartment and grabbed a bag of chocolate chip cookies from the cupboard in the kitchenette, pleasantly surprised that Jason hadn't gotten to that bag yet.

He pounded on Bella's door.

She answered with a puzzled expression on her face. "What's all the commotion?"

Harold grabbed her hand. "Come on. We have some work to do." He dragged her to the stairwell and practically pulled her up to the sixth floor.

"What's going on, Harold?"

"We have to save Abner Dane from jumping off the roof," he puffed. On the sixth floor landing they came to a door that led to the roof.

Harold grabbed the handle but found it locked. "I need you to open this door."

"Okay." Bella waved her hand and the door creaked open.

"Come on." Harold led the way up some final stairs to the roof. He could see the back of Abner, perched on the cement railing that went around the edge of the roof. "Can you put a spell on him so he won't jump or fall off if startled?"

Bella waved her hand again. "Done."

Harold approached Abner, "Hey, Abner, I've brought you a whole bag of chocolate chip cookies."

Harold rattled the bag of cookies. "Get off the edge and come have a treat. All the chocolate chip cookies you can eat."

Abner didn't move.

Harold approached and reached up a hand. Finally, Abner took it and Harold pulled him down to safety.

Abner collapsed in a heap, covered his eyes and began crying. Harold leaned over the parapet and called down. "Detective Deavers, Abner's safe, but send up the EMT crew."

148

"Abner tried to jump but couldn't." He continued sobbing. "Abner wanted to join the two women who died."

"Why did you say you killed the two women?" Harold asked. "Abner doesn't know. It just popped into his head."

Bella put her arm around Abner. "Why don't you relax and have a cookie."

Abner moaned. "Abner doesn't deserve to live." Harold tore open the bag and handed him a cookie.

Abner scarfed it down in one bite. Then he turned pleading eyes toward Harold. "Can Abner have one more cookie?"

Harold gave him another.

Abner munched this one more slowly, wiped a crumb off the corner of his mouth and looked longingly at the bag. "Abner thanks you. Can Abner have a third cookie?"

"Eat as many as you want." Harold put the bag down next to him.

The man reached for another cookie, took a tentative bite and clutched his chest. "Abner doesn't feel very well." He toppled over, gasping for breath."

"Do something!" Harold shouted to Bella.

"My magic can only move or hold things. I can't cure people, other than with a few potions I can mix. I'd have to go to my apartment."

Harold heard footsteps pounding up the stairs and two EMTs emerged from the doorway, carrying a stretcher.

"He's having some kind of attack," Harold shouted. The EMTs began ministering to Abner.

Detective Deavers shot through the door, gasping for breath. "Phew. A lot of stairs. What's happening?"

"We talked him down and gave him some cookies, but then he had an attack of some kind."

The EMTs checked Abner's breathing, put an oxygen mask on his face, lifted him onto the stretcher, adjusted straps around him and headed toward the stairs.

Harold reached toward his bag of cookies.

"Wait," Deavers said. "Don't touch anything. I want to talk to each of you. I'll meet you in your rooms."

As Harold and Bella headed down to the fourth floor, Harold tried to piece it all together. "Bella, Abner initially said he killed the two women. I can't buy that. Then afterwards he couldn't explain why he had made that statement."

"Right. He's crazy but not the killing kind of crazy. Something doesn't make any sense here."

Harold put his key in the lock of his door. "Remember, he interrupted our meeting with Atherton and Martha."

"Unfortunately, that jerk Atherton wouldn't let him speak."

"Yeah, too bad we didn't have a chance to hear him out."

Bella hugged his arm. "Then he stages this stunt on the roof."

"And without the cookies and the assistance of a pretty witch he might have actually jumped and killed himself."

Bella grimaced. "If he doesn't recover, we may never know what was going on in his mind."

CHAPTER THIRTY-ONE 🦇

Harold waited in his apartment for Detective Deavers to appear. Instead the door shot open, and Jason galumphed into the room. He kicked off his shoes, one hitting the couch and the other sliding into the entertainment center. "We had a great hike, Grandpa."

"I hope you didn't find any more bones."

"No modern ones. Let me show you what I dug up." Jason reached into his jeans and pulled out a fossilized shell. "This is a brachiopod."

"How do you know?"

"We studied these in school last year. They're pretty common in Colorado given that this land used to be underwater. I heard a siren on the way back. Did I miss anything exciting while I was gone?"

"You mean other than the man trying to jump off the roof of the building?"

Jason's eyes grew wide. "Omigod. What happened?"

"A man named Abner Dane, whom I've spoken with before in the dining room, threatened to commit suicide. He said he had killed the two women who disappeared. Bella and I...uh...talked him down."

Jason grinned. "Cool, Grandpa."

"Yeah, I guess it was. Bella used her skills to get us through a locked door to reach the roof and prevented him from falling. Unfortunately, he had some kind of attack, and the EMTs took him away."

"Wow. Is he okay?"

"I don't know. We'll have to wait to hear what happens at the hospital."

"I'm starving."

151

"You can grab some snacks in the cupboard in the kitchenette."

Jason strolled over and grabbed a bag of cookies. He tore them open and prepared to take a bite, when something struck Harold.

"Wait! Don't eat that."

Jason pulled the cookie away from his mouth and sniffed it. "Is it poison or something?"

"It's possible. I gave the man on the roof some cookies out of my cupboard, and then he collapsed."

"Yuck." Jason dropped the cookie onto the counter and threw the bag alongside. "I guess I'll stay hungry."

Harold slammed his hand on the counter. "How dare someone try to poison our food? Detective Deavers will have someone look at the snacks to make sure they're okay."

"I'm gonna take a shower." Jason headed toward the bathroom.

Harold went over to the discarded cookie and sniffed. It smelled like oatmeal, nothing out of the ordinary.

Seething, Harold paced around his living room, waiting for Deavers. Shortly, when the detective arrived, Harold resisted the urge to offer him a cookie. Instead, he showed him the bag lying on the kitchenette counter. "Someone may have poisoned these cookies. I brought a bag up to the rooftop, and Abner Dane had his attack right after eating some cookies. My grandson was going to eat a cookie from another bag when I warned him to put it down. Check these as well as the ones from the roof."

"The crime scene investigator is already collecting the evidence on the roof. Hold on a minute." He punched in numbers on his cell phone. "Yeah, let me speak to Pat Wilkie...Pat, when you get done up there come to apartment 493 in the Back Wing. There's something else for you to take a look at...good, see you in a little while." He snapped it closed.

"Can I offer you anything, Detective?"

"I think under the circumstances, I'll pass. Now tell me what made you take cookies up to the roof."

Harold let out a sigh. "When I first met Abner Dane, he stopped by my lunch table in the dining room. He gobbled down all the cookies left on my table. Knowing that, I figured I might be able to lure him back from jumping with an offer of his favorite—chocolate chip."

Deavers gave an eye roll. "Apparently it worked. He came off the ledge."

Harold didn't bother to mention the assistance provided by Bella. He figured the detective wouldn't appreciate that nuance, and he'd already had his problems with Bella leaving the interrogation room and getting into his car. No sense making him more suspicious of her actions. "So I opened the bag of cookies, and Abner had eaten two when he keeled over. When I returned here and offered my grandson a cookie from another bag, I made the connection. Who would be sneaking into my apartment and poisoning cookies?"

"We don't know for sure that's the case, but assuming it is, have you made some enemies in your short stay here?"

Harold thought for a moment. "Only some residents of the Front Wing and a member of the retirement home administration."

Deavers whipped out his trusty notepad. "Names?"

"The two people on the residents committee, Atherton Cartwright and Martha Kefauver, and the Executive Director, Winston Salton, would be on my persons-of-interest list."

Deavers jotted a note and then looked at Harold. "What did Abner Dane say to you as you were talking him off the roof?"

"He acted very strange. Earlier he indicated he killed the two missing women, but I have a hard time buying that. On the roof he said that statement just popped into his head."

The detective nodded. "I'm not convinced either. If Abner survives, I'll have a long chat with him to see why he made that statement."

"I tried to get him to say more on the roof, but he refused. Then he ate the cookies and keeled over."

Right then a knock sounded on the door.

Harold stepped over and opened the door to find a young woman in black slacks, white blouse and black jacket with her hair tied back.

"You're at the right place, Pat," Deavers called from inside.

"I'm here to collect some evidence." Pat strode past Harold.

"Bag all the cookies on the kitchenette counter," Deavers said. "But don't eat any of the evidence."

Pat exhaled loudly. "Right."

"You'll find some additional bags in the cupboard," Harold said.

"We're not going to eat anything from that stash after what happened to Abner. I'll have to buy some new snacks for my grandson."

"Did I hear something about new snacks?" Jason emerged from the hallway, rubbing his still wet hair with a towel. He wore shorts and a T-shirt.

"Not yet. We're donating what we have to the police, but I'll make a trip to the store to get you something new later today."

"Good. I'm starving."

Harold snorted. "You're always starving. We'll go to dinner after the police have finished here."

"Pat, dust the counter and cupboard for prints as well. Mr. McCaffrey, I have your prints on file but not your grandson's. I'd like to ask permission to collect his prints. That way we can eliminate his from the ones we'll find in the kitchenette."

"It's okay with me if Jason doesn't mind."

"Cool. I've never had my prints taken."

Pat gave Deavers a kit, and he proceeded to ink Jason's fingers and roll each one onto a card.

"You can wash off the excess ink with warm water and soap," Deavers said.

"Cool. Grandpa, maybe I should get a tattoo now as well."

"No!"

Jason chuckled. "Just kidding." He sauntered off to the bathroom while still inspecting his fingers and mumbling, "Cool."

Within fifteen minutes Pat had completed her work, and she and Deavers departed. It was only then that Harold wondered if any of Jason's prints had been inadvertently left in Hattie's apartment. Too late to worry about that.

Harold and Jason took the elevator, and inside Jason pointed to the schedule on the wall. "There's a trip to the zoo tomorrow."

"Probably not the best thing for us with all that's been going on around here."

"Come on, Grandpa."

Harold thought for a moment. It might be a good diversion for Jason, and there was nothing to do right now with Deavers following up. "You really want to go?"

"Yeah. I haven't been there since my folks took me to the Zoo Lights around Christmas when I was ten. I love animals."

"It says we should gather in front of the building at ten. I'll see if Bella wants to join us, that is, if she's willing to get up early."

"I bet Tomas would like checking out the wild dogs. I'll mention it to him after dinner. We can have a regular Back Wing party."

When they stepped out of the elevator, Pamela Quint was standing there. Her eyes lit up at the sight of Harold and Jason. "Good to see you gentlemen."

"We're going to the zoo tomorrow," Jason said. "Want to come."

"I haven't been to the zoo in years. Sure, why not?"

"In front of the building at ten," Jason said. "This is cool. We'll have quite a crowd."

"I'll call to make the necessary reservation for the trip," Harold replied. "Yes, we'll give the Front Wingers quite an experience."

That evening the phone rang, and Harold answered to hear a teenage boy's voice asking for Jason.

Harold handed the phone to his grandson and listened as Jason said, "Hey, Carl...yeah...that would be cool...let me check with my grandfather." He placed his hand over the mouthpiece. "My friend Carl from school wants to know if I can come over tomorrow to spend the night."

"Do you want to?"

Jason shrugged. "I guess. But there's so much happening around here."

"I'll let you off duty for one night."

Jason put his mouth to the phone again. "That works...cool...we're going to the zoo but will be back by then...see ya." He hung up the phone. "Carl and his mom will be here at 5:30 tomorrow."

"You'll have a busy day. First the animals at the zoo, and then you can catch up with your friend."

Jason twitched. "I guess. I don't know if I should leave you alone."

"I have all my Back Wing friends to take care of me."

CHAPTER THIRTY-TWO 🦇

The next morning at ten o'clock the Back Wing contingent of Harold, Jason, Bella, Tomas and Pamela gathered in front of the building while a group of Front Wingers huddled off to the side making every effort to ignore them.

"They act like we have a contagious disease," Pamela muttered. "A bat should go shake them up a little, but I don't want to mess up my hair."

Bella yawned. "It's their problem, not ours, dear. We're going to have a fine trip to the zoo no matter what people we have to put up with in the van. It's awfully early for an expedition."

"I've been up for hours," Tomas said. "I had to walk myself."

Jason left the group and wandered off into the grass to pick up a rock lying there. Harold moseyed over to join him. "What did you find?"

"I thought it might be quartz but it's not." Jason dropped the rock.

Harold heard a pop, a buzzing sound and looked down at his pants leg to find a hole right through the cuff. "Uh-oh, the Perforator got me again."

Another pop, whizzing sound and Jason jumped. "What's that?" Harold pointed to a hole in Jason's jeans. "He shot you too."

"Shot?"

"There's somebody with a BB gun who likes to shoot at pant legs. My friend Ned Fister calls him the Perforator."

Jason scowled. "Look at that hole. These are my best new jeans. When my mom gets back, she's going to kill me."

"Don't worry, Jason. I'll cover for you."

Harold and Jason returned to rejoin the rest of the Back Wingers as a white van pulled up. On the side was a logo of a purple mountain with large green script letters proclaiming, "Mountain Splendor."

All the Front Wingers quickly scrambled in and took the front seats. Then Harold noticed Ned Fister off to the side. He didn't seem to be in any rush to fight for the front.

"Taking in the animals today, Ned?" Harold asked.

Ned rubbed his wrist. "Yeah, I decided to take a break from gardening. My arthritis is acting up. Besides, the zoo has great flower displays this time of year. Gives me new ideas on what I can do at Mountain Splendor."

"Your buddy the Perforator punctured my pants and my grandson's."

"With me taking the day off, he had to try some other targets. I hope they catch that jerk one of these days." Ned headed into the bus.

"Guess it's the back of the bus for us," Bella said, winking at Harold.

"This way we can keep our eyes on our adversaries," Harold replied. Harold and Bella sat on one side with Pamela and Tomas on the other side in the second to last row. Jason stretched out in the last row.

Once everyone had taken a seat, the driver, a young man who didn't look much older than Jason, stood and announced. "We'll be heading directly to the zoo. Last chance if anyone is hungry, thirsty or needs to use the bathroom."

Several Front Wingers tittered. Pamela elbowed Tomas.

"I'm good," he said.

"I'll be dropping you off at the main zoo entrance. I'll hand out the admission tickets, so take one and only one. You're on your own once you get off the bus. I'll be picking you up at the same place at exactly three P.M., so no stragglers."

"What about lunch?" someone called from the Front Wingers.

"Lunch is on your own. You'll find a number of snack bars at the zoo. Fasten your seatbelts and we'll be off." He ducked into the driver's seat and started the engine.

"We don't have any seat belts," a voice called out. "We're all going to die," another voice murmured. "No we're not. We're going to the zoo."

"This is the first retirement home excursion I've been on," Bella whispered to Harold.

"Really? I'd thought you would have gone on numerous trips."

"Back Wingers aren't encouraged to go on outings. And I don't usually get up at this gawd-awful hour in the morning."

Harold noticed that Atherton Cartwright and Martha Kefauver sat right in front of Pamela and Tomas. Martha loudly announced, "I'm a zoo patron. My dear departed husband contributed an enormous amount of money to zoos. Back in Chicago they even named the Kefauver Bat House after him."

"Obviously for an old bat like his wife," Tomas said.

"I heard that," Pamela said holding her hand to her ear. "Watch who you call an old bat."

"Sorry," Tomas replied. "I didn't mean to insult the bats."

Martha harrumphed and adjusted her straw hat, which looked like it had been stolen from a dairy horse.

"I think this will be a very entertaining trip," Harold said.

Bella snuggled close against him. "I imagine Atherton and Martha will have some unique experiences today."

"Uh-oh," Harold said. "What do you have in mind for them?"

Bella had a mischievous gleam in her eyes. "Oh, I don't know, but I'm sure there will be some interesting opportunities at the zoo. We'll have to see what transpires."

When the van pulled up to the zoo entrance, all the Front Wingers clambered out first, pushing and shoving like little kids.

"Look at them scattering like rats," Tomas said.

"All the better for us," Pamela replied. "We can take our time without being burdened by the hoity-toity."

Tomas suddenly grimaced and ran off to the restroom. When he returned, they each took a map and went through the turnstile.

"We're appointing Jason as tour guide," Tomas said. "Where to first?"

"To the left." Jason pointed. "The giraffe house."

There, they found half a dozen giraffes munching on hay. One baby sat on the floor with its legs splayed to the sides.

"Man, look at those necks," Jason said

Harold noticed Martha Kefauver standing in front of them by the railing.

"This place stinks," Martha announced.

Bella wiggled her nose and Martha's straw hat went sailing through the air and landed against the bars where one large giraffe stood. It stuck out its tongue, grabbed the hat with its teeth and pulled it into the cage.

"Hey," Martha shouted. "My hat."

By this time the last edge of the rim had disappeared into the giraffe's mouth.

"Why Martha Kefauver," Bella called out. "Don't you know you're not supposed to feed the animals? And you of all people, being a zoo patroon, should know better."

"It's patron."

Bella smiled. "Oh, sorry."

Martha stomped out of the giraffe house. "What next?" Tomas asked

"Snakes, spiders and the Komodo dragons in the Tropical Discovery Building." Jason rubbed his hands together. "This should be cool."

They entered the building and found an area where a curator held a tarantula for people to touch. Jason immediately stepped up to take a turn. When the hairy creature crawled over his palm, he laughed. "It tickles, Grandpa. You want to try it?"

"That's okay."

Atherton Cartwright stuck his nose through the crowd. "That's disgusting." He turned and started walking away.

Bella wiggled a finger. Suddenly, the tarantula flew through the air and landed on top of Atherton's white head.

"Oh, Atherton," Bella called out. "Someone of your stature and reputation shouldn't be trying to steal animals."

He stopped abruptly. "What are you saying?"

A group of children giggled and pointed at him. "What's the matter with you obnoxious kids?"

"You have tarantula poop on your shoulder," a little urchin called out. Atherton brushed his shoulder and then made a face. The tarantula crawled over his ear. Atherton jumped a foot and the tarantula continued down his shoulder and onto his arm. A squeal unbecoming a man of any age escaped his throat.

The curator, a woman in her thirties in a brown uniform dashed over. "Sir, please return the tarantula." She reached out and it crawled onto her palm. "Shame on you, sir. And in front of the children."

"Some people just don't know how to act in public," Bella said. "I'm so embarrassed for our retirement home."

Atherton looked around with wild eyes and dashed out of the building.

Ned Fister came up to Harold. "Quite a performance from old Atherton. Couldn't have happened to a nicer guy."

"He certainly knows how to make a scene. You want to join us?"

"Nah. I enjoy wandering around on my own. Like I told you before, in addition to seeing the animals, I have lots of flower displays to check out."

The Back Wing five-some continued on, and Jason found the room with the Komodo dragon. "Wow. How'd you like to have one of those for a pet?"

"No thanks," Harold said. The scaly creature reminded him of Atherton Cartwright.

Around a corner they came to a cave behind glass with vampire bats hanging from the ceiling. Most remained motionless, but one flapped its wings.

Pamela let out a long sigh. "My cousins."

"Are you a vampire bat?" Jason asked. "Of course. It's the best kind."

"Cool. You drink blood."

"I particularly like dog's blood." She grabbed Tomas's arm, and he jumped.

"Let's get out of here before she gets any more crazy ideas." Tomas led the way outside into the bright sunlight.

"Next on the agenda," Jason announced as he looked at the map, "is Wolf Pack Woods, especially for Tomas."

"Ah, at last."

They stopped at the railing to watch a pack of wolves pace around a rock and grass habitat. One wolf stopped and scratched behind his ear.

Tomas also scratched behind his ear. "Too bad Kendall isn't here. He'd get a big kick out of this as well."

"I don't see any bald wolves," Jason said. "Kendall would certainly stand out in that crowd."

"He had to sleep in today. Had a late night, and besides it would be hard for him to navigate the distances here with his walker."

They continued through the zoo, seeing elephants, rhinos and a hippopotamus.

"I'm hungry," Jason said. "Lunch time."

They went to the Samburu Grille to order food. When Tomas's turn in line came he said, "Make my hamburger raw...I mean...rare."

Jason ate a cheeseburger, fries, large drink and most of Bella and Pamela's meals.

"No food goes to waste with that kid," Tomas said. "Oops, I forgot." He dashed off to the restroom.

"Good thing they have lots of facilities around here," Harold said.

"Hey, there's Alex from my school," Jason pointed to a boy standing in the food line. "Bella, will you do some tricks for him?"

"No way."

"Aw." Jason shot up and went over to jabber with Alex.

Harold watched the two boys wave their hands in the air as if they were Italians meeting each other after a long separation.

In a few minutes Jason returned and sat back down. "He's with a pretty lame crowd. Just his sister and mother. No witches or shape-shifters."

"Good thing," Harold said.

After lunch they rode the railroad and carousel and strolled over to the aviary.

"I wouldn't mind flying around up there," Pamela said.

"With your poor sonar, you'd be bumping into birds and branches," Bella said.

"I beg your pardon." Pamela tapped her ear. "Since I started using a hearing aid, I do much better."

"Haven't seen Atherton or Martha recently," Harold said. "No great loss," Tomas replied.

"They do provide entertainment opportunities for Bella." Harold squeezed her hand.

She put her other hand to her breast. "Me? I don't know what you're referring to."

As they passed Monkey Island, Harold stared up into a tree where one monkey launched itself from one branch to another. He suddenly remembered how close Abner Dane had come to flying off the roof of the retirement home. What had gotten into that crazy guy? And why had he made the statement that he had killed the two women? He realized he hadn't yet heard about Abner's condition. He'd call Detective Deavers when they got home.

He stopped to watch two monkeys grooming each other. They ran their fingers through each other's hair, collecting bugs. These two jumped down to the ground where a smaller monkey was eating pieces of banana.

Harold's attention was pulled to the sound of Atherton Cartwright and Martha Kefauver laughing. What were those two up to?

When he looked back at the monkeys, the two larger monkeys grabbed the food away from the smaller one and scampered back to an overhead branch.

Harold squinted at these two bullies. The prissy expressions on their faces reminded him of the laughing Atherton Cartwright and Martha Kefauver.

This clicked with him. There was something not quite right with the way Atherton and Martha acted. He suspected they were somehow involved in the shenanigans at Mountain Splendor. Was it his male intuition at work? A great insight? Heartburn? He'd have to noodle on this when he had a chance.

At three, everyone convened by the curb, and the white van pulled up. Once again the Front Wingers grabbed all the front seats.

"Some people never change," Tomas muttered as they headed to the back of the bus and plunked down on the seats.

The driver was still in a chipper mood and counted all the heads before announcing, "All accounted for. No one fed the crocodiles, I guess."

"Lucky for you," someone in the front grumbled.

A number of the Front Wingers fell asleep on the trip home, and Atherton and Martha remained remarkably quiet.

Bella leaned toward Harold. "The bragging and complaining seems to be reduced on this go around."

"Maybe they're gaining some wisdom in their old age."

CHAPTER THIRTY-THREE 🦇

B ack in their room Jason dropped onto the couch. "Keeping up with all the old fogies wear you out?"

"Nah. I thought I'd rest for a few minutes before I play catch with Tomas. After that Carl's mom will be picking me up." Jason yawned and closed his eyes.

"Just don't fall asleep."

But Jason was already snoring.

Harold chuckled and stepped over to check his answering machine, where he found a message Detective Deavers had left requesting a meeting of the residents committee at five P.M. in the Front Wing lounge. He hoped there was good news on Abner's condition.

With a few minutes to spare, Harold lay on his bed thinking over all that had happened within the last week. If only Jennifer had lived, he never would have become involved in all of this. He'd still be living with her in their house. He let out a deep sigh. He had to accept reality. Things had changed, and he'd have to make the best of them. He'd met some interesting characters here at Mountain Splendor and had a chance to get to know his grandson better. He had to be grateful for that.

Finally, he roused himself. As he entered the living room, Jason popped up. "Wow, I must have zonked out."

"As I told you, we old people are hard to keep up with."

"In your dreams, Grandpa."

"Can you entertain yourself for a few minutes? I had a message that I need to attend a short meeting downstairs."

"Sure. Pamela Quint told me to stop by before I go play Frisbee with Tomas. She's going to tell me all about vampire bats and show me how to hang from the ceiling."

"Just don't fall down."

Jason headed off to Pamela's room, and Harold took the stairs down to the first floor. He found Bella and Detective Deavers already seated. He joined them just as Atherton Cartwright and Martha Kefauver stormed into the room as if on a mission from the Pentagon. Harold did a double take. Rather than their usual garb they wore sweat suits and slippers. He chuckled to himself. These two Front Wingers were trying to prevent any chance of wardrobe malfunctions during the meeting.

Once everyone had taken a seat, Deavers cleared his throat. "Thank you for joining me on such short notice. Things have heated up around this place, and I felt it was necessary to convene this group again."

Martha let out a tired sigh. "I know, Detective. To successfully complete your work, you need Atherton's and my assistance."

He fixed her with his stare. "No, that's not what I'm saying. I need the help of this full group."

"What Martha means," Atherton stopped to sniff in the direction of Bella and Harold, "is that some of us are better prepared to provide useful assistance to the constabulary rather than *cause* more trouble."

Harold figured Atherton was getting cocky because he had no zipper or shoe laces for this meeting.

"I expect all members of this committee to contribute, and Mr. McCaffrey and Ms. Alred have proven very capable to date. Let me give you a brief update. First of all, in addition to the two murdered women and the kidnapping of Mr. McCaffrey's grandson, we have the attempted suicide of Abner Dane."

"He was a certifiable fruitcake," Martha said.

"Irrespective of his mental condition, he tried to kill himself. Through the efforts of Mr. McCaffrey and Ms. Alred, he was talked off the ledge. Unfortunately, he subsequently had an attack and was taken to the hospital."

"How's he doing?" Bella asked.

"I'm sorry to report he didn't make it," Deavers replied. "And initial autopsy results from the coroner indicate he had been poisoned."

Harold and Bella exchanged questioning glances. "Poisoned?" Atherton arched an eyebrow.

"Yes. Cyanide in cookies from Mr. McCaffrey."

Martha raised her chin. "That's what we told you, Detective. These Back Wingers are up to no good. Mr. McCaffrey obviously killed Abner."

Deavers held up his hand. "That isn't quite the situation. It appears someone else poisoned several bags of cookies in Mr. McCaffrey's kitchenette."

Harold's heart pounded in his chest. His intuition had been correct. It was a good thing he hadn't let Jason eat that cookie. Here he had been entrusted with the care of his grandson, and Jason had come within a bite of being poisoned.

But what if he hadn't taken the cookies to Abner? Harold had rescued him only to inadvertently contribute to the poor man's death. But then Jason would have eaten cookies out of the tainted bags. He gave up the mental ping-pong game to refocus on what Deavers was saying.

"Do you have any evidence of who may have placed the poisoned cookies in Harold's apartment?" Bella asked.

"Yes. We're working on that. In addition to what has happened earlier, please ask around to see if anyone saw someone going into Mr. McCaffrey's apartment."

"We wouldn't know, Detective." Atherton turned his chin toward Martha, and she nodded in agreement.

"We never go…there," Martha added.

"Really? Well, that's interesting," Deavers said, "because we found Mr. Cartwright's fingerprints on Mr. McCaffrey's kitchenette counter."

CHAPTER THIRTY-FOUR 🦇

The plot thickens, Harold thought at the revelation that Atherton's fingerprints had been found in his apartment. When had he been there? Had he kidnapped Jason? Did he poison the cookies? Could he be a prime mover in all the crimes committed at Mountain Splendor? Harold's gut feeling at the zoo regarding Atherton and Martha might be panning out.

"I...uh...must have been there during an open house." Atherton snapped his fingers." That's it. A week ago I... uh...was on a committee that toured a selection of apartments. That must have been right before Mr. McCaffrey moved in and his was one of the one-bedroom apartments vacant for viewing. I...uh...must have put my hand on the counter then." He stopped babbling.

This sounded to Harold as pathetic as the excuse he'd used to convince Deavers of why his fingerprints had been found in Hattie Jensen's apartment.

"I thought you never went to the Back Wing," Deavers said. "Well... uh...I never intentionally go there. The open house was a
different situation..." His mouth dropped open. "How did you have my fingerprints anyway?"

"We had them on file." Atherton paled. "Oh."

"His statement doesn't make any sense," Harold said. "I've wiped the counter several times since I moved in. He obviously snuck into my apartment recently."

"That the case, Mr. Cartwright?" Deavers asked.

"I'm not going to sit here and be insulted. Come on, Martha." Atherton grabbed her hand and lifted her out of her chair. They headed toward the exit, but after a few steps both of their sweat suit pants flopped to the floor.

Martha screeched and tried to swat Atherton's hand away.

Atherton's momentum carried him forward, he tripped and fell flat on his face, pulling Martha down on top of him.

"Get away from me!" Martha slapped him. She stumbled to her feet, pulled her sweat pants up with one hand, harrumphed and shuffled out of the room.

Atherton regained his feet and performed a similar grab, lift and shuffle.

"Old people," Bella said with a sigh. "It's like a three-ring circus around this place. You never know what will happen."

"Yeah," Harold added. "It's amazing. They don't make elastic waist bands like they used to."

"Anything else you have for me?" Deavers asked, looking toward the ceiling as if pleading for the gods to deliver him from this place.

"If Atherton was in my apartment, how did he get in?"

"Maybe he stole a master key," Bella replied. "Detective, can you tell us more about Atherton and Martha?"

"I'm not at liberty to divulge anything else at this time. Any more comments from you two?"

"I think you've pumped the turnip dry for the time being," Harold replied.

Deavers put his notepad in his jacket pocket and stood. "If that's the case, I have another interview here that I need to tend to."

Bella stood, took Deavers hand and leaned close to him. "Thank you for working so hard to find who is responsible for all these awful crimes, Detective."

A half-smile crossed Deavers face. "How unusual. It's not often I get thanked for questioning people."

Bella returned the smile. "Some of us here," she nodded toward Harold, "want to see all of this resolved."

Deavers turned and left the lounge.

Once he was out of sight, Bella motioned Harold over. "Here's something for us to take a look at." She held up Deavers's notepad.

"What? How'd you get that...oh." Harold wagged his finger at Bella. "Another of your little tricks."

"All in the interest of justice. Aren't you dying to see all the comments he writes on his notepad?"

Harold wanted to feign nonchalance, but instead he grabbed the notepad out of Bella's hand and opened it.

"Hey, we can look at this together."

They sat back down and began perusing it.

"Here's something interesting." Harold tapped a page. "Deavers found Abner Dane's fingerprints in Frieda Eubanks and Hattie Jensen's apartments. I was convinced Abner had nothing to do with the disappearances and murderers of the two women. Did Abner really play some role in what happened to them?"

"As Churchill said, it's a riddle wrapped in a mystery inside an enigma."

Harold turned away from Deavers' hen scratching for a moment. Too many pieces of this puzzle hadn't fallen into place yet. The two murdered women—one a neat freak and one who could be on the hoarders TV show. Frieda and her gambling debts and trying to blackmail Rachel Kunz. Hattie willing all her money to Mountain Splendor. The kidnapping of Jason. Abner Dane and his suicide attempt and then being poisoned by cookies from Harold's cabinet. The suspicious Winston Salton, Atherton Cartwright and Martha Kefauver. All of these pieces had to tie together somehow. He felt as if a solution buzzed over his head like an angry bee, but he couldn't pull it back into the hive.

Bella patted Harold's arm. "A penny for your thoughts."

"Sorry. This will take much more than a penny. I'm thinking over all that's happened. There are so many unanswered questions around this crazy place."

"And here's another one you may have missed while off in Never Neverland. Read this." Bella pointed to a sentence on the notepad.

Harold gawked. "What? It says no fingerprints were found on my kitchenette counter."

"Exactly. Deavers was testing Atherton, who failed. He tricked the slimy dilettante into admitting he'd been in your apartment."

"I'll be darned," was all that Harold could muster.

"Atherton went into a snit fit as a diversionary tactic. I suspect he was up to no good even though Deavers uncovered no fingerprints."

"Do you think he poisoned the cookies?"

Bella sucked on her lip for a moment. "It's possible. Also, he could have been the one who kidnapped Jason since he was in your apartment at some time. And I wouldn't put it past Martha, the big phony, to have helped him."

"Is there anything else I missed while daydreaming?"

"One other significant item. Deavers has been exploring a connection between Frieda Eubanks and organized crime. He knows she was in significant debt to some wrong kind of people."

Harold rubbed his chin. "Maybe that note we found in Frieda's book was a threat from the mob. That's a whole new direction. So some gambling types could have killed Frieda."

"Again possible, but wouldn't they be more interested in getting their money back than killing her?"

Harold wiggled his foot nervously. "Unless it was meant to send a signal to others to pay up or else."

"But even if that had been the case, it wouldn't explain what happened to Hattie Jensen. Hattie wouldn't have been gambling big bucks."

"No, but Mountain Splendor sure benefits from her demise. I'd like to understand Winston Salton's role in Hattie changing her will. And her diamond ring is missing. Another of the unsolved puzzle pieces."

"Harold, aren't you glad you moved here? Your boring life living by yourself has changed so much with all this mystery."

"To say nothing of the interesting residents I've met in the Back Wing."

Bella winked at him. "That too."

"Are you two going to sit there yakking all day?" a woman's voice inquired.

Harold looked up to see Rachel Kunz standing next to his chair with three other women. All had their arms crossed. He blinked. "Huh?"

Rachel tapped her foot and glared at them. "You're sitting in the chairs we need for our bridge game. Now move it."

"I do believe we're being kicked out," Bella said. Harold and Bella stood and left the lounge.

Once out of earshot of the four women, Bella said, "We should find Detective Deavers anyway and return his notepad. I suspect he's in the administrative area."

"Why would you think that?"

"My superior detecting skills and noticing he had left a note about an appointment with Winston Salter."

They went to Winston's office and found Deavers sitting there.

Bella knocked on the open door. "Oh, Detective, you left something in the lounge." She stepped in and handed him the notepad.

He patted his jacket and flinched. "What? How'd you get that?"

Bella gave her angelic smile. "As I said, you left it in the lounge when we spoke earlier. I thought you'd want it back."

"I didn't leave it there. I put it back in my jacket pocket."

"No, Bella's right. We found it in the lounge. You must have accidently dropped it. These things happen."

Deavers scrunched up his nose. He wasn't buying.

Harold's head jerked at the sound of a loud crash, and a Frisbee flew through the window, spraying glass onto the credenza behind Winston. He stared at the blue disc as it skidded to a stop on the hardwood floor. "Uh-oh."

"Where'd that come from?" Winston shouted.

Running footsteps could be heard, and Jason raced into the room. "I'm sorry. I threw the Frisbee too hard and it broke your window."

"Why you juvenile delinquent," Winston sputtered. "You've destroyed Mountain Splendor property. Detective, arrest this young thug."

"What a minute," Harold said. "Jason admitted his mistake. He didn't try to run, hide and deny it. I'll make restitution for the expense."

"You don't need to do that, Grandpa. It was my fault. I'll pay out of the money I've earned from washing cars."

"It's...it's not that simple." Winston jabbed his right index finger at Jason. "He should be punished. We can't allow young criminals to roam the grounds."

"He's staying with me and has caused no other problems," Harold said.

"We're going to instigate a new rule." Winston slammed his hand down on his desk. "No overnight visitors under twenty-one."

"Then you may end up with a vacant room."

"Make that two," Bella added.

"Make that three." Tomas trotted into the office.

Harold stared intently at Winston. "Rather than losing paying customers, I think you should accept Jason's apology, and we'll reimburse you for the expense of replacing the window. You don't need to overreact."

Winston glared back for a moment and then lowered his eyes. "I guess it's not worth losing three residents over."

"I'm sorry." Jason hung his head. "It won't happen again."

"It better not," Winston growled, picking up the Frisbee and putting it in his desk.

Bella, Tomas, Jason and Harold left the office.

"It was an accident, Grandpa, but I'll be more careful."

"This kid can really fling a Frisbee," Tomas said, putting an arm around Jason. "But in the future we'll go out into the open space, away from the building."

"Good idea," Harold said.

"Wow, that guy really freaked out over a broken window," Jason said. "He practically foamed at the mouth."

"Kind of like Tomas after some bad meat," Bella added. "Nah. Even I don't ever look that rabid."

"Winston Salton is under a lot of pressure with all the problems happening around here," Harold replied. "And it's obvious occupancy rate is a hot button with him."

"It's going to get worse," Tomas added. "Earlier, I overheard a group of Front Wingers discussing how they intended to move somewhere safer."

Bella laughed. "That's why your threat of more rats jumping ship worked, Harold. Let's hope Detective Deavers gets to the bottom of all of this soon, so this place remains financially solvent. I don't really want to move somewhere else."

"I'd hate to see Mountain Splendor shut down," Tomas said. "Where else could all of us live together? Without a Peter Lemieux and his tolerance for all kinds of people, we wouldn't have been able to find a retirement community."

"I think we'd better redouble our efforts to assist Detective

Deavers," Bella said. "Tomas let's you and I round up the regulars for a meeting later this afternoon. We have some work to do."

CHAPTER THIRTY-FIVE 🦇

Back in the apartment Harold checked his watch. "Jason, you better get ready. Your friend will be here to pick you up in a few minutes."

Jason put his pajamas, toothbrush and change of clothes in a backpack.

"Aren't you going to pack your vampire book?" Harold asked. "Nah. We'll be too busy, and Carl isn't into vampires. Too bad. I could really tell him some interesting stuff."

"I wouldn't suggest spreading rumors of what goes on around Mountain Splendor."

"I wouldn't do that. I'll keep that between you and me, Grandpa." Bella materialized through the wall. "What are you two up to?"

"Hi, Bella. I'm going to spend the night with my friend Carl. Will you keep an eye on Grandpa while I'm gone?"

"He's a hard one to keep track of."

"Just make sure he doesn't get into any trouble while I'm gone." Bella laughed. "Who takes care of whom around here?"

The three of them headed downstairs and out the front lobby.

Their timing was perfect as a silver SUV drove up and stopped in front of the building.

"Are you sure you want me to leave you alone with all that's going on?" Jason asked.

"You go have a good time. Bella and I will keep things under control here."

"I don't know…"

"Go!"

They moved down the walkway to the waiting vehicle. Jason

didn't have his usual light step. He whispered in Harold's ear, "Are you sure?"

"Yes. Enjoy yourself."

Carl's mom, a young woman with shiny black hair, lowered the driver's side window. "I'll bring him back mid-day tomorrow."

"We have nothing planned. Just call or leave a message if plans change." Harold realized he would miss Jason. He had become used to having someone else sharing his apartment.

At the sound of a click, the back of the SUV rose. Jason threw his backpack in, pushed the button to close the back and climbed in the backseat. Carl turned from the front seat and gave Jason a knuckle bump.

With Bella standing next to him, Harold watched as the car drove away. What a positive spirit a teenager added to this place. Even if it entailed throwing Frisbees through the retirement home director's window.

Harold pivoted toward the building. He heard a pop and a buzzing sound and his pants brushed against his leg. He looked down to see a hole. "Darn Perforator."

"Huh?" Bella looked puzzled.

Another pop and whizzing sound, and the bottom of Bella's slacks smacked against her leg.

Harold pointed to a hole in her slacks. "There's someone who shoots a BB gun. He hit both of us."

"Why of all the gall." Bella looked up the hillside, stuck out her arm and shook her index finger. "Come on." She grabbed Harold's hand and dragged him up the grassy slope.

"He's probably long gone, Bella. If he can see us to shoot, he'll spot us coming."

"Oh, don't be so sure."

They came to a section of pine trees.

"I imagine he stood behind one of these to shoot. Like maybe right there." Bella pointed at a silver gun barrel protruding from the side of a sturdy pine tree.

A young man stood holding a gunstock, his mouth and eyes frozen wide open. He reminded Harold of a revolutionary war statue. "Well done, Bella. The police haven't been able to catch this guy."

"They just don't have the right tools. What shall we do with him?"

Harold regarded the young man. He had long blond hair flowing out from beneath a Broncos cap, stood approximately five-foot-ten and was probably in his late teens. "I think some punishment that will encourage him to change his behavior."

"Good idea." Bella wiggled her nose and the BB gun flew out of his hands, turned one-hundred-eighty degrees until it pointed at the perpetrator. "Harold, why don't you check to see if he has any identification?"

Harold strolled over and removed a wallet from the kid's back pocket. "We seem to have caught Stanley Huggins, a student at the School of Mines." He slid the wallet back into to the young man's pocket.

Bella snapped her fingers, and Stanley unfroze. His eyes widened as he became aware of his BB gun hanging in the air and pointing at him.

"Now, Stanley, it seems you have been causing some problems around here with this BB gun of yours," Bella said. "What you have been doing is not acceptable. What do you have to say for yourself?"

"I...I want my gun back."

Bella shook her head. "It's not going to happen, Stanley. I think you have several choices. You can either join the military and put your sharpshooter skills to another use, or you can give up harassing people at Mountain Splendor or anywhere else."

"I haven't hurt anyone."

"Not yet, but you've been a pain in the you-know-what." She pointed to her pant leg. "I don't appreciate the hole in my favorite slacks." She waved her hand and the BB gun fired, knocking the cap off Stanley's head. His mouth dropped open. Then the gun began to shoot holes in his baggy T-shirt and jeans.

Stanley gasped, turned and ran up the hillside. One last shot caught him in the butt. He squawked, rubbed his behind and kept running.

"I don't think he'll be a problem any longer," Bella said. The gun sailed over to her and she grasped it. "Let's head home."

Back at Mountain Splendor, Bella wiped the gunstock with her handkerchief and dropped the BB gun into the dumpster.

CHAPTER THIRTY-SIX 🦇

L̲ater Harold joined the gathering in the Back Wing lounge. Bella
called the meeting to order. "Thank you all for coming."

"I want you to know I woke up early for this meeting," Bailey said.
"I hope the lack of sleep doesn't disturb my digestion."

"No, stick with the Nordic blood and you'll be fine," Viola said.

Bella raised her hand. "Enough chit chat. As you know, there've
been some very unusual events taking place here at Mountain
Splendor."

"I know," Kendall Nicoletti said. "Those two dingbats came running
out of the Front Wing lounge earlier today and tripped over my
walker. Their sweat pants fell around their knees. Martha Kefauver
actually wore knickers. And Atherton Cartwright had boxer shorts
with hearts on them."

"What'd he say?" Pamela asked.

"Something about boxing tarts," Alexandra answered.

"Listen up people." Bella clapped her hands. "If we could focus
for a moment. We have two murders, a kidnapping and a poisoning
to help the police solve. It's imperative that all this get resolved so
Mountain Splendor stays open. You don't want to be forced to find a
new home, do you?"

"No way," Bailey replied. "I like having takeout next door. I don't
want to traipse all over town to get dinner. Let's hear Bella out."

"Thank you, Bailey. I'd like to ask each of you to help out in the
investigation. The police need our assistance."

"As if they'd ask us," Viola said.

A background of voices muttered in agreement.

Bella clapped her hands together again. "No, they haven't officially asked the whole Back Wing for assistance, but we're going to help. With all the...uh...special talent in this room, we can do a great deal to aid the police investigation."

"Who do you want me to bite?" Bailey called out. "That won't be necessary."

"I'll cast a spell on all the bad guys." Warty waved his wand in the air. "I'll turn them into frogs or toads."

"Um, Warty, I think you will better serve by watching," Bella said. "We need lots of eyes to figure out what's going on around here. Now I have a few assignments to pass out. Alexandra, would you be willing to spend more time in the Front Wing lounge?"

"Sure. I have a whole collection of new couch patterns I want to try out anyway. I can change them hourly."

"Just don't make it too obvious when people are in the room. And Pamela can you turn on your hearing aids?"

"What?"

Kendall poked Pamela in the ribs. "Turn on your hearing aids."

"Oh. I hate these little beasts."

"Just do it," Kendall said.

Pamela tweaked behind her ears. "Okay, they're on."

"Good. Pamela, can you hear me better now?"

"Loud and clear, dear."

Bella nodded. "Pamela, I want you to position yourself in the rafters of the dining room before each meal...with your hearing aids on. Listen in on conversations. You may be able to overhear something useful."

"I'm on it like white on rice. I might as well get started since it's almost dinner time." She dashed out of the room.

"Next assignment. Viola and Bailey, I want you to hang around the reception area. Take turns so it doesn't appear too obvious. Check the comings and goings and see if you spot anything unusual."

"I'll even wear my choppers," Viola said. "If I can find them." She began searching through her purse. "Who took them this time?"

"No one took them," Bailey said. "They're under your chair. Must have fallen out of your purse."

"Thanks." Viola reached down, retrieved her false teeth and jammed them in her mouth.

Bella continued. "And, Viola, if anything important happens, write it down so you don't forget."

"Write what down?...just kidding."

"Tomas and Kendall, I'll need you for some surveillance."

"Don't forget me," Warty called out. "I'm ready for action."

"Well, why don't you position yourself by the parking lot? Watch people coming and going."

"Perfect. If one of the perps drives up, I can change him into a bat."

"That's not necessary, Warty," Bella said. "We already have a bat. Just watch. You don't have to change anyone into anything." Warty scowled. "You're wasting all my special talents."

"What about you, Bella?" Tomas asked.

"Harold and I will visit some specific rooms in the Front Wing. We'll need you and Kendall to be watching and alert us if the residents return."

"I'll trip them with my walker if necessary," Kendall said. "I'll bite them on the ankle," Tomas added.

"No violence needed. We want surveillance, not assassinations."

"There's a concert in the dining room tonight at seven-thirty," Harold said. "Assuming two of our suspects go, that will be the perfect time for a little investigation. The four of us can meet outside the dining area at 7:15 to finalize plans."

The meeting adjourned, and Harold headed down to grab a quick dinner. As he ate his pork chop by himself, he noticed a bat hanging in the center of the room near the chandelier. A woman began squawking and pointed to the ceiling. She grabbed a waiter by the sleeve and waved her other hand. He disappeared and shortly a maintenance man appeared carrying a long stick. He stood on a chair and poked the stick toward the ceiling. The bat took off and flew out of the room. So much for Pamela's surveillance.

After dinner Harold retrieved Bella and they stopped by Pamela's room.

"Did you learn anything before being rudely kicked out?" Harold asked.

She adjusted the curls of her hair. "Some people don't know how to treat a lady. I did overhear one interesting conversation. The old hearing aids were in fine fettle."

179

"Yes?"

"Well, I got the lowdown on several things. A woman named Sandra Vickery was speaking with her tablemates."

"I met her the night I first arrived here," Harold said. "She sat at a table of people that never invited me back."

"Typical. Anyway, she had some very uncomplimentary things to say about Frieda Eubanks. Said she was always trying to con money from people and deserved to die. The other people at her table didn't disagree."

"That definitely fits with what we know of Frieda," Bella said. "And here's the other interesting tidbit." Pamela leaned forward and cupped her hand to whisper in a conspiratorial tone. "One of the other women at the table said that Frieda had been trying to steal Hattie Jensen's diamond ring. Hattie avoided Frieda whenever she showed up. How do you like them apples?"

Harold looked at Bella. "When we found Hattie's body she wasn't wearing a ring. I even mentioned that to Detective Deavers."

"You're right." Bella tapped the kitchenette counter. "I didn't make the connection at the time, but we had heard before that Hattie wore that diamond ring all the time. Someone took the ring before we found her body in the storage bin."

"And one final thing for you two detectives," Pamela said. "When the comment was made about Hattie's ring, Sandra turned as white as a sheet, covered her mouth and dashed out of the dining room. I would have followed her, but I wanted to stay at my post. Not that I lasted too much longer after that."

"Strange behavior." Harold pursed his lips.

"Probably worth some further investigation," Bella said. "We may have to check out Sandra Vickery's apartment as well tonight."

"I'll look up her room number in the directory," Harold said.

"You should be safe checking her apartment this evening." Pamela looked around as if to verify that no one had snuck in to eavesdrop. "Earlier, all four people at the table said they planned to attend the concert. Sandra should be safely ensconced in the musical scene."

"And we know what the ring looks like," Harold said. "It's a big diamond surrounded by rubies."

"You have a good memory," Bella replied. "Yeah, I still have all my brain cells functioning."

Bella gave a satisfied nod of her head. "I think we have our work cut out for us tonight. Maybe we can put the puzzle pieces together."

CHAPTER THIRTY-SEVEN 🦇

Harold and Bella positioned themselves like sentinels on either side of the door to the dining room at seven-ten. The place had been converted into an auditorium with potted ferns adorning a wooden platform and dining room chairs aligned in rows facing the impromptu stage. A group of musicians in black suits and dresses scraped chairs into place and sat down on the platform. They began tuning their instruments.

The early birds arrived at exactly seven-fifteen to get the best seats for the concert. Atherton and Martha strolled in arm-in-arm. Sandra Vickery dashed into the room by herself at seven-thirty.

Harold signaled to Bella, and they headed back to get Tomas and Kendall, who were waiting in the Back Wing lounge.

"Here's the plan of attack," Harold said. "In checking room numbers for our targets, I've discovered a very interesting pattern. All three suspects that we want to check out tonight are on the sixth floor. It turns out that Atherton and Martha's rooms are on either side of Hattie Jensen's room."

"Kind of like Viola and me impinging upon you." Bella smiled.

"Exactly. And the plot thickens. Sandra Vickery's room is right across the hall from Hattie's room."

"Hmmm. Our suspects had Hattie surrounded."

"What do you want us to do?" Tomas asked.

"Kendall, can you position yourself near the Front Wing elevator on the second floor? If you see the concert ending or any of our suspects heading to the elevator, jump on the first elevator going up and get off on the sixth floor."

"I don't exactly jump anymore," Kendall replied.

Harold gave a dismissive wave of his hand. "You know what I mean. Tomas, you wait by the elevator on the sixth floor. Do you have your cell phone?"

"Right here, Harold." Tomas waved it in the air.

"Good. If Kendall appears or you see anything suspicious give me a call. You have my number on speed dial, right?"

"Right again."

"Okay, let's deploy."

Bella grabbed Harold's arm. "I feel like I've joined Special Forces." Kendall found a chair near the elevator and plopped down, keeping his walker at ready. Harold, Bella and Tomas caught a green elevator to the sixth floor.

They exited and Tomas found a place to sit. "Much nicer decorations than in our wing. They have real paintings versus our prints. I've never been here before and probably never will be again."

Harold and Bella headed down the hallway. "Where do you want to start?" Bella asked

"Let's try Sandra Vickery's room." Harold pulled latex gloves out of his pocket and handed a pair to Bella. "Let's not leave any fingerprints for Detective Deavers to find."

They both slipped on the gloves.

Bella checked to make sure no one was in sight and disappeared through the wall. The door clicked and opened.

Harold did a quick scan of the hallway and ducked inside. He turned on the light and found a living room, neatly furnished with a leather couch and entertainment center larger than his own. A collection of DVDs filled one shelf.

Bella went over and picked up several. "Her taste runs to romantic comedies, chic flicks and tear-jerkers."

"I'm more interested in finding if her taste runs to stealing diamond rings. Let's look around." Harold began opening cupboards in the small hallway while Bella went into the bedroom. He found nothing more than spare sheets and towels.

"Harold, come here."

He stepped into the bedroom.

Bella pointed to a large wooden jewelry box. "This bears investigation."

Mike Befeler

"Have you opened it yet?"

Bella patted his arm. "No. I was waiting for you. It's locked."

"But no problem for the Bella I know."

She waved her hand and the box popped open. "Imagine that. It seems to want us to look inside."

A collection of earrings rested on the top shelf of the jewelry box. Bella lifted it out, and the space below held bracelets and necklaces. She sorted through everything. "No rings."

"Darn. I thought this might be it."

"No, I imagine the ring, if she took it, would be in some special hiding place. We'll have to keep looking."

Harold paced around the bedroom. He opened the dresser drawers and rummaged through, finding nothing other than T- shirts, blouses and undergarments.

Bella checked the closet. "Nothing."

Harold went through the bed, checked the mattress and lowered himself to the floor to peer underneath. With no success, he remade the bed to hide any evidence of their search.

"We haven't checked the kitchenette yet," Bella said.

They looked through the cupboards, and Harold opened the small refrigerator. Two cans of soda, a package of cheese and a bottle of pickles. In the freezer compartment he picked up something wrapped in butcher paper. It felt like a piece of frozen meat. He almost put it back but decided to unwrap it, revealing a piece of chicken breast. He turned it over and something sparkling caught his eye. He chuckled. "I do believe I've found some ice on ice."

CHAPTER THIRTY-EIGHT 🦇

Harold examined the ring with its large diamond and accompanying rubies. "So Sandra ended up with Hattie's ring. Have we located Hattie's murderer as well?"

Bella crinkled up her eyebrows in concentration. "I don't know. How would Sandra have hoisted the body into the storage bin? And why did Hattie will everything to Mountain Splendor?"

"Yeah. I figure Winston Salton as a primary suspect in Hattie's death. He's big enough to carry the body and sure benefits from the bequeath. He could have manipulated Hattie to change her will and then dispatched her." Harold returned the ring to its hiding place and rewrapped the chicken. "I think Detective Deavers may want to have a talk with Sandra Vickery. Let's go have a look at Martha and Atherton's apartments."

After Harold peeked out the door, they quickly exited. Bella did her thing at Martha's door and let Harold in.

This apartment had a large bookshelf in the living room. Harold scanned through several titles finding classics and histories of the American Revolutionary War. On one shelf rested pictures of horses and a number of ribbons and medals.

"Obviously, Martha used to horse around," Harold said. Bella rolled her eyes. "Please."

In the bedroom they found a mounted photograph of Atherton Cartwright, inscribed, "With all my love."

Bella rolled her eyes again. "What's with this guy? Does he hand these out to all the women on this floor?"

"I don't know, but it has the same inscription as the one we found in Hattie's apartment when we were snooping there with Jason."

Harold lowered himself to his hands and knees and checked under the bed. No boxes with hidden treasure. He brushed against the bed skirt and something pricked him. He looked carefully and removed a cocklebur which he deposited in the trashcan by the dresser.

They continued searching through the whole apartment. In the kitchenette they only found a bag of corn chips in a cupboard, a bottle of green olives in the refrigerator and a can of cleanser under the sink. The bathroom cabinet had lots of shampoo, conditioner and skin moisturizers.

"What a disappointment," Harold said. "Nothing incriminating. With Martha hanging out with Atherton, I hoped we'd find something to link her to one or more of the crimes—maybe even a bottle of chloroform."

"Let's move on," Bella said. "I'll take a short cut through Hattie's apartment and meet you at Atherton's door."

Harold watched her vanish through the wall. He'd never get used to this special skill of Bella's. Still, it certainly came in handy when investigating.

He let himself out the conventional way, first checking to make sure the coast was clear and proceeded two doors away.

Bella ushered him into Atherton's apartment and closed the door. "I took a quick gander around Hattie's bedroom on my way here. Guess what?"

"You obviously saw something?"

"It's what I didn't see that interested me. The picture of Atherton we noticed before wasn't on the nightstand any longer. The one in Martha's room is probably the same one we saw earlier."

Harold let out a disgusted groan. "He recycles pictures of himself rather than giving out multiple copies, I guess."

"That means he's been in Hattie's apartment."

Harold clicked his tongue as he looked around Atherton's living room—a sleek blue couch that would make Alexandria envious, a glass coffee table with a recent issue of *GQ*, a bookshelf with a collection of law and architectural books.

One thing caught his eye. On a table by the curtains stood an architectural model of a four-story building with a large glass entryway. It was labeled, Mountain Splendor Casino. "What the heck is this?"

Bella came over and stared closely at the model. "A casino? I don't get it."

Harold walked around the model and inspected it from all sides. "Is this a hobby of Atherton's or something else?"

"I don't know. Let's check the rest of the apartment."

Bella stepped into the bathroom and opened the medicine cabinet. She gasped. "There...there's a bottle of chloroform in here."

"Bingo. I think we may have found who kidnapped Jason. Let's see what else we can uncover in this slimeball's place."

In the bedroom Harold saw a four poster bed and a desk.

Bella tried the desk drawers, but they remained locked. She wriggled her nose, and the drawers popped open. "Oh, look, we have access now."

Harold groaned. "Remind me never to let you near a bank vault." He pulled open a drawer and began riffling through papers. "Here's an application to the Colorado Gaming Commission. Wow. Paperwork to open a casino. How can that be? Only the towns of Black Hawk, Central City and Cripple Creek are allowed to have casinos in Colorado."

Bella stepped nearer and looked over his shoulder. "This is really strange. What was Atherton up to?"

Harold picked up a photocopy of an old map. "Look at this. It shows a Cheyenne Indian settlement in what's now Golden." He leafed through and scrutinized another document. "Hmmm. This indicates only two Indian casinos in Colorado—the Sky Ute Lodge and Casino in Ignacio and the Ute Mountain Casino in Towaoc."

Harold thought back to the one time he and his wife Jennifer had stopped at an Indian casino. They had been on their way from Colorado to Las Vegas for several days of shows, laying in the sun at the Bellagio pools and gambling. They needed a restroom break so they stopped at the Moapa Tribal Casino off Interstate 15. Jennifer gravitated quickly into the gaming area, and he had followed. They played video poker for fifteen minutes. Jennifer won twenty-five dollars, and he lost ten dollars. Typical of his gambling experience. Jennifer had the touch, but he was exactly what the casinos loved—a losing gambler. Too bad he never had Bella's skills to make the machines, dice, roulette wheels or cards deliver.

Bella grabbed another sheet of paper. Her mouth dropped open. "This...this is a copy of a deed, giving land to the Cheyenne tribe."

Harold looked at the document and compared it to the map. "I'd say that we're standing on Cheyenne land. That means—"

Harold felt a rush of air and heard a door slam. He turned to find Atherton and Martha dashing into the bedroom. His mouth went dry.

"Martha, you know what to do," Atherton shouted. Martha fired a Taser and Bella collapsed.

Atherton grabbed the paper out of Harold's hand.

Harold put his hands up to defend himself, but Atherton slapped them aside and punched him, knocking him to the floor. Harold lay stunned, holding a sore jaw.

Martha disappeared for a moment and returned holding a bottle and a towel. Before Harold could shake off the blow and rise, Martha poured contents from the bottle onto the towel and thrust the towel over Bella's face. Bella was out for the count.

Atherton grabbed a roll of duct tape and bound Harold's hands behind his back. Harold tried to resist, but he was too weak from the blow, and Atherton was too strong for him. Then Atherton wrapped tape around his legs. Once he had Harold secured, he did the same to the unconscious Bella.

"What are you doing here?" Harold asked. "You were supposed to be enjoying yourselves at the concert."

"Intermission. I saw a guy with a walker acting suspicious around the elevator, so we decided to come up here to check."

"Did he get on the elevator with you?"

Atherton laughed. "Nope, I gave him a little shove and closed the door."

"Did you see anyone on the sixth floor when you got off the elevator?"

"No. The place was empty."

So much for his surveillance team. All his careful plans had been for naught. Harold wondered what had happened to Tomas.

"I think your snooping has put you in a world of trouble. Martha, what do you think we should do with these two?"

"Since the warning and the poisoned cookies didn't work, maybe we need a more permanent solution."

"You mean like how you killed Hattie Jensen?" Harold asked.

"I had nothing to do with Hattie's death," Atherton said. "What a waste. I was getting her all lined up to leave me her money when she disappeared and then showed up dead. Her inheritance would have been very financially beneficial."

"You definitely miscalculated. She left all her money to Mountain Splendor."

"What? There's no way I'm going to let that happen. I want this place to go bankrupt and soon."

"So you can build a casino here."

"Hey, Martha, this guy has a good idea for us. Too bad he won't be around to lose his money at craps." Atherton slapped a piece of duct tape over Harold's mouth.

Harold tried to piece it together. Hattie's money going to Mountain Splendor. Had Winston Salter killed Hattie? But Harold had more important issues to worry over. He had learned too much about Atherton who apparently had no qualms when it came to kidnapping and poisoning.

Harold was glad Jason was out of danger tonight, but he and Bella were in big trouble. He couldn't move to do anything useful, and Bella had no way to use any of her special abilities when knocked out by chloroform.

CHAPTER THIRTY-NINE 🦇

After Atherton and Martha left the room, Harold could only hear murmurs as they spoke in the living room. He struggled to move his arms, but the duct tape wouldn't budge. *How could he get out of this predicament?* The door opened and closed, and all remained silent for a few minutes. Harold's cell phone jangled. He twisted but couldn't reach it with his bound hands. It stopped ringing. Was that Tomas finally calling? If so, too late to do any good. He'd been blindsided by Atherton and Martha with no backup plan to cover such an eventuality. He tried to push his hands as far apart as possible, but the duct tape held fast. He was stuck.

The apartment door opened and closed, followed by a squeaky sound. Soon after, Atherton appeared pushing a laundry cart. He picked up Bella's unconscious body and dropped it into the laundry cart as if he were tossing in a rag doll. The guy had obviously stayed in shape. Then he lifted Harold and pushed him in on top of Bella.

Harold landed with a thump. Bella let out a moan but didn't move. He wriggled to the side to keep from smothering her. A sheet went over his head. Great. No one would be able to see them. Then he felt the laundry cart move. One wheel definitely needed to be oiled. They squeaked along and came to an abrupt stop. Fear mingled with frustration that he was helpless to do anything for Bella.

Several minutes later he heard a ding and then the cart moved a short distance ahead and shook to a stop. They must be in an elevator. He felt a bump, and he could sense a downward motion. Another ding and the cart jiggled and squeaked along again. It tilted forward, and Harold figured they must be going down a ramp. The temperature became slightly cooler. A gentle breeze shook the sheet.

190

Bella moved beside him. Then he heard a burst of snapping sounds and the duct tape released from around his hands, legs and mouth. Bella whispered in his ear, "What's going on, and where are we?"

"Atherton and Martha are abducting us," he whispered back. "We're in a laundry cart, and I think outside Mountain Splendor."

Harold wished the Perforator would show up with a bazooka and take care of Atherton and Martha. He pictured an explosion with body parts flying into the air. *Stay focused.*

At that moment he heard an automobile screech to a stop.

"I have an idea," Bella said. "Hold on tight. I'm going to capsize this thing."

The cart went over, and Harold tumbled out with Bella right behind him. He banged his elbow on something hard and blinked. An overhead lamppost shed light on asphalt. He found himself lying in the middle of the parking lot.

"Grandpa," came a shout.

Harold sat up to see Jason running toward him. Out of the corner of his eyes he caught a glimpse of Atherton and Martha climbing into a black car. The engine gunned, and it shot out of the parking lot missing Harold by inches.

Jason helped Harold and Bella to their feet.

Warty came running down the steps waving his wand. "I'll turn that car into a coat." He pointed his wand and a streak of lightning shot out and hit a bush right behind the disappearing black car. The bush turned into a giant taco.

"Oops."

Bella shook her head in disgust. "A lot of help he is. In addition to being a poor shot, Warty has always been dyslexic."

"What are you doing here?" Harold asked Jason.

"I was too worried about you, so I came back. Carl's mom just dropped me off. What happened to you?"

"I'll tell you in a minute, but first I need to call Detective Deavers." Harold reached for his cell phone, looked up the number he had stored and hit the green button. The phone rang and cut over to voicemail. "Detective, this is Harold McCaffrey. You need to call me ASAP. Atherton Cartwright and Martha Kefauver tried to kill

Bella and me. They're also responsible for kidnapping Jason and poisoning the cookies."

"Wow, so that's what happened," Jason said. "Did they kill the two missing women as well as doing that other stuff?"

"They wouldn't admit to that. There's a lot of this that doesn't make sense. I'm still trying to piece it all together."

Warty shook his wand as if trying to loosen the right magic and smiled at Bella. "Anyway, I saw it all happen. I even memorized the license number of the car."

"The black car?" Bella asked.

"No, the silver car that dropped the kid off."

Harold smacked his forehead. "That was the car driven by the mother of Jason's friend. The black car is the one that Atherton and Martha took off in."

Warty frowned. "Oh. Didn't get the license for that one."

Tomas came running out of the building. "There you are. I called your phone, but you didn't answer. I saw two people pushing a laundry cart out of the hallway. I waited for a while and decided to check it out."

"Where were you when they first showed up?"

A sheepish look came over Tomas's face. "I'm sorry. I had an emergency and needed to use the restroom."

Harold realized it hadn't been the best choice to put someone with incontinence on critical surveillance duty.

They headed inside and spotted Kendall approaching with his walker. "I tried to get on the elevator," he said.

Harold held up a hand. "Don't worry. I understand Atherton Cartwright shoved you out of the way."

"Yeah. The big lug caught me off balance. I fell flat, and by then the elevator door had closed. It took forever for another elevator to come. When I got up there, Tomas said he hadn't seen anything, so I came back down."

Harold shook his head. He and Bella had survived even if Atherton and Martha had escaped. Detective Deavers would hopefully be able to track them down. Now he had one other mission for the evening.

"I need to find Winston Salton right away," Harold said.

"He was in the concert," Kendall replied. "I saw him schmoozing with people while I waited by the elevator.

Harold turned to Bella. "I may need your special powers on this. I need to confront Winston and do it quickly."

Bella hugged his arm. "I'll be happy to be your enforcer."

"What about me?" Jason asked.

"This guy may be a murderer. No sense all of us going to speak with him. I don't want to put you in danger."

"I'll keep an eye out to see if he draws a gun or anything and warn you so Bella can zap him. How's that?"

"He might as well come with us," Bella said. "You don't want to leave him alone with everything that's going on around this place."

"Okay, okay." Harold waved his arms in the air. "I'm outnumbered. Let's go wait in the dining room for the concert to wrap up."

They took the stairs to the second floor and entered the dining room, finding three open chairs near the back of the room. They scooted in as a violin concerto played on. Harold looked around the room. Some people watched with rapt attention. Others had fallen asleep with heads to the side. One woman in front of him snored while drool leaked out of the corner of her mouth. Tough crowd to entertain.

"What kind of music is this?" Jason whispered. "Classical."

"I've listened to classic rock but not anything like this before."

"It's a good education for you."

At the end of the number some people clapped while others jolted wake. The musicians stood and took a bow. Then people limped, shuffled and staggered out of the room. The woman in front of him continued to snore until another woman shook her shoulder.

"What?" The woman lurched forward. "Come on, Gertrude. Time to go."

"But I was enjoying the concert."

Harold spotted Winston Salter in his dark suit shaking hands with one of the violinists. When he turned and headed to the exit, Harold waved his troops forward, and they intercepted him at the door.

"Mr. Salter, I need to speak with you."

Winston looked at his watch. "It's pretty late. Can it wait until the morning?"

"No. This is urgent. It concerns the future of Mountain Splendor." Winston let out a sigh. "All right. Let's go to my office." The four of them walked to the administrative area, and Winston unlocked the main door followed by the door to his office.

As they sat down, Harold decided how he would approach this conversation. "I appreciate your making the time for us. This is very important. First, how well do you know Atherton Cartwright?"

"He's been an active member of several resident committees for the last two years and currently serves on the Board of Directors for Mountain Splendor. He has stayed very involved and assisted with a number of zoning and legal matters we've encountered."

"That's interesting. Has he ever discussed selling this property?"

"He did mention one time being approached by a syndicate that had some ideas on developing this land."

Harold exchanged a glance with Bella. "That fits. I think he had his own agenda, and it didn't include living in his apartment here in the long run. Did you know he wanted to drive this facility into bankruptcy and replace it with a casino?"

"What? That would go against his fiduciary responsibility as a Board member. Besides there's no way a casino could be built in Golden."

"Actually there is," Bella said. "It turns out this is Native American land, and a treaty gave it to the Cheyenne tribe. Legally, they could build a casino here."

"Yeah, that has actually happened in a number of places before," Jason added. "I studied Native American rights in school this last year. There are casinos all over the country now. Many tribes have become very wealthy because of casinos."

Winston put his head in his hands. "Great. Someone is trying to buy this property out from under us. That's all I need on top of everything else."

"Like needing to find money to keep this place solvent," Harold said. "That has been a challenge lately with all the expenses."

"And this gets to the heart of what I want to discuss with you," Harold said. "Hattie Jensen willed all her money to Mountain Splendor. Given your financial struggles, that's very convenient. Is that why you killed her?"

Winston's head popped up. "What? I certainly didn't kill her."

In all his years of selling insurance Harold had become a good judge of human character, lying and obfuscation. He pointed a finger at Winston. "You manipulated her to leave all her money to the retirement home."

Winston visibly sagged like a deflated balloon. "Oh, hell. It's all going to come out anyway. I plan to resign. Yes, I convinced Hattie to leave her money to Mountain Splendor. I thought that might be the salvation of this place, but with everything happening around here, I'm afraid we won't be able to maintain our occupancy rate to keep it solvent. But I had nothing to do with Hattie's death. I have no idea who killed her."

Harold studied him closely. Winston was telling the truth.

Then another thought struck Harold. *Yes. That's who the murderer might be.*

CHAPTER FORTY

They left Winston Salton in his office writing his letter of resignation.

"We have someone else we need to speak with," Harold said. "Follow me." He led Bella and Jason to the sixth floor of the Front Wing.

Bella arched an eyebrow. "Back here again?"

"Yes. We need to have one more interview this evening."

He strode down the hall with Bella and Jason on his heels and knocked on the door of Sandra Vickery.

In a moment the door opened, and Sandra stood there still in her satin dress from the concert. "Yes?"

"We need to talk," Harold said, pushing his way into her room with Jason and Bella following.

She wrinkled her nose and sniffed. "You're the man who mistakenly sat at our table for dinner one time. What gives you the nerve to pound on my door and barge in here at this hour? And who are these other people?"

"We're part of a committee helping with the investigation into the deaths of Hattie Jensen and Frieda Eubanks."

Sandra put her hand to her visibly paling cheek. "I don't understand."

Bella closed the door behind her. "I think you understand perfectly well since you stole Hattie's diamond and ruby ring."

Sandra slumped onto the couch and put her hands over her face.

Fitful sobs emerged from behind her fingers.

Jason disappeared for a moment and returned with a box of tissues. He handed one to Sandra, who dabbed at her cheeks.

Bella kneeled in front of the distraught woman and looked in her teary eyes. "We need to learn exactly what happened."

"It's…it's a difficult situation." Sandra sniffled.

"Let me make this easier for you." Bella reached out and took the woman's hands. "We know you have the ring. Did you kill Hattie?"

Sandra shuddered. "Of course not."

Harold watched the exchange. Sandra wasn't a murderer. But she was still hiding information.

Bella released her hands. "The police will think you did. Theft isn't as serious a crime as murder."

Sandra looked up with red-rimmed eyes and wiped away another tear. "I only took the ring. I did nothing else."

"And how did you get your hands on the ring?" Bella asked.

Sandra looked at Bella, then at Harold and Jason. "This is hard to discuss."

"We're listening," Harold said.

Sandra gulped. "It all began when I heard a noise outside my apartment an evening last week. I looked through the peep hole in my door and saw Hattie running out of her apartment. Frieda came charging out right behind her, leaving the door wide open. I cracked my door and saw them disappear down the stairs. Curious, I entered Hattie's apartment. I noticed something sparkling on the rug under the couch. It was Hattie's ring. I picked it up and stuck it in my pocket." She sobbed, unable to continue.

"Take your time," Harold said.

Sandra nodded and took a deep breath. "I shouldn't have kept it, but I did. Curiosity got the better of me again, and I went into the stairwell. Looking down, I saw Hattie lying in a clump on the basement floor. She had either fallen or been pushed. Frieda picked her up and threw her over her shoulder like a sack of flour." She snuffled again. "Frieda was quite strong, you know."

"Yes, she lifted weights," Harold added. "Then what happened?"

"I heard a door open and close and knew she had exited at the basement level. I descended the stairs and followed. When I reached the basement door, I peered out just as Frieda disappeared into the storage area. I waited until she came out again, noticing that she no longer carried her bundle, and ducked out of sight behind a stack of chairs. Once she left, I went into the storage area."

"How did you get in?" Jason asked.

"Don't you know? Everyone's room key also opens the storage area."

"I didn't realize that," Harold replied.

Sandra dabbed with the tissue again. "It took me ten minutes looking around that creepy place, but I finally spotted Hattie's body. She was dead and had been left in a bin." She covered her eyes.

Jason pulled a fresh tissue out of the box and handed it to Sandra.

She blew her nose. "Then I went back to my apartment, locked the door and hid the ring."

"Did you later kill Frieda?" Harold asked.

Sandra flinched. "Of course not. I stayed away from her. She scared me, and I didn't want to have anything to do with her. Then I heard she had disappeared."

"Why didn't you report finding Hattie?" Bella asked.

"Are you kidding? I had her ring. The police would have thought I killed her. I waited until someone else found the body. I…I don't feel very well. I need to lie down." She put her feet up on the couch and closed her eyes.

"Sandra?" Harold said.

She smacked her lips twice and began snoring. "Now what do we do?" Jason asked.

"I don't want to leave her alone here with the ring," Harold said. "I'm going to try Deavers again. He opened his cell phone and called. This time the detective answered. "This is Harold McCaffrey. In addition to the information I left you in an earlier message, we know who caused the death of Hattie Jensen and have located her ring. Get right over to Mountain Splendor before the evidence disappears. We're in room 620 of the Front Wing."

After Harold completed the call, he looked at the sleeping woman and then at Bella. "What do you think of her story?"

"I believe she's telling the truth."

"I thought Atherton or Winston or Sandra might have killed Hattie, but it appears to have been Frieda, either directly or indirectly."

"But we still don't know who killed Frieda."

Harold tapped his chin. "If Detective Deavers can track down

Atherton and Martha maybe they will have some connection to the second murder. We've at least put some of the puzzle pieces together."

CHAPTER FORTY-ONE 🦇

When Deavers entered Sandra's apartment, the detective was all business. He whipped out his notepad. "I need to speak with each of you individually, starting with Mr. McCaffrey. Please come with me into the bedroom."

Harold joined him and described what had happened with Atherton and Martha. "Those two were involved in some sort of conspiracy to turn Mountain Splendor into a Native American casino. They abducted Bella and me. Also, they apparently went into my apartment, kidnapped Jason and put poison in the cookies that Abner Dane ate." Then he explained about the ring and what Sandra Vickery had told them regarding Hattie and Frieda.

After Harold had completed his account, Deavers jotted a note on his pad and looked up. "Got it." Then he asked Jason to join him. Finally, Bella had her turn.

"What happened to you and Bella?" Jason whispered in Harold's ear. "I'll fill you in after the detective leaves."

When they all gathered again in the living room, Harold said to Bella, "I hope you corroborated my story."

Bella ran her hand through her disheveled hair. "What I remember of it. Being chloroformed, I missed part of the whole episode."

Jason said, "I didn't have too much to tell. Only coming back and finding the two of you in the parking lot."

Deavers snapped his notepad closed. "All of your accounts are consistent."

"That's good." Then Harold pointed to the sleeping Sandra. "You'll want to interrogate her, Detective."

Deavers made a call to put out an APB on Atherton and Martha.

Then he shook Sandra awake. He showed his identification and asked Harold, Bella and Jason to step out into the hall while he questioned Sandra.

They left, and Bella said, "No sense standing here. Let's use Atherton's apartment. She went through the wall and let the other two in.

Jason stood on one leg and then the other. "This is so cool. We're helping solve the murders and all the weird stuff going on around here."

"Some of it," Harold replied. "It appears Frieda wanted Hattie's ring. Apparently, Hattie dropped it under the couch to hide it from Frieda and tried to escape. She either fell or was pushed down the stairs by Frieda. We still don't know what happened to Frieda. Most of the other pieces fit together."

"Well, we can't do all the work." Bella nudged Harold. "We need to leave some of it to Detective Deavers."

"I'm sorry you missed spending the night with your friend," Harold said to Jason. "I hope you'll have another chance to do that."

"No problem. We would have played boring videogames all night. It's much more exciting around here."

"That's what I told you and your dad originally. Remember, I said you'd have some unique experiences when you stayed with me."

"And I didn't believe you. Boy, was I wrong."

Harold heard Deavers muttering in the hallway and opened the door. "We're in this apartment, Detective."

"What are you doing here?"

Harold, Bella and Jason stepped out into the hallway. "The door was open so we decided to sit down rather than standing here waiting for you, Detective."

He scowled. "I didn't see any doors open when I first came down this hallway."

She shrugged. "I guess you missed something."

"I know what I saw."

"Did you recover the ring?" Harold asked.

"Yes. Ms. Vickery showed me where it was and gave me a full statement."

"When you get a search warrant you'll find some very interesting documents in this apartment," Bella said, pointing to the open door.

Deavers eyed her warily. "That you just happened to see."

Bella smiled. "Exactly, and we couldn't resist looking at them."

"Right, the door was open, you invited yourselves in and the documents popped into your hands, practically begging you to read them."

"You're very perceptive, Detective."

Deavers rolled his eyes. "Anyway, thanks for the information. We'll be going over this place in detail tomorrow. I'll be asking for Mr. Salton's cooperation as well."

"You'll probably need to work with someone else," Harold said. "He's resigning. I think the pressure must have been too much for him."

Deavers shook his head. "I imagine being around all of you would do that."

CHAPTER FORTY-TWO 🦇

The next day Peter Lemieux called an all-residents' meeting in the dining room. Harold pounded on Bella's door to wake her up, because he figured she wouldn't want to miss it. Harold, Bella and Jason took seats near the back of the room and waited for the meeting to start.

Bella yawned. "This better be good to give up my beauty sleep."

"You look pretty good," Jason said.

"Well aren't you a kind young man."

Jason leaned close to whisper to her, "I figure I have to stay on the good side of a witch. I don't want you turning me into a coat or taco like Warty tried to do."

"If I aimed a spell, I wouldn't miss."

"That's right," Harold said. "She nailed the Perforator."

Jason's eyes widened. "You found that jerk who shot a hole in my jeans?"

"She took care of him good. He won't be causing problems any longer."

Jason bounced in his seat. "Ooh, ooh. Did you turn him into a toad or something?"

"Hopefully I changed him into a more responsible member of society. Sshh. The program's going to start."

Peter picked up a microphone and thanked everyone for coming on such short notice. "I'm sad to report that Winston Salter has resigned as Executive Director of Mountain Splendor. I will be acting director until the Board makes a decision on a permanent replacement."

The room erupted in cheers. Peter gave a bashful smile. "Now, Detective Deavers would like to make some comments."

Deavers straightened his tie and stepped forward. "We have made progress in the investigation we've been conducting here at Mountain Splendor. I would like to ask your cooperation on one further item. We're seeking Atherton Cartwright and Martha Kefauver. They disappeared last night."

A murmur ran through the crowd.

Deavers held up his hand. "This isn't like the disappearance of Hattie Jensen and Frieda Eubanks. Mr. Cartwright and Ms. Kefauver have not met with foul play. They are wanted for questioning. If any of you see them, please let Mr. Lemieux or me know immediately." He placed a stack of business cards on the table in front of the room. "My phone number is here. Thank you." He sat down.

Peter went back to the microphone. "You'll see a number of people from local law enforcement in the building today. It's part of their ongoing investigation. I can assure you we're doing everything we can to resolve the problems we've encountered. I know some of you have had concerns, so I'm instigating a price reduction policy for the next two months. We'll take twenty percent off your regular monthly fees during this time."

"That'll buy me a new set of dentures," one woman said.

"Once you get them, don't bite anyone, Mildred," the woman sitting next to her added.

"I hope you don't cut the amount of food we can eat by twenty percent as well," came another voice

Peter chuckled. "There will be no reduction of services. This is merely a thank you for staying at Mountain Splendor. I want to encourage all of you to continue in residence here, and you have my personal commitment to make this the best retirement community in Colorado. I'm also offering a finder's fee of a thousand dollars for anyone you recommend who moves here."

"Hey, Mildred. That'll buy you an additional set of dentures if you lose a pair."

"Nah, that'll give me some spending money. I'll make a Wal- Mart run."

Peter cleared his throat. "Please continue to live here and encourage any of your friends to join us as well. Now I'd like to open it up to questions."

204

A hand in the second row waved. "Yes?"

A woman stood up and leaned on a cane. "How can you assure us that there won't be reoccurrences of the dreadful events of the last week?"

Peter looked thoughtfully at the woman. "I can't make any guarantees. But I know this. Detective Deavers and his associates are doing everything possible to bring the perpetrators to justice and to eliminate the threat of any future occurrence. You also have my word that the administration at Mountain Splendor will do everything in our power to make this a safe and enjoyable place to live. As of this morning, we have added three people to the security staff, and the Golden Police Department has assigned an officer to spend part time here for the next month. I will have an open door policy so any of you can stop by at any time to speak with me, voice your concerns and give me your suggestions. I will be onsite around the clock for the duration of the time I'm acting director. You can come to my office during working hours or my apartment after hours. I'll be living in apartment 213 in the Back Wing."

"Back Wing?" a voice shouted.

"Yes. I know there has been some animosity between the Front and Back Wing. That needs to stop. Members of the Back Wing have been instrumental in assisting the police investigation and in resolving the problems we've encountered. Unfortunately, some of the problems have been caused by people living in the Front Wing. The people who had been representatives of the Front Wing on the residents committee helping the police have...uh...become suspects. I will need to ask other members of the Front Wing to help in the future."

"Who were the Front Wingers on the committee?" someone asked.
"The people Detective Deavers mentioned earlier: Atherton
Cartwright and Martha Kefauver," Peter replied.

"I never liked that snotty Atherton Cartwright and stuck-up Martha Kefauver anyway," a voice called out.

"Let's try to remain positive. I would ask all of you to be open-minded and work together through this period of transition. Again, thank you all for being at Mountain Splendor and feel free to stop by to see me at any time."

The meeting adjourned, and Harold approached Deavers who stood in the front of the room speaking with Peter Lemieux. "Detective, I have a question. I remember that Abner Dane's fingerprints were found in the apartments of Hattie Jensen and Frieda Eubanks. Given all that happened yesterday, Abner being in those apartments doesn't make any sense."

Deavers eyed him warily. "How did you know that? I don't remember mentioning it to you?"

Uh-oh. "Uh...a little wit...bird must have told me."

Deavers shook his head as if trying to shake some order into it. "However you found this out, I had the same reaction. In checking around I learned an interesting fact about Mr. Dane. It turns out he wandered through the halls, and whenever he found an open or unlocked door, he went inside. Kind of like some of you last night."

Harold winced.

"Also, we found a master key in Mr. Dane's pocket right before he died. That's what he probably used to gain access to the roof. Speaking of which, how did you get through the locked door to reach the roof, Mr. McCaffrey?"

Harold twitched. "Um...the door must have been unlocked."

"No, Mr. McCaffrey. It's an automatic locking door. It swings closed and then locks."

"Maybe Abner had wedged it open."

"Not when I got there. It was locked and closed. I had the head of housekeeping with me to open it."

Harold forced a smile. "That's how you arrived so quickly. Housekeeping is very helpful around here."

"Speaking of which, housekeeping reported two master keys disappearing over the last several weeks. We can account for one of them, the one Abner Dane used. Any ideas on the other one?"

Harold wrinkled his brow. "No. I don't have a clue."

Deavers regarded Harold thoughtfully. "I thought I'd ask. Anyway, regarding Mr. Dane, he didn't do any harm, but he liked to handle people's knickknacks. His fingerprints are probably in nearly every room in this facility."

"Thanks for the clarification. Any signs of Atherton Cartwright or Martha Kefauver?"

"Not yet, but we'll find them."

CHAPTER FORTY-THREE 🦇

Bella came back with Jason and Harold to his apartment. As Harold unlocked the door, Viola came out of her room.

"Why are you going into our meeting place, Bella?" Viola asked. "You've forgotten again. We don't meet here anymore. This is Harold's room now."

"Who's Harold?"

Harold waved to her. "Hi, Viola."

Viola squinted at him. "You look familiar."

"We're neighbors now, and this is my grandson, Jason, who you've met before as well."

"Oh yeah. I remember seeing that kid around here. I thought he worked for housekeeping. Well, I'm off." Viola headed down the hall.

Once inside, the adults had coffee and Jason a cup of hot chocolate. "Peter Lemieux will make an excellent director," Bella said. "The Board would be wise to make it a permanent position."

"He'll have some major challenges keeping this place financially solvent."

"This will all blow over. Once the police apprehend Atherton and Martha and solve Frieda's murder, things will get back to normal. Peter knows how to run this place cost-effectively without reducing the needed services."

"Who do you think killed Frieda Eubanks?" Jason asked.

Harold looked up at the ceiling for a moment. "She had lots of enemies. She was blackmailing several people, had a gambling problem, ended up in debt. I suspect that someone she blackmailed decided to solve the problem permanently."

"Maybe Frieda owed money to the mob, and they whacked her," Jason said.

"We found that note in Frieda's apartment asking for $25,000, but most likely the people she owed money to wanted to get their money back."

"Maybe she planned to use that note to blackmail someone else," Jason said.

Bella tapped her shoe on the carpet. "That's possible. When Frieda killed Hattie, she was probably threatening her for money and definitely wanted her ring."

"Then one night later, Frieda disappears," Jason said. "And she ends up dead in the open space."

"I bet it ties in to what Atherton was doing with the casino," Harold said. "I haven't put it all together yet. Hopefully, Detective Deavers can find Atherton and Martha and wring the truth out of them."

"This is so cool, solving crimes," Jason said.

"Your detective career will soon be over, young man. Your mom and dad return tomorrow to take you home."

Jason's face fell. "Aw, I don't want to go. Can't I stay here?"

Harold broke into laughter. "Is this the same kid who didn't want to be stuck with old people a week ago?"

Jason looked indignant. "I didn't know all the cool people living here and all the weird stuff going on. Home will be boring after this."

"You're welcome to visit any time."

Jason rubbed his hands together. "Yeah, I'll have to come back regularly. And you'll have to tell me all the new mysteries that pop up."

"Hopefully, the crime spree is over," Harold said.

"I think we'll have to have a little party for Jason tonight, seeing as he's leaving tomorrow," Bella said. "I'll gather everyone in the Back Wing lounge. If you'll excuse me, I'll get preparations started." She disappeared through the wall.

—

After Harold and Jason ate their meal of steak, baked potatoes and peas in the dining room, they adjourned to the festivities in the Back Wing lounge.

A large banner hung on one wall proclaiming, "Jason, come back again." Bailey arrived with a tray of green and red Jell-O shots. She set it down on the table right next to a bowl of Warty's punch, which bubbled and steamed.

"Remember, only green ones," Harold said. "Can't I try a red one, please?"

"No."

"Aw, Grandpa."

"And don't drink any of the punch either. You've tried enough new things this week like being kidnapped, chloroformed and tracking down murderers."

Jason smiled. "Yeah. I've had a great time."

"Not exactly my idea of fun," Harold said.

Jason elbowed him. "You can't fool me, Grandpa. You've been enjoying all this excitement as well."

Harold started to deny it and caught himself. His grandson was right. He certainly had liked having Jason around. The young pup added a new dimension to his life. And they both had become caught up in all the intrigue. Certainly better than sitting on the couch and watching the wallpaper. And he had to admit, some unique characters inhabited this place. As if to demonstrate the point, Kendall changed into a werewolf and began howling at the big globe light overhead.

"Howl, howl, howl," several people chanted.

Kendall howled again and then broke into a coughing jag. "I don't have the throat for much of that anymore. I need something to drink." He went over to the refreshment table and began lapping from a bowl of water.

Warty came up to Harold and Jason. "There you are. I have some new magic to show you. Watch, I'm going to change that empty vase into a bouquet of flowers." He waved his wand and the vase turned into a rock.

Warty tapped his wand on his hand. "Must be a bad wand. I really don't need a wand. I can use my finger." He pointed toward a couch. "I'm going to change that green couch into a woman."

Poof. Alexandra Hooper stood there.

Warty's mouth dropped open, and he stared at his finger. "It actually worked."

Alexandra stepped over. "No, you doofus. I wanted to join the party."

Harold watched the crowd, chatting and enjoying themselves. He'd made some interesting friends in the short time he had lived here. Nothing he would have expected to ever experience in his lifetime. How his view of living in a retirement community had changed over the course of a mere two weeks. He guessed he wasn't too old to learn new things after all.

And then there was Bella. He saw her across the room, and she smiled at him. He felt a pitter patter in his chest. He had never met a witch before but was glad he had met this one.

Tomas tapped a glass with a knife. "I want everyone's attention. I have a present to give Jason." He handed him a wrapped package.

Jason tore it open to find a gold Frisbee.

"It's to replace the confiscated one that went through Winston Salton's window. This one even glows in the dark. You can play with it night or day."

"Cool."

"Remember. Throw it in open fields and not near windows."

Harold strolled over to where Bella was speaking with Viola. "Ah, the two people who used to use my living room for a meeting place."

"Meeting place?" Viola wrinkled her nose.

"You've forgotten, dear, but for a while you and I met in the room between our apartments."

"That's right. Then something happened." Bella patted her arm. "Harold moved in."

"And now we have to talk at parties instead. You never invite me into that room anymore, but I saw you visiting earlier today." She put her hand to her mouth. "Now where'd my false teeth go?"

"I thought you had them over by the refreshments."

Harold, Bella and Viola walked over to the food and drink table. "I don't see them," Harold said.

Bella pointed. "There's something in Warty's punch."

210

Viola stuck her hand in and fished out a set of false fangs. "How'd they end up in there?"

"I don't know," Bella said. "But you should rinse off any of the punch before you put them in your mouth."

Still holding the dripping false fangs in one hand, Viola patted her hair with her other hand and gave a toothless smile to Harold. "If you ever get tired of Bella, I'm available."

"Don't even think about it, Viola, or I'll turn your false fangs into spiders."

"Yuck. I hate spiders."

After the celebration Harold and Jason returned to their apartment. "Thanks for letting me stay here while my folks took off on their boring trip."

"Again, you might want to keep some of the exciting events to yourself, so your parents will let you visit again. If they find out all the things that happened here, you'll be grounded until you're thirty-two."

"Not to worry, Grandpa. My lips are sealed." He ran his thumb and index finger across his mouth. "And you'll have to let me know what Detective Deavers comes up with when he finds Atherton Cartwright and Martha Kefauver."

Those two still being on the loose bothered Harold. Wherever they had gone, he expected they were up to no good. "Hopefully everything will get resolved soon."

Harold tucked his grandson in and adjourned to the bedroom to read. When he turned off the light, he tossed and turned before falling into a restless sleep. He dreamed of walking in the open space and coming to the spot where Frieda's remains had been found. He looked down and saw cockleburs all over his pants. Then he partially awoke, and another image formed into his mind. A cocklebur in Martha Kefauver's apartment. His eyes shot open, and he mumbled, "Martha."

"That's right," came a woman's voice.

Harold rubbed his eyes and in the dim light saw Martha Kefauver standing over his bed with a handgun aimed at him. He pointed at her. "You killed Frieda Eubanks."

"Well, if you aren't the amateur sleuth. And too nosy for your own good. It's too bad Atherton didn't take care of you and your grandson before. But he's a useless worm anyway. I have to clean up after him all the time. I won't have to worry about his incompetence anymore. He's dead like you're going to be shortly. This time I'll do it right."

Harold suddenly felt wide awake. Here was a lunatic threatening him in the middle of the night. He had to keep this woman talking while he figured out what to do. Then another image returned. He had seen a brochure for an Indian casino in Frieda's apartment. And Atherton had been messing around with Native American casino finagling. Frieda had been blackmailing people. It all clicked. "I bet Frieda found out about your Indian casino scheme and threatened to blackmail you and Atherton. She had a number of blackmail attempts going on."

"That worthless cow. We returned her ransom note and agreed to pay her the money she wanted. Atherton was supposed to meet her in the open space and kill her. He wimped out. I had to go do it myself. Now I'll have to take care of all the loose ends."

"How did you get into my apartment?" Then the answer to his question came to him. "You stole a master key. Detective Deavers indicated one was missing. That's how you got in my apartment to kidnap Jason and poison the cookies."

Martha cackled. "You're on your game. Too bad it won't help you one bit."

Harold spotted his walking poles just out of reach in his closet. If he could only reach one and distract Martha long enough to whack her over the head. He inched toward the closet.

"Stop right where you are." Martha leveled the gun at him. Harold's heart began thumping. "Where's Jason?"

"He's sleeping in the living room. I think it's time to wake him up, so he can enjoy the festivities. Move."

Harold couldn't reach his walking pole. That strategy wouldn't work. He let out a deep sigh and padded into the living room with the gun-toting Martha right behind him. He could see Jason on the couch in the ambient light from the nightlight in the hall.

"Wake him up," Martha commanded.

Harold shook Jason. "You need to get up. We have company." Jason sat up. "It's still dark."

"Martha Kefauver has returned."

Jason squinted. "Holy shi…shitake. She has a gun."

"Now you two line up against the wall."

"My knee has a cramp," Jason blurted out. "I don't think I can move."

"Get a move on, kid, or you'll have a hole in your knee or other assorted places of your body."

"Is she going to shoot us?" Jason gasped. "Don't tempt me."

Jason scooted over and stood by the wall.

"That's better, kid." She waved the gun at Harold. "Now move over next to your grandson."

Harold joined him.

Jason fidgeted and began tapping on the wall. "What are you doing?" Martha asked.

"I'm nervous." He thumped again. "Well, cut it out."

"I have to go pee."

"Too bad."

Jason stood on one foot and then the other, tapping the wall.

"I told you to quit that." Martha pointed the gun right at Jason's forehead.

"Okay, okay."

Harold heard a whooshing sound, and Bella appeared.

Martha flinched but then regained her composure. "Where'd you come from?" She aimed the gun at Bella. "You can line up with your friends right over there. I'll make a clean sweep tonight."

"I don't think so." Bella pointed a finger at Martha.

A snake crawled out of the barrel of the gun, wound around and began crawling up Martha's arm. She let out a shriek and dropped the gun. The snake continued up her arm as she swatted at it, tripped and fell to the floor.

Jason scrambled over, picked up the gun and with a shaky hand pointed it at Martha. "Don't move, scumbag!"

Bella turned on the light. The snake turned into duct tape and wound itself around Martha's arms and body from her waist up to her neck until she looked like a mummy.

"Isn't that a pretty sight," Bella said. "All packaged and ready for the police."

Harold reached for the phone and called Detective Deavers.

CHAPTER FORTY-FOUR 🦇

While they waited for Detective Deavers to arrive, Harold decided to do some of his own interrogation. "It looks like you and Atherton worked together but then had a falling out. He try to cut you out of the casino action?"

A sneer crossed Martha's face. "Ha. Atherton thought he was so smart setting up that scam. But he would have blown all the money anyway. I figured out how to siphon it off. It's always fun to scam a scammer."

"He seemed awfully surprised that Hattie left her money to Mountain Splendor rather than to him."

"He thought he was God's gift to women but failed to entice that little mousey woman into turning her cash over to him. He sure read her wrong. I should have known better than to rely on Atherton. What a loser."

"I bet he couldn't follow directions very well."

Martha let out a burst of air as if trying to rid her lungs of smoke. "That's an understatement."

"Why'd you keep bothering my grandson and me?"

"You were snooping around and getting too close to our operation."

"But things fell apart between you and Atherton. That's when you killed him."

"I'm not saying another word." She shut her mouth.

When a blurry-eyed Deavers arrived, Bella displayed her handy work. "Detective, here's the murderer of Frieda Eubanks."

Martha struggled to move to no avail. She forced a smile. "Thank heavens you're here, Detective. You won't believe what happened to me. I was minding my own business, and these insane people attacked me."

"And would you care to explain why you showed up in my apartment to threaten me with your gun?" Harold asked.

"That's not my gun. It belongs to Ather...it's not mine."

Harold grinned. "So you brought Atherton's gun. Wasn't that convenient? Did you also use it to kill him?"

"I...I...I'm not saying any more." Martha clamped her mouth shut.

"Martha is like a switch," Bella said. "She operates in two modes. Wide open yammering and closed jaw."

"Let me explain what happened, Detective," Harold said. "I awoke to find Martha in my apartment pointing a gun at me. After threatening me, she confessed that Atherton Cartwright hadn't been up to killing Frieda Eubanks, so she stepped in to commit the murder. She also implied she had done something to Atherton. She and Atherton were involved in a scheme to try to buy this property and turn it into a Native American casino. She was responsible for other crimes committed at Mountain Splendor including working with Atherton to kidnap Jason and to put poison in the cookies in my apartment."

"Then she tried to kill my grandpa and me."

"Quite a list." Deavers turned toward Bella. "And when did you show up?"

"Just in the nick of time."

"That...that woman did something strange. A snake came out of the gun before I could shoot. Then I ended up in duct tape. There's something suspicious about her. She's not normal."

"I thought you weren't going to say anything more," Harold said. "Oops."

"In addition to being a killer, I think she has a tendency to hallucinate," Bella said. "Poor woman. Being a murderer causes her to act out her wildest fantasies."

"She...she did something weird. These people are lunatics."

There was a knock on the door. Harold stepped over and opened it to find two police officers standing there.

Deavers waved them in. "Please escort this bound woman to the county jail. Process her, and I'll be there later to question her."

"I hope you process her like a cheese," Bella said. Deavers chuckled. "Oh, we will, Ms. Alred. We will."

After Martha had been taken away, Harold parted the curtains and stared downward. He noticed a black car parked near the entrance to the building. "Come here, Detective."

Deavers stepped over.

Harold pointed toward the parking lot. "That appears to be the car Atherton and Martha escaped in the other night."

"Worth checking out," Deavers said.

They went to the red elevator, took it to the first floor and trooped out to the parking lot.

Deavers looked through the window and tried the handle. "It's locked. I'll have to get a search warrant."

"You don't need that if the trunk is open showing incriminating evidence, do you, Detective?" Bella asked.

"No, but the trunk is locked."

Bella turned away from Deavers, wiggled a finger and the trunk popped open. "Oh, looky. The trunk is open after all."

They all moved around to the back of the car. Atherton's body lay on its back in the trunk with a huge exit wound in the center of his forehead.

CHAPTER FORTY-FIVE 🦇

The next day Deavers stopped by and asked to speak with Harold, Jason and Bella. They all gathered in Harold's living room.

"I want to thank you for your assistance in this investigation," the detective said. "Half of the residents' committee was very helpful in solving the crimes committed at Mountain Splendor. Unfortunately, the other half of the committee committed many of the crimes."

"I'm sure you've collected boxes of evidence from Atherton's room, Detective." Harold said.

"Yes, we've gone through all the papers on the Indian casino scam and have the details sorted out. That model casino was quite interesting."

"The guy had big plans," Harold said.

"It turns out this isn't Native American property. The so-called treaty was a forged document. This was all a ruse to buy the property and try to set up a casino under false pretenses. Martha manipulated the scam, unbeknownst to Atherton, and milked money from him that he planned to use for legal and filing fees. When he finally caught on to the fact that she was conning him, she shot him. Then she returned to get revenge on you and your grandson, Mr. McCaffrey. I think she intended to dispose of a trunk full of bodies."

"And fortunately Bella showed up to save us, as she said, in the nick of time." Harold took her hand and squeezed it.

Bella leaned against Harold's arm. "I didn't think we needed to lose any more residents. We already have too many vacant rooms with Hattie Jensen, Frieda Eubanks, Abner Dane, Atherton Cartwright and Martha Kefauver no longer residing here. And besides you've been a very good neighbor." She squeezed his hand back.

"And speaking of Martha, what's happening with her?" Harold asked.

"She has a new temporary room in the county jail before a more permanent home in the state penitentiary after her trial. We have significant evidence linking her to the murders of Frieda Eubanks and Atherton Cartwright. She tried to claim that Atherton killed himself, but it's pretty difficult to shoot yourself in the back of the head in such a way that the bullet exits right through the center of your forehead and your body neatly falls into the trunk of a car and then the lid slams itself."

"And I bet the gun she brought into my apartment was the one used to killed Atherton and Frieda," Harold replied.

Deavers gave a devilish grin. "For a retired insurance salesman, you put things together pretty well. Another interesting fact we learned about Martha Kefauver. That's not her real name. She assumed the identify of a woman with that name who died several years ago. Her real name is Betty Hoop."

"How'd you track that down?" Harold asked.

"When we fingerprinted her, we found a match. Betty had a long rap sheet of scams and embezzlement with numerous outstanding warrants for earlier crimes. Martha, AKA Betty, will be locked up for the rest of her life."

"I gather she's not a Daughter of the American Revolution," Bella said. Deavers chuckled. "She's more a Daughter of the American Reprobates. Her parents emigrated from Europe to the US in the 1930s under suspicious circumstances. You could classify them as a two-bit crime family. She followed in their footsteps — all con artists."

"And I bet all her horse awards were fakes," Bella said.

Harold smiled at Bella. "Probably purchased from a pawn shop. You had her pegged from the outset. You made a statement that she was a phony, and you were right."

—

After Deavers left, Harold received a phone call that Peter Lemieux wanted to stop by to speak with him. While they waited, Bella levitated Jason and floated him around the living room, making him swoop and dive like a model airplane.

"This is so cool, Grandpa. You should try it."

"That's okay. I've done enough flying in my day."

When Peter knocked on the door, Bella lowered Jason to the couch. He stretched out as if he were a lounging teenager.

Peter came to a brisk stop. "Oh, good, I'm glad Bella's here as well. That'll save me another trip. I want to thank all of you for your help in solving the murders."

"Just part of our civic duty," Harold said.

"This is a cool place," Jason said. Then he frowned. "Is it going to stay open so my grandpa can keep living here?"

"As a matter of fact, yes. I was concerned that people would start bolting after all that has happened, but it seems the residents have rallied around yours truly. We have no new cancellations, two people who had given notice have decided to stay, and three residents have recommended friends, who may move to Mountain Splendor. I plan to do some advertising, and I think within several months we'll have the occupancy level back to where it should be."

"Good news," Harold said. "My home is safe."

"And it isn't going to be turned into a casino," Bella added. "The gamblers will have to keep going up to Black Hawk and Central City."

"It gave me quite a fright that we might lose the property," Peter said. "Detective Deavers explained the scam that Atherton and Martha tried to perpetrate. And to think of the steps they took. But I also want to check with you, Mr. McCaffrey. Since we have several vacant apartments now in the Front Wing, do you want to move?"

"Not on your life. I like it here just fine."

"Okay. We'll be repainting after the various families remove the possessions. I'll see if we can put some of the new prospects there as soon as possible."

"Won't there be a stigma that murderers or victims lived in some of those apartments?" Bella asked.

"Might be. But some people also think that kind of history is interesting. You never can tell how potential residents will react."

"And you don't have to publicize who used to live there anyway," Harold added.

"That too."

"I have one question for you," Harold said to Peter. "Anything."

"Why have you been so tolerant of the...uh...unusual lifestyles of members of the Back Wing?"

Peter chuckled. "I've never told anyone, but my mother is a little different and may soon need a place like the Back Wing." He shook Harold's hand. "Thanks again for all your assistance."

That afternoon Jason had finished packing and had his suitcase stashed in the living room ready for his departure. At the sound of a knock on the door, Harold opened it to find his son Nelson and daughter-in-law Emily, looking tanned and relaxed.

Jason's father announced, "We've come to retrieve our long-lost son."

"Hi, Dad. Hi, Mom." Jason stepped closer and hugged them.

"You ready to head home?" his dad asked. "Do I hafta?"

Nelson arched an eyebrow. "What? You weren't that anxious to stay here in the first place. Why the change of attitude?"

"That was before I met all the cool people here. Grandpa has some of the best friends. He even has a girlfriend."

"She's not my girlfriend." Harold scowled.

Jason grinned. "I don't know. You two acted pretty cozy in that laundry cart."

"What laundry cart?" Nelson gawked.

"It's a long story." Jason winked at Harold. "I had a super time, Grandpa."

"You come back and visit again."

"How about next week?" Jason asked.

"We'll see," Nelson replied. "Grab your stuff and let's get going. Thanks, Dad, for taking care of Jason. We had a terrific second honeymoon."

Harold accompanied his family downstairs and watched them drive away. He realized he would miss Jason. Ah, the wonders of youth. All that energy sure added to the excitement around the place. But even without Jason, there was a lot happening at Mountain Splendor. He hadn't been bored since he set foot in here.

Harold spotted Ned Fister off in the garden digging up some withered plants. He stepped over. "Beautifying the place again, Ned?"

"Absolutely. There's enough work to keep me out of trouble for the rest of the summer and fall. I hear you helped rid Mountain Splendor of some of our less desirable residents."

"Word gets around fast."

"Hey, this is a retirement home. What better things do people have to do than pass on the latest interesting poop? And I haven't been hassled by the Perforator lately. You do something to convince him to change careers?"

"Could be."

Ned guffawed. "There have to be a number of interesting stories there. You going to tell me all the particulars?"

"Sure. I'll meet you for dinner, and we can catch up. A lot has happened. It may take the whole meal to give you an accurate account."

"Sounds good."

Harold returned to the building and took the slow red elevator up to his apartment. After unlocking his door and entering, he stood and looked out the window. The "M" on the hillside, instead of standing for School of Mines, now could stand for murder, mayhem, mystery, malevolence, or even melodrama.

Another thought occurred to him. The "M" might instead stand for the majesty of being alive. He wanted to play golf again. He could retrieve his golf clubs from Nelson's garage. Yes, the idea of getting out again appealed to him. As he had discussed with Bella, he looked forward to teaching her the game.

Harold felt a pair of arms go around him. "Bella, where did you come from?"

"I snuck through the wall a while ago and listened from the bedroom when your son and daughter-in-law came to pick up

222

Jason. I've been waiting to speak with you. What's this that you don't have a girlfriend?"

Harold turned around to face Bella. "I thought we might try for more than that."

ABOUT THE AUTHOR

Mike Befeler is author of six novels in the Paul Jacobson Geezer-lit Mystery Series, two of which were finalists for The Lefty Award for best humorous mystery. He has six other published mystery novels: *Death of a Scam Artist*, *The V V Agency*, *The Back Wing*, *The Mystery of the Dinner Playhouse*, *Murder on the Switzerland Trail* and *Court Trouble*; an international thriller, *The Tesla Legacy*; and a nonfiction book, *For Liberty: A World War II Soldier's Inspiring Life Story of Courage, Sacrifice, Survival and Resilience*. Mike is past-president of the Rocky Mountain Chapter of Mystery Writers of America. He grew up in Honolulu, Hawaii, and now lives in Lakewood, California, with his wife, Wendy. If you are interested in having the author speak to your book club, contact Mike Befeler at mikebef@aol.com. His web site is http://www.mikebefeler.com.

CPSIA information can be obtained
at www.ICGtesting.com
Printed in the USA
FSHW022158021219
64697FS

9 781948 338448